Your Love Is Wicked and Other Stories

By
Jim Fraiser

PublishAmerica
Baltimore

Hardcover 978-1-4512-9861-1
Softcover 978-1-4489-3978-7
PUBLISHED BY PUBLISHAMERICA, LLLP
www.publishamerica.com
Baltimore

Printed in the United States of America

For my son, Paul James Fraiser

ALSO BY JIM FRAISER

M is for Mississippi: An Irreverent Guide to the Magnolia State

Shadow Seed

Mississippi River Country Tales

For Love of the Game: The Holy Wars of Millsaps and Mississippi College Football

Majesty of the Mississippi Delta

The Delta Factor

The French Quarter of New Orleans

Majesty of Eastern Mississippi and the Coast

Camille

Vanished Mississippi Gulf Coast

Whiskey with Chaser

The Garden District of New Orleans (due 2010)

PRAISE FOR OTHER BOOKS BY JIM FRAISER

Whiskey with Chaser

"Reminiscent of *Cape Fear*. Chilling for its gritty realism! A great read."
Charles Wilson, best selling author of *Extinct* and *Embryo*.

"The latest must read from Mississippi's Renaissance man."
Martin Hegwood, best selling author of *Big Easy Backroad* & *Jackpot Bay*

"A well-written, high octane thriller with a welcome dose of substance. Lean prose, dark humor, gritty realistic dialogue and a terrifying plot."
Greenwood Commonwealth

The French Quarter of New Orleans

"Fraiser's learned text provides an intelligent, enlightening look at one of America's most charming areas."
Publisher's Weekly

"It belongs on every New Orleans coffee table. Fraiser's well researched and sprightly history is an inviting volume."
New Orleans Times Picayune

"Fraiser, a Mississippi novelist and popular historian, has a pleasing prose style, unpretentious and informative, and proves a pretty good scholar to boot."
Mobile Register

Majesty of the Mississippi Delta

"Fraiser presents the right mixture of history and folklore with insightful text."
Library Journal

"Fraiser's text is lively and anecdotal....Readers will love the stories. It's a pleasure."
New Orleans Times Picayune

Shadow Seed

"Fraiser makes the story move, but its characters' relationships moved me. I highly recommend *Shadow Seed* to our viewers."
Alan Katz, *New Orleans Cox Cable TV*

"A crafty legal thriller...producing suspense and introspection with clever dialogue, providing plenty of depth and humor. A well-told, genuinely Southern drama."
Oxford Eagle

Camille

"Fraiser knows how to tell a story, with suspense building throughout...An inspiring tale."
Delta Magazine

"Fraiser brings his lawyer's eye for detail and experienced in-depth research to his historical fiction. Through pure craftsmanship, he keeps the readers enthralled."
Judge Robert Evans, author of *The 16th Infantry: Civil War Letters & Reminiscences*

Mississippi River Country Tales

"This book can do nothing but add to Jim Fraiser's growing reputation as a Mississippi writer who knows how to tell stories."
Former Mississippi Governor William Winter

"Nowhere has one author put together so diverse and comprehensive collection of stories about the [Deep South] region."
The Clarion Ledger

"Reads like a first rate historical novel. It's simply a darned good book."
Charles Wilson, best-selling author of *Nightwatcher* and *Game Plan*

"A fast paced and easy to read history. An enjoyable collection of stories."
Northeast Mississippi Daily Journal

Vanished Mississippi Gulf Coast

"Fraiser's writing is clear and concise; in [his] snapshots of architectural and cultural treasures Fraiser is at his best. He has compiled an interesting study of this region."
Louisiana History Journal

"This is a tour-de-force of coastal communities devastated by Katrina. I recommend it to our readers, who will enjoy Fraiser's narrative, non-fiction style."
Mississippi Libraries Magazine

"From local history to current culture, this book is perfect

for natives and tourists alike."
Mississippi Magazine

"Intriguing to those who enjoy history and informative to those studying the Deep South. A romantic slice of life... the reader can almost see his characters."
Victorian Homes Magazine

"Hollywood is reading: Vanished Mississippi Gulf Coast by Jim Fraiser...A truly majestic book of what existed before and after Hurricane Katrina devastated that beautiful area."
Jill Jackson's HOLLYWOOD, King Features Syndication, Inc.

Contents

Author's Note

Americans generally believe that their awe-inspiring technology will preserve them despite their almost total surrender of morality, reason, decency and common sense. It won't.

They have apparently convinced themselves that their glorious history—their preservation of democracy and freedom at home and abroad—will preserve them forever despite the dark clouds massing on the horizon. It most assuredly will not.

The pages of world history are cluttered with the remains of once-great civilizations that entertained such outlandish notions. The Greeks, Romans, Spanish, French, Japanese, British and Soviet empires, to name a few, all convinced themselves this fallacy was fact. History proved them wrong.

Most Americans believe that if their country falls it will do so because of the shenanigans of their politicians in Washington. But it is in their own day-to-day choices that their eventual destruction or salvation lies.

But every re-telling of this drama (or comedy, depending upon your perspective) requires an appropriate stage upon which to play out. Although a few are set elsewhere, most of these stories are set in Greenwood, Mississippi, the cotton capital of Mississippi's fabled Delta. The "Mississippi Delta" is a flatland region bounded on the east and west by the Mississippi and Yazoo rivers, respectively, with Memphis occupying its northernmost point and Vicksburg its southernmost site. Greenwood, easily the most flamboyant town in that region, is home to Staplcotn and Viking Range Corporation, significant corporate sources of its wealth, as well as the world's most fertile and lucrative soil outside of Egypt's Nile Delta.

Founded in 1848, this charming hamlet is renowned for its confluence of three pulchritudinous rivers, ancient red brick downtown streets, the Viking Cooking School, the Alluvian hotel, an elegant bookstore and historic blues museum. It boasts a lovely boulevard graced by towering oaks and turn-of-the-century, white-columned Neo-Classical and Colonial Revival mansions, the site of an unprecedented Civil War battle that pitted a Union warship flotilla against Confederacy infantry and artillery, 1960's Civil Rights landmarks denoting another people's valiant struggle for freedom, a magnificent Beaux Arts style courthouse replete with the state's most unique Confederate monument and tetra-style clock tower, an ancient swing bridge called Old Keesler Bridge, a concrete and steel structure spanning the Yazoo River near where Stephen Collins Foster penned *Way Down Upon the Yazoo River* (later changed to *Way Down Upon the Sewanee River*). The graves of Confederate officers, groundbreaking bluesman Robert Johnson and, a few miles to the east, the last great Choctaw chief, Greenwood Leflore, lie in silent testament to the historical and cultural significance of the jewel of the Mississippi Delta.

Suffice it to say, Greenwood serves as the ideal setting for any kind of fiction. Her world class boutique hotel, refashioned from the shell of the old Hotel Irving that once accommodated visitors during Greenwood's rise to prominence as the worlds largest, inland long staple cotton market, and its renowned restaurants such as Lusco's, the Crystal Grill and Giardina's, many of which offer eclectic and southern-fried cuisine in prohibition-era-style dining-in-the-booth atmosphere, would prompt any writer to populate his or her fiction with the bizarre and enigmatic characters you'd expect to frequent such locales. There's no need for resort to fantasy to populate fiction; one need only recall one's friends, neighbors and fellow townspeople in Mississippi hamlets such as Greenwood, Tupelo, Oxford, Laurel and Bay St. Louis.

So, to the question of why set most of these stories in Greenwood and other similarly flamboyant Mississippi locales, I say if you're going to make gumbo, why not use the best seasoning and create the most flavorful incarnation available?

AUTHOR'S SECOND NOTE

Several of these stories, in whole or in part, were previously published in the same or similar form in my non-fiction books, novels, produced plays or magazine and newspaper articles.

Before the Storm, During the Storm and *After the Storm* previously appeared in the novel, *Camille*.

Apologies to Dante, Mother of the Crime, Heal Thyself and *Old Times Not Forgotten* were excerpted from the novel, *Shadow Seed*, reprinted as *Whiskey with Chaser*.

The Pitch and *A Second Monkey Trial* are adapted from the nonfiction book, *M is for Mississippi: An Irreverent Guide to the Magnolia State*.

Affaire de Honor, Cancel My Request, and *The Ultimate Disgrace* are adapted from the nonfiction book, *Mississippi River Country Tales*.

Apologies to the Bard and *The Apology* are adapted from articles previously run in the Jackson Northside Sun and Jackson Business Journal.

Parts of *Recipe for Disaster* are excerpted from *Mississippi*

River Country Tales and the forthcoming *The Garden District of New Orleans*

My How Times Is Changed includes excerpts from the *Delta Magazine* short story, *The Star that Set on the Delta.*

History Lesson is drawn from the novel, *The Delta Factor*, reprinted as *Whiskey with Chaser.*

The Drinking Party is adapted to prose format from my original play of that name.

OLLIE G. MOHAMMED

We found your brick on the Walk of Champions today. It's in Section III, row 39, number 4. You'd have loved the day even more than the brick. Not that there's anything wrong with your brick, dedicated as it is to you from your pals. Still, it's not much of a memorial to life lived like yours. All-star athlete, A student, worked your way through college and grad school, taught computer science at UCLA, helped program the computers that sent Voyager to Saturn, made a million by the time you were forty. Donated thousands to worthy causes every year. And the best pal any of us ever had. But then you never cared for accolades, either receiving them or handing them out, did you? You were just happy to be.

But now…How's the song go? "Another brick in the wall"? Or the sidewalk, in your case. You don't even get a wall. People trod on your brick like they never did on you.

Hmmff. You were anything but another brick in the wall. A real one of a kind; anyone would admit that. An odd egg would be a kind way of describing you. All your ridiculous expressions— "that's wicked," meaning 'that's good,' for one. Yelping "Godfrey Daniels" instead of cursing in public, for another.

But nothing said 'you' like your irritating habit of assuming different personas in public just to embarrass your pals. Like the time you 'became' Ollie G. Mohammed and argued the case for Islam in New Orleans' St. Louis Cathedral during a tour I had arranged for us. Just to get my goat, thank you very much.

Oh, yeah. Politically incorrect described you to T. And God knows I loved you for that.

But you died and that's it. Now the brick honoring you is just one of hundreds lining a sidewalk that nobody really notices on the way to a ballgame that the fans care about more than they do the religion they practice the next day.

Anyhow, like I was saying, the day itself was perfect for you—seventy five degrees, the sun a veritable ball of fire searing across a cloudless sky casting a molten sea of bronze over the rolling hills of Oxford and the majestic oak-laden Grove. Two of the wives brought barbeque in your honor and Ole Miss whipped LSU by three touchdowns. Yeah, you'd have loved it. Our oak groves echoed into the evening with rousing choruses of "Hotty Toddy" and barely discernable strains of "Dixie" from the brass band marching down University Avenue; the air throbbing with a profusion of scents from sweet Kentucky bourbon to hamburgers sizzling on portable grills.

Well, you know how it was. Nobody enjoyed football weekends more than you. Even when we lost games by three touchdowns, which we mostly did while you were alive. Of course, we're having a great year now you're gone. Won the West in baseball and went to the NCAA's in basketball. Another New Year's Day bowl for the Rebs, I'm sure. And you missed it all.

Or at least I assume you did. *You* always insisted you would. No heaven, no hell, according to you. And now the Grove, just like you imagined it would be if...I mean....I just....

Can you tell me one damned thing? Why the hell did you have to die at Christmas? I know, I know. Glad to have missed it. That's what you'd've said. You hated Christmas. Ebeneezer Scrooge and Scientific American all rolled into one. Hard core atheist and proud of it. But God, how I miss those absurd Solstice Cards you sent out every Christmas. Solstice cards, for heaven's sake. A true believer to the end.

You know, I can't help but laugh about the time you joined us for Christmas dinner back in '97. Me and Suzi, our little girls, my sister and her drunk boyfriend, the Cliftons and their new baby boy. I've never seen anyone roll their eyes so many times during dinner. Hell, there's a picture in my scrapbook from that very night where you're looking askance at me, rolling your eyes as if everyone at the table had just broken wind in unison. Fluttering those eyelashes that all the girls said were so beautiful. What the heck were they talking about? Beautiful eyelashes, for God's sake.

Anyhow, you declared you'd never do Christmas dinner again. No curse words or oaths to the pagan gods. Nothing like that. But you damn sure meant it. Never came back. Your word was your bond, just like they say. Even if you worshiped at altars I never understood and conducted yourself as if you cared less what anyone thought about you.

Like the time at Greenwood High, the big baseball game against Greenville. You stole second base twice, each time going back to retrieve your hat after if fell off and sauntering into second base before the throw arrived. Showing up the catcher unmercifully, provoking him into making two costly throwing errors in the late innings. Then, when he took me out at second base during a double play attempt and carved up my shin with his spikes, you took my throw at the bag a few innings later and nailed him between the eyes as he barreled into second. Then, just to show up his replacement, you stole second, third, and on a low, outside pitch, home to win the game. Never seen anything like that at any level. Major leagues, little leagues, anywhere.

But you always extracted a price for your loyalty, didn't you? Like our freshman year at Ole Miss when I drove you to Tupelo to tour Elvis's house, and you picked the smallest, most crowded room in which to opine in your loudest possible whisper that it was a shame a guy with so much talent killed himself with drugs, booze and fried peanut butter and banana sandwiches. I thought those Elvis fans were going to kill us. Then we went to Johnnie's Drive Inn and you crowed about how you'd die for their barbeque sandwiches, and why didn't Elvis OD on barbeque instead of the bananas. Why did you do such things? Did you think you were going to convince the world to give up liquor, cigarettes, fried bananas and Jehovah just on your say-so?

But what I'd most like to know is why you never wanted children. I know you told your true love she was a Christian and you were an atheist and you didn't want to screw it up for her, what with the kids and all. But damn! With a raving beauty like that you marry her quick and hash those things out later. At least that's what I would have done. But not you. No, sir. Too honest for that, weren't you? Hey, I understand. You cared about her too much to lie, I guess.

But hating Christmas? Really? Just because a few misguided fundamentalists claim there were dinosaurs on Noah's Ark, that the world was created in six days and Moses parted the Red Sea rather than slogging through the Sea of Reeds doesn't mean you shuck the whole thing, does it? Does it?

Sure, Christmas is blatant commercialism and relatives you can't stand, but....What the hell's wrong with Santa Claus, for God's sake? The kids' eyes on Christmas morning when they spy the presents under the tree....What in the Dickens is wrong with that?

Well, I guess it was for the best, wasn't it? Nobody to leave behind. Nobody to care. Well, no family, anyhow.

Bah, humbug and all that. But that didn't stop you from eating your share of my turkey and dressing during our big Christmas dinner, did it, Mr. Integrity? And yes, I remember that you did declare that it wasn't as good as the barbeque at Johnnie's Drive Inn.

But not a drop of alcohol did you drink at your one Christmas dinner. Booze wasn't rational enough for you, was it? Never drank and never ate anything bad for you. Except barbeque, of course. Figure that one out, huh? Not one beer in your life, salads for lunch, tennis at night and walking the golf course three times a week and always on weekends, and you ate barbeque every time we passed a rib joint.

Hell, I thought we were going to die that time we happened upon that "Mississippi Barbeque" joint in Watts, the most dangerous ghetto in Los Angeles. At least for white people who're actually from Mississippi, I'd imagine.

Yeah, sunny Los Angeles, the year we flew to LA for our annual pals' baseball trip. Ollie G. Mohammed didn't miss an opportunity to offend everybody in Dodger Stadium when, I casually mentioned to you during the seventh-inning stretch that you ought to read Kierkegaard or Pascal or some other philosopher who could explain the finer points of religion to you in terms you could understand. Good grief! I swore I'd never make that mistake again.

But that was nothing. You were just setting us up for the marquee performance of the trip.

When we were trapped in the Dodger Stadium parking lot, in the back of Section G, where fifty thousand fans were lined up in their cars trying to get home after the game. Ever the creative problem solver, you suggested that I get out and walk behind the car into the offending lane of traffic, fall down and fake a heart attack. Block traffic long enough for the guys to back out the car and whip into the exit lane. You knew I'd do it, too, because we all assumed you had another plan if that one didn't work. You wouldn't hang your pal out to dry, would you? Never did. Not once in fifty-five years. Never would have if you'd lived to be a hundred.

So I did it. But we hadn't counted on the Los Angelinos making such a big to-do about my heart attack. They were Yankees after all, weren't they? So, of course a crowd quickly gathered around me asking if I needed help. Now I'm lying there, still as stone, thinking, "ain't this great, I'm damn sure going to jail, now."

But there you came, clad in your Ole Miss baseball jersey, shouting, "out of my way, I'm a doctor." You gave me CPR, your version of course, replete with a vigorous mouth-to-mouth resuscitation that was a deeper, wetter kiss than any I had in college, just because you knew I couldn't do anything about it at the time. Then you announced to the gaping crowd, "We gotta get this man to a hospital. Back up, there, and let this car out." The crowd parted in great waves as if Moses had just waved his magic staff. The boys backed into the lane, threw open the back door, and you tossed me on the seat, dived in on top of me, and we burned rubber into the exit lane, just as this bamboozled Ohioan or Minnesotan said in a distinct nasal tone, "Hey, wait a minute. That guy wasn't a doctor!"

We laughed about that for an hour, drank copious beers (except for you, of course) and then played whiffle ball from midnight to three AM when you hit the game winning homerun and you and I whooped it up like we had just won the World Series. Only you, pal. Only you.

But, and this is so very like you... None of your shenanigans, not even endless barbeque, could kill you, could it? Took a bad ticker from day one. Congenital the docs said. A bomb waiting to go off. Took you out on Christmas day, too. Oh, yeah. Ring one up for the Christmas gods, I say.

Your pal Slade's taking your demise very hard. Thought he was going to cry when we found your brick in the Grove. But he's honoring your memory in appropriate fashion. Keeps gaining weight but when we rib him about it, he scoffs and says he outlived you.

Your pal Jodie's new baby looks just like him, but he named the boy after you. When we asked him why, he said because you told everybody he was out of his mind for having another kid at his age, and so figured to name the boy after you just to get you back. And then you surprised everybody and died. But he told us today in the Grove you weren't going to get out of having a kid named after you just because you died, or some other silly excuse like that.

I just hope you were right when you declared there was no Hell. You always said you couldn't believe in Hell because you knew your father was roasting down there if anybody was. Were you serious about that? I never knew your dad, dying young like he did. Anyhow, I sure hope you aren't down there right now saying, "Godfrey Daniels, it's hotter than I thought."

Well, anyhow, this is what I really wanted say. We were walking to the game after finding your brick on the Walk of Champions when we saw these four guys tossing beer bottle tops at the brick sidewalk on up ahead of us. Then we noticed a few were doing it behind us. A whole fraternity of 'em, I guess. They were tossing their caps, scrambling onto the sidewalk to see where they landed, and scoring the results in some crazy competition. We asked what they were doing, and they said they were playing Bottle Cap Toss. Players got the most points when their caps landed on someone famous, fewer for landing on somebody one of them had known and zip for landing on anyone else. Points were deducted for landing on a blank brick. And undoubtedly in consideration of their drunken state, they suffered disqualification for missing the sidewalk entirely.

At that moment one of their bottle caps landed right on your brick. You know, I'd like to tell you that we told them who you were and they hand-slapped and high-fived each other like they had just won the BCS National Championship Game, with the winning points coming from landing on your brick.

But that's not how it happened. Life was only like that when you were around. I told them you weren't anybody famous, and of course none of them had ever heard of you. Although one of them did seem rather happy that your brick wasn't blank and it didn't cost him points.

So what if they hadn't heard of you? They were ridiculous frat boys, all dressed exactly alike in their khakis and blue blazers; rich frat boys who probably hadn't worked a day in their lives, were drunk out of their minds, and undoubtedly planned on going to church with their families the next day. They were nothing like you.

They'd never know who you were or what you meant to us. To me.

Yeah, they were nothing like you. But it was hardly their fault. Nobody's like you. Or ever will be. But hey…That's what so great, and so very terrible, about the way God made us, isn't it? That's never been clearer to me than it is right now.

Godfrey Daniels! I wish Ollie G. Mohammed was here to tell me that I have no idea what the heck I'm talking about.

BEFORE THE STORM

Drew Stone awoke to the sound of incessant hammering outside his second story bedroom window. Rubbing the sleep from his eyes, he peered to his left where his wife, Carole, slept soundly beside him. A glance at their bedside clock confirmed that he'd overslept by thirty minutes. He'd told Stevie the night before they'd finish the tree house first thing in the morning, and around the Stone house, first thing had always meant 0700 hours.

Once accustomed to the habit of early rising, Stevie had taken to it with a passion, especially where projects like tree houses were concerned. And with the exceptional heat and humidity they'd had to contend with all summer, they both learned to gettheir outside work done early each morning.

The hammering continued as Stone bounced out of bed and flung open a window.

"Stevie!"

The boy's face appeared in the larger of two tree house windows. "Yeah, Dad?"

"How's it going, Son?"

"Almost finished, Dad. Come on up!"

"All right. Give me a second."

"Great."

Ten minutes later, the elder Stone, clad in khaki pants and grey, crew neck t-shirt, climbed the wooden plank steps he'd hammered into the trunk of their front yard's great live oak tree three months earlier, and hoisted himself through the opening onto the floor beside his son. Stevie set aside his hammer and squatted beside his dad.

"Looks great, doesn't it?"

"Sure does, Stevie." Stone ran his hand across the rough-edged boards in the treehouse walls as he scanned the ceiling, noting that it was a few nails from completion.

"You've done good work here, Son. This is really something to be proud of."

"Thanks, Dad. Heck, making it with you was half the fun."

Stone quietly savored the moment. Before long, he realized, Stevie and his fellow fifth graders, like little Steve Haas next door, would grow out of their childlike devotion to their parents and take their first steps toward manhood and parent-free independence. But for now, this tree house had been the ideal summer-long project that had brought them even closer than before. For that, Stone silently thanked his grandfather and his father for starting and then passing down the Stone family tradition of father and son tree houses.

"Yeah, it was fun, wasn't it," he said, ruffling Stevie's short-cropped blond hair. "I think I enjoyed making this tree house even more than the one I built with my dad in Florida, when I was your age."

"Cool," Stevie replied. "Uh...Dad?"

"Yeah?"

"Where did you find those boards we used? What kind of wood are they?"

Stone regarded the near finished roof with a deep sense of satisfaction. This was the moment he'd been waiting for—the moment he'd foreseen ten years before they'd even begun their tree house project—when he'd salvaged several boards from his family home in Florida the week after his grandfather died.

"Those are cypress," he replied. "I brought them all the way from Key West. They were part of your grandfather Drew's house. My childhood home."

Stevie pondered the revelation as he held a solid piece of cypress in his hands. "Wasn't granddad killed by a storm?"

"A hurricane, yes," Stone nodded pensively. "The great Labor Day hurricane of 1935. The one I told you about last Christmas."

"I remember. Why didn't he get away? From the hurricane, I mean?"

Stone lay a cypress board on his lap, running his hand back and forth across the grain as he leaned against the rear tree house wall. "You grandfather was a carpenter, Stevie, but he also did some volunteer work for a local hurricane brigade. He died trying to save us—my mother, your Aunt Margaurite, and me— from that hurricane. The worst storm to hit Florida in all recorded history."

Stevie considered his father's words for a moment. "Where do hurricanes come from?" he asked.

"Well, they're tropical disturbances formed when two opposing currents of air come together over a warm ocean. They become hurricanes when their winds reach speeds of at least seventy-four miles per hour. They usually form during late summer and early fall, when the ocean's waters are warmest. They move across the Atlantic Ocean and sometimes make landfall in the Americas."

"Why're they called 'her-a-canes,' and why do they give 'em girls' names?"

Stone grinned and resisted the temptation to make a joke at the fairer sex's expense. "The name comes from a Spanish phrase meaning 'evil spirits,' and an Indian word meaning 'big winds.' Weathermen like to give them their girlfriends' names. Sort of a tradition, like sailors giving ships women's names, or pilots naming airplanes."

"But why?"

"You'll find out later."

"Well...How bad can hurricanes be? As bad as tornadoes?"

"Well, you probably don't remember much about Betsy, since you were away at your aunt's in Laurel when it hit the coast five years ago, but a hurricane puts out more energy in a day than is released by 400 hydrogen bombs. They can blow a house away, carry a car for miles, and drive a straw into a tree trunk."

Stevie's face lit up like a light bulb. "Wow!" he exclaimed. "Is the hurricane coming here?"

Stone turned to face his son. "Who told you about the storm?"

"Shelly Fourcade, when we went riding yesterday afternoon. She said it wasn't gonna come here, though. Do *you* think it will?"

"I don't know, Son. The weatherman doesn't seem to think so."

"Rats."

"What's more," Stone observed, his voice brimming with optimism as he scanned the peaceful, light blue gulf sky, "I haven't seen any of the usual hurricane warning signs last night or this morning."

Stevie cradled a hammer in his hands. "What signs are those?" he asked excitedly.

"Well, let's see," Stone mused, trying to concentrate despite the oppressive humidity, which he realized was worse this morning than it had been all week. "Increased swells in the gulf, cirrus clouds on the horizon, a brick dust sky. Oh, yeah," he added, wiping newly formed beads of sweat from his brow, "and the barometer falls dramatically."

"Shoot," Stevie grumbled, acutely aware that he had seen none of those signs all week, although he wasn't at all certain what a barometer might be, or how he would know if he saw one falling.

"Well," his father continued with a sudden air of solemnity, "if it does come here, you won't be around to see it, because your mother and I'll be packing you off to Laurel. This coast is no place for young'uns when the devil winds blow."

"Aw, Dad," Stevie whined, sounding as disappointed as he might have been if his father had told him not to expect Santa Claus for Christmas. "Would I hafta go away?"

"Yes, Son, you would. Didn't you get enough excitement checking out the ghosts at the Pirate House yesterday?"

Stevie's mouth hung open in surprise. "How did you know about that," he asked, a hint of embarrassment evident in his voice.

"Your buddy Steve told me, when I went next door last night to tell his family goodbye before they left for their family reunion in Mobile. Miss Myrt said you and Steve took Shelly to the Pirate House, trying to scare her with the ghost of the pirate Jean Lafitte."

Stevie looked sheepishly at his father. "Yes, sir," was all he said.

"Well did you? Scare her, I mean?"

Stevie shook his head as he twisted the hammer between his fingers. "Naw. She wasn't scared at all. And we didn't see any ghosts."

Silence reigned for a moment, until Stevie ended it with another question. "Dad, did pirates really hole up at that house? And attack ships when hurricanes came?"

Stone smiled as he recalled the old 1802 planter's-type cottage with broad, columned front gallery, located several miles westward up the beach road near the dividing line between Waveland and Bay St. Louis. True enough, it had always been rumored to house the leader of an infamous band of Gulf Coast pirates who supposedly ran treasure through a tunnel under the beach to a cellar in the house. But historical accuracy aside, Stone recognized in the tale an opportunity to give his son what the boy loved as much as a midsummer's baseball game—a swashbuckling pirate story with the War of 1812 thrown in for good measure.

"Well," he began, in hushed tones for dramatic effect, "it *was* once the home of the dreaded pirate, Jean Lafitte, and Lafitte and his bloodthirsty buccaneers sent many a gulf sailor to Davy Jones' Locker. But in 1815, Lafitte joined up with General Andy Jackson to defeat the British at the Battle of New Orleans and keep America free. He and his men were heroes, not villains. At least when they lived around here."

"But our teacher told us something about somebody, pirates maybe, attacking British ships in the bay, right out there," Stevie said, pointing across their front lawn toward the beach road, out into the gulf.

"It wasn't pirates attacking the British, Stevie. It was the people of Bay St. Louis, in 1814, before the big land battle at Chalmette. They fought against the British navy occupying the gulf, right out from downtown. They delayed the British long enough for Jackson to get his men ready to win the Battle of New Orleans."

"And did a woman really whoop the British in that battle, like Shelly said?"

"Yes, Son, she did. Just when the mayor was ready to surrender Bay St. Louis to the British fleet, a local woman snatched a soldier's cigar and touched of a cannon that scared the British away."

"Wow," Stevie cried. "That must have been really cool."

"I'll bet," Stone agreed. "But nothing your mother couldn't have done, I'm sure."

"Mom?" Stevie laughed. "No way. Mom would have—"
"Drew!"

Stone turned to see his wife, Carole, leaning over the rail of the second floor wrap around gallery of their two story Spanish cottage. "Yes, hon?" he shouted.

"Telephone. It's Jerry Saucier, from your squadron."

"What's he want?"

"They want you at the base in two hours. And Joe Necaise wants to meet with you and Jerry before that."

Stone knew what the message meant without even having to ask. He and his co-pilot, Jerry Saucier, would fly a reconnaissance mission into the monster later that day. And he was equally certain why Joe Necaise wanted to meet them before they took off. Necaise, an experienced hurricane reconnaissance navy pilot stationed in Miami, had, while on loan to Stone's air force reserve squadron at Keesler six years ago, trained Stone for the hurricane reconnaissance missions he'd later command when Keesler fielded its own air force reconnaissance team. He knew that Necaise had flown one of the last two days' reconnaissance missions into the storm, and assumed that he'd caught a late night jet to Biloxi for a briefing with Colonel J.C. Patterson at Keesler. Now his mentor would brief him on the dangers he would face in this swiftly strengthening hurricane.

"Drew?"

Stone exhaled heavily. "Sorry, hon. Tell Saucier I'll pick him up at his house in thirty minutes."

"Will do."

As Carole resumed her watercolor painting on the gallery, Stone turned to face his clearly disappointed son.

"Do you have to go, Dad?"

"Sorry, Stevie," Stone replied, patting the boy's shoulder. "When Uncle Sam calls, your daddy has to answer."

"Is this about the hurricane?" Stevie asked.

"Yes. You know I pilot a Hurricane Hunter plane from Keesler Air Force base in Biloxi."

"Yeah, Dad. Hurricane Hunter..." Stevie repeated, fingering his lip as he tried for the thousandth time to picture it in his mind. "That's way cool, Dad. But...Do you really have to fly right into the middle of the hurricane?"

"Into the eyewall, yes. The only place we can get the information we need about the storm is right inside its eye."

"Wow! But won't you be scared when you do that?"

"Naww," Stone grinned. "I've got the best plane and the

most experienced crew in the world. We'll be just fine, Stevie, I promise you. It's the people on the ground who don't get away from the storm wherever it makes landfall who have every reason to be scared."

"Sheesh."

"Well, anyhow, I've got to go. Why don't you finish the roof for me, pardner."

"Can I? That'd be great! Thanks a lot, Dad."

"And if this storm blows over, I'll take you to see the new *Fantastic Four* movie in Biloxi tonight. What do you say?"

"That'd really be great, Dad," Stevie said, leaning over and embracing his father.

Stone held the boy tightly, sensing with unexpected clarity that this could well be one of the last times, until grandfatherhood, that he would hold unbridled childhood innocence in his arms. He patted Stevie on the back and climbed down the tree house steps. As he reached his home's front door, he turned and looked back up at Stevie, already hard at work hammering nails into cypress boards, putting the finishing touches on the roof. *I wish this could last forever,* Stone mused, treasuring what should have been nothing more than a typical father-son moment, but which his job as a hurricane hunter made all the more precious for being all the more tenuous. Stevie was everything he had ever hoped for in a son, and no matter what the future held, it could never deny him that.

WITNESS EXCUSED

Even though she wore a dark brown pinstripe suit rather than her black judicial robe, and despite the fact that they were meeting in her private office rather than her courtroom in the Leflore County Courthouse, Judge Seetha Markham made certain that Jerry Lang entertained no misconceptions about the current pecking order in the Greenwood, Mississippi, legal system.

"Make no mistake, Mr. Lang," she said, "you *will* be representing Henry Watts, just as surely as today is Wednesday. I made the appointment this morning on the record and that appointment stands. I don't give a damn what his uncle wants. I probably shouldn't have told you what he said."

"But if City Councilman Watts wants his nephew represented by a black attorney, then why not just—"

Markham gaveled her desk with the palm of her hand. "I run this courthouse, not Harry Watts."

"I know that, Judge, but—"

"Oh, come on, Mr. Lang," Markham coaxed, her ebony skin taking on a noticeably brighter sheen in the glow of the soft sunlight breaking through the curtains and cascading across her face. She leaned back in her plush, black leather chair. "Watts is waiting for you at the Detention Center. Go brown nose him a bit. Who knows? Win this case and good old Uncle Harry might just run you for mayor next year."

Markham rose and strode resolutely around her desk, leading him toward the door of her private chambers. "I told Watts if he wanted an African-American attorney, he could always hire one. But on court appointments, I decide the attorney. "

Lang stopped in the hall and turned to face Markham. "Judge, if he's not willing to pay, then he—"

"Oh, Councilman Watts knows you're the best. He's getting you, and for free! He really owes me on this one. He knows that and I know that, but he'll never say it. Of course, he'll try to ruin you if you do lose. Or at least make you look as much as possible like an uncaring racist."

"Either mayor or picket signs in my yard, huh?"

"Come to think of it, you may really have a chance to win this one. You can see from the file there that they've got very little hard evidence against your client, other than the eye witness. No damning lab tests, as yet. Just the car he was driving."

Lang shook his head as he flipped through the court file. "What a solid citizen my client is.... A crack addict with a youth court record for violence."

Markham grinned broadly in her office doorway. "You don't have to put him on the stand and give the D.A. an opening on that."

* * *

Monday morning's *Greenwood Commonwealth* featured a fat, front page headline about the Henry Watts murder case. Lang reclined in his dark-blue, faux leather office chair and smiled as he read a report that he had been unavailable for comment over the weekend. After meeting with Watts in the jail and issuing witness subpoenas for the forthcoming preliminary hearing he had returned to his fishing lodge on Moon Lake for the weekend, capital murder charge notwithstanding. The fishing had been above average for a mid-March Mississippi warm spell. If Uncle Watts didn't think enough of his nephew to come out of his pocket for a paid attorney, Lang had decided, he wasn't going to lose out completely on a prime fishing weekend just to hold the bastard's hand. The buzzing phone turned his thoughts back to the office.

"Yes?"

Jill Savery's voice brimmed with barely restrained impatience. "A woman's here to see you."

Lang frowned. How many times had he told his secretary to use the client's name to the client's face? Clients, much like doctor's patients, liked to believe that their lawyer considered them to be more than just a life support system for a bank account.

"*Who* is here to see me, Jill?"

"A Miss Sheryl Gores."

"I beg your pardon?" The eye witness in the Watts murder case was waiting in his reception area?

"A Miss Gores. Shall I send her back?"

He wasn't sure. As a general rule, prosecution witnesses usually avoided defense lawyers as vigorously as lawyers ducked life insurance salesmen. And when cornered, opposing witnesses could be terribly unpleasant, to say the very least. But this opportunity to jump start the Watts defense by interviewing the prosecution's star witness was too good to pass up. She must have something interesting to say, he mused, having hunted him down right after the sheriff had served her with his subpoena. "Yes, by all means," he said, "send her back."

"Yes, sir."

He buzzed his secretary back a second later. "Is she on her way?"

"Of course."

"Is she armed?"

"No, but I have some mace in my purse. Buzz me back if she starts kicking your butt."

"Smartass."

"Chickenshit."

Lang hung up the phone. He hated it when Jill spoke to him that way. He made a thousandth mental note to never again mess around with the hired help.

He heard a forceful knock.

"Come in."

The door flew open. Framed in the doorway was a thin, stringy-haired, ornery looking young woman.

"Hello, Ms. Gores. I'm Jerry Lang. Please have a seat."

Gores seated herself, crossed her arms and legs. "I know who you are, Mr. Lang. You represent the nigger that killed that old Baucomb woman."

"Hmm." *Oh, great,* he thought. I've got a dumbass in the jail and now a redneck in my office.

"I want you to know that—"

Lang silenced her with a raised hand. "This is rather awkward for me, Ms. Gores. You, a prosecution witness, I, representing only my client's interests...."

Gores frowned. "I don't need no lawyer with me, if that's what you's worried about. What I got to say is 'tween you n' me."

Lang leaned back in his chair, hands folded in his lap. That'll work, he thought to himself, carefully restraining the urge to smile. "Fine. You've been duly advised. Now, what may I do for you, Miss Gores?"

"I need to talk to you, Mr. Lang."

He nodded.

She chopped wood nervously with her right foot. "The nigger. I want to talk to you about that nigger you represent."

"Henry Watts."

"I know the fucker's name."

"Look, Miss Gores, I wish you wouldn't use that disrespectful language. I'm not going to—"

"No, it's okay. I got to tell you 'bout your *client*."

"As you wish. Just ease up on the N word, okay? Let's conduct ourselves in a civilized manner if at all possible, shall we? May I fix you something? Water, a Coke?"

"I ain't here to drink your water, Mr. Lang. There's somethin' you got to know."

"And that is?"

"Are you gonna represent that.... that…"

"I've been appointed," he said more sternly than he intended, "to represent Mr. Watts, yes."

She shook her head in disgust. "You lawyers, you represent anybody who'll pay the freight, huh?"

"We don't approve of the crime, Miss Gores. We simply represent the accused person's right to a fair—"

"You try to get him off, right? You-"

Lang silenced her with a firm wave of his hand. "It's an abstract concept, Miss Gores. Preserving a man's right to a fair trial. Everybody deserves a fair trial under the Constitution. It's a lawyer's responsibility to see that his client gets one. A fair trial, that is. I'm sure you understand."

"I'm sure I don't give a shit. Are you good at it?"

"What?"

"You gonna get this sack of shit off?"

He lowered his head. "Miss Gores, his name is Henry Watts. As I said before, you shouldn't…"

Gores rolled her eyes angrily. "You gonna win his case, Mr. Lang? He splattered that old woman's brains all over her kitchen. You gonna walk that bastard after that?"

"Perhaps," Lang frowned, "our talking wasn't such a good idea, after all, Ms. Gores. Maybe you should—"

This time Gores raised both her hands, her eyes flashing fire one moment, then cooling to dark, round embers the next. "No. It's okay. I ain't gonna have a conniption. I got to tell you what I come to tell you."

He glanced at his watch. "Tell me what?"

Her expression softened. "Hey, I know you're a busy man, Mr. Lang, but you got to know! If that bastard gets out, he's gonna cut my throat! I swear it!"

"Beg pardon?"

"He told me! Black bastard called me from the jail! Called me at my apartment, you see! I lived right next door to him. Uh, huh. Two doors down from that old woman he kilt. Saw him drivin' away in her car that night. I don't know how he found out. Told me on the phone that if I testified at the preliminary hearin' this Friday, he'd kill me. Carve me up like a Thanksgiving turkey! I ain't making this up, Mr. Lang!"

"Have you told the police that Mr. Watts threatened you?"

Her eyes narrowed, her jaws tightened. "Hell, yeah. The cops don't give a shit. They say he ain't never goan' get out. But, Mr. Lang... If you walk him, he'll run me down and cut my throat." She paused. "And that ain't all he said he'd do."

"What else did he threaten to do?"

Gores crossed her arms, her foot bobbed up and down. "I don't want to talk about it. You're a lawyer. You been around. You can figure it out. That nigger is dangerous, Mr. Lang."

"Then why come to me, his lawyer? What did the nig...." Lang exhaled impatiently. "What did Mr. Watts say he'd do to you? I can't help you if you don't tell me the whole story." Or the whole truth.

"He said he'd rape me, that's what he said! And not just the natural way. Is that what you wanted to hear? He said he'd stick it up my ass all the way to next Tuesday! Okay? You got the picture now? He's crazy, Mr. Lang! He's crazy, and dangerous as hell!"

For the first time he noticed her slightly masculine quality, the kind he had occasionally seen in some lesbians, female golfers, and women lawyers. Hers, though, was the raw-boned, hard-working, self-supporting country girl brand of mannish quality that he'd often found occasion to admire. Whether by enduring pregnancy alone or supporting a worthless husband and several screaming kids, these iron magnolias earned their stripes every day.

Now his job required him to set the devil incarnate loose upon this blameless woman. And why? For witnessing the aftermath of the heinous murder of yet another ill-fated woman. Such times made him wish he did something more frivolous for a living, like renting umbrellas at the beach or teaching education courses to half-asleep coeds at Ole Miss. He had to say something. "Calm down, Miss Gores."

"*I'm calm!*"

"Well, I'm confused."

"What?"

"Sure. I mean...Most eyewitnesses want to get out of testifying, they tell the D.A. they made a mistake. Misidentified the witness."

"I gave the cops a statement. Watts knows that."

"Maybe you were wrong. It was dark and you were across the street from the man you saw coming out of the victim's house. Maybe you can't see that far at night."

"I can see the moon at night, Mr. Lawyer. How far is that?"

"I..."

"Look, I saw what I saw. And I told the cops. Watts knows it. If I don't testify the cops will nail me. If I do, Watts will kill me. You got to let me off the subpoena. "

"I see."

"Do you?" She whipped a subpoena out of her oversized, macramé purse and fluttered it in the lawyer's face. "Let me out of this summons to the p'leminary hearing. He'll see me at the hearin' when I testify! If he gets out he'll cut my throat. I swear it!"

"Look, Miss Gores... Watts won't be able to get to you, much less get out of jail."

"That's what the cops told me, but Watts ain't talked to you or the cops like he done talked to me. He'll do it, Mr. Lang. I know he will!"

"He has no bail, right now. Even if the court sets one there's no way he could make it. He's indigent. He couldn't possibly afford bail. And an out and out dismissal looks pretty unlikely, right now."

"I ain't takin' no chances. No way! I ain't gonna be there at the p'leminary hearin.'"

"The police can protect you," he said, half-heartedly. Hell, let her fly the coop if she that was what she wanted to do. A win by default was still a win in his book. If Gores dumped her subpoena, the case against his client would fail. Watts would walk free, wouldn't have any reason to hunt her down, and everybody, including Gores, would be happy. He knew it but he couldn't say it. Not to the star witness against his client.

Her face reddened. "The cops'll protect me all right. Jus' like they protected that old Baucomb woman."

"That was different. Besides, you're under subpoena. You've no choice but to be there. Or Watts' case will be dismissed."

"The hell you say!"

"The Supreme Court says. *Davis v. Mississippi* made it crystal clear: if a defense-subpoenaed eye-witness fails to appear at a preliminary hearing, the police may not offer her testimony through hearsay evidence, and any case based substantially on the missing witness's statement must be dismissed. That's the law."

"That ain't right! I just can't testify at that hearin'!"

"You're preaching to the choir, Miss Gores. I don't want you to show up, either. Hell, I subpoenaed you hoping you wouldn't show up. But I can't release you from the subpoena. My client has an absolute right to cross-examine any witness against him and..."

"You want him to walk, don't you, you bastard? You don't care 'bout his cons'tutional rights! You just wan'ta win his case, like this is some kinda fuckin' football game or somethin'."

"Please, Ms. Gores, I don't see the need for—."

She rose suddenly, waving a finger in his face. "You want him to walk right out of that courtroom, don't you, you—"

"I'm required to represent my client's best interests! That's the law."

"Then the law sucks! They could release him that day, and I could be hit over the head and raped that night! Is that what you want, Mr. Big Shot Lawyer? Are they payin' you enough for that?"

"I... Miss Gores.... I just can't release you. Can't you understand that? What if I were representing you?"

"I bet you'd release any witness if it was *your* ass on the line like mine is right now. You damned lawyers! You look out after yourselves just like them doctors do, don't you?"

"No. I mean...Well, yes, of course we do, in a sense, but—"

"If it was *your* ass, it'd be different!"

"No, it wouldn't."

"Let me off the summons. He'll kill me if he sees me in court."

"I can't."

"If he walks," she said, squinting angrily, aiming a bony finger like a pistol, "whatever he does is all on you." That said, she turned on her heels and scurried out the door before he could utter another word. A slamming door told him the interview was over.

He considered his change of fortune for a moment then pressed an intercom button. "Ms. Savery?"

"Yes?"

"You hungry yet? I hear the Crystal Grill got in some fresh Red Snapper this morning."

"You gonna piss *me* off like you did that redneck bitch?"

"I'm offering to buy you the best lunch our fair city has to offer. Are you going to argue with me about that?"

"My mamma didn't raise a fool, boy. Let's go while the getting's good."

"Vamanos!"

APOLOGIES TO DANTE

John Kitchens phoned Richard Farris as soon as the three olive-skinned men in the dark suits hit the sidewalk outside his downtown Greenwood office.

"Can you meet me for a drink?"

"When?"

"Right now. It's important."

"Sure. On condition that we meet at the Alluvian bar."

"Must we, Richard? They're usually packed right about now. It's after four on a Friday, you know. Let's go to the Flatlands Grill, or CiCi's Delicatessen on the Boulevard."

"Only at the Alluvian, John. It's the ideal locale for your counterfeit soul. The bar serving Mississippi's most impressive and expensive boutique hotel erected in the area of that state renowned for poverty, a bartender and part-time interior design advisor who wears too much makeup, a large mirror over the bar that forces you to look deeply into your own soul, and, most significantly of all, that little sign on the bar, 'Greenwood the Cotton Capital of the World', standing proudly beside the tiny statute of bluesman Robert Johnson... Such a vintage contradiction in terms, symbolizing as they do both the enormous cotton wealth in this town and the ever present pseudo-glorification of the black man upon whose back those white fortunes were made. Anyone could see that the Alluvian Bar is precisely where you belong."

"No way, Richard. Your clients, my employees, they all drink there. How about the Cotton Club in Ramcat Alley? You can have a shoe shine, we can find a cozy table far from the poker game, quaff a cold brew and hash out my problem in relative privacy."

"The Alluvian bar, John, or find another shoulder to cry on."

Kitchens gave a resigned sigh. "I suppose beggars can't be choosers," he groaned. "See you there, hard ass."

Moments later, seated at a small table in the window of the Alluvian Bar facing the red-brick-pocked Howard Street, Kitchens ordered a whiskey for his friend. "All right, Richard," he began, a hint of trepidation evident in his voice, "here it is. Don't interrupt me and just let me get it all out."

Farris sipped his drink and nodded congenially.

"I made a big loan last year. The man had impeccable credit. I made enough off that transaction to buy a new Lexis for me and a diamond ring for Sally. Thing is, I knew he had a shady background..."

"Oh?"

"All right. No getting around it. Word was he was in the Dixie Mafia. But, hey, I'd heard that about our mayor, too, and I knew that was horsepucky. So what? The only issue was whether the loan was good business. No risk to the bank, that is. God knows, the bank certainly didn't object to the loan. They wanted a few more interest-sucking millions in the kitty just like any other bank."

"Ah, yes," Farris grinned, "the American word for 'kosher' is 'profitable.' I'm with you, John. Pray, proceed."

"Right. Anyhow, it went off without a hitch. And everything's been hunky dory for the past few months. Then, well...I started reading newspaper reports about the proposed casino where the Tallahatchie and Yalobusha meet to form the Yazoo..."

"Of course. The area near old Fort Pemberton where in 1862 our local boys gave the Yankee navy an unprecedented thumping. Now they're planning to clean up again, this time at invading tourists' expense." Farris raised his hands and mimicked the headlines of a newspaper. "'The *Star of the West Still a Big Gamble,*" he snorted. "Great name for the casino. Ought to attract the Sons of Confederate Veterans and descendants of ex-slaves with equal force. Capital idea. Proceed."

"Star of the West Casino, yes. The Delta's next great tourist attraction. The directors bought the land, snatched up the permits, the legislature approved the resort status request, and the city fathers got right on board in return for a big tax bump to the school system, which, within a year, shot up to level three academic status for the first time since integration in 1971."

"Yes, yes, and the stars were shining brighter at night, too. I understand. Get on with it, John."

"Right. So anyhow, I began noticing that everyone who had tried to wreck the project, the lady who refused to sell her land at any price, the city councilmember who opposed gambling on religious grounds, even the *Commonwealth* reporter covering those stores, met with foul play. Murdered during a house burglary, run out of office due to a sex scandal based on nefarious proof, and run out of town with a libel lawsuit, respectively."

Farris sat up straight in his chair. Kitchens had garnered his full attention.

"It took me a while to put two and two together," Kitchens continued. "Then I asked the Dixie Mafia point man about it."

"You didn't."

"I did."

"John, I never really thought that anything you said would interest me more than the legs of the new waitress working here on weekends. Obviously, I was wrong. What happened next?"

"He told me in no uncertain terms that I didn't want to make any waves."

"You're not a Navy man, after all."

"Well, you know how I am. I don't like to be threatened."

"Who does? Of course, those who really hate it rarely do business with the mafia."

"I though this guy was different. He seemed like such an upstanding young man when he came in asking for the loan."

"I hope you weren't too terribly surprised by the way he turned out. Or did you honestly believe that this *particular* criminal was innocent?"

"Look, Richard, this is serious business."

"Oh, most certainly it is, now. It wasn't serious business when your patron and his fellow hoods redecorated that Victorian house with an old lady's blood, or when a few of your fellow citizens got run out of town on a rail. But when *you* discovered that your patron was responsible for it all, and *you* could be in danger from your own patron, then suddenly it became as serious as a rich uncle's heart attack."

"I'm not in any danger unless..."

"Unless what?"

"Unless I call the loan like I threatened to do."

Farris leaned back in his chair, any eyebrow arching imperiously toward the ceiling. "John, I am impressed. Such a stellar show of conscience! Such courage in the face of certain death."

"Thanks for that."

"Such remorse for sins you've committed, for innocent lives you've sacrificed in the name of lucre. Good heavens, is a date with Father Flannery in the confessional just over the horizon?"

"Richard! Please."

"What do you plan to do?"

"That's what I'm asking you! What should I do?"

"Obtain satisfactory employment, for starters. Quit loaning money to hoods. Stop denying loans to small businesspeople and farmers who seek only to earn an honest living with the sweat of their brows. Quit loaning money, period. Usury is a sin, John. Don't you own a Bible?"

Kitchens shook his head in disbelief. "Hey, I'll give up my devil when you give up yours. At least I'm not a lawyer."

Farris laughed aloud. "Well, John, that proves it."

"Proves what?"

"Proves you don't own a Bible. Or have you forgotten that when Our Lord lost his temper for the first and only time in recorded history, it was the bankers, not the lawyers, he bullwhipped out of the temple. Thus endeth the Sunday school lesson."

"Aw, cram it, Richard. Meanwhile, I need your damned advice."

Farris stretched out his long, lanky legs, placed his hands behind his head, and said, "Then I believe we should begin by discussing my fee."

"I'll buy the frigging drinks, jackass. Now get serious about helping me, here."

"You're asking me what I think you should do?"

"Of course."

"Well, to begin with, do you have a legitimate basis to call the loan? I'm sure the hoods have plenty of collateral in money, property and sold souls in high places."

"Doesn't matter. All loans for such exorbitant amounts come with clauses that give me extraordinary discretion. I could say the casino business is too big a risk in the newly depressed economy. I could publicly start connecting the dots between my "patron" and those killings, scandals and other matters, more of which would surely surface after I went public..."

"No doubt. If they've killed half as many folks as Tiger Woods has nailed sexy babes, you'll have enough people singing to fill the chorus at First Baptist Church."

"Right. The point is, there's no issue there. I can pull the plug anytime I want. Or I could simply phone the FBI and tell them what I know. Once they launched an investigation and leaked it to the press, the bank president would step in and call the loan himself. He could never hang me up for making a questionable loan in the first place, since the collateral was more solid than gold bullion. The bank president, a staunch Presbyterian, would love to order me to call that loan. He'd probably give me another raise."

"Unless he cares more about living than you do. But what if he does care, John, and won't call the loan himself? Then it's back to being up to good ole John to pull the plug and send the new version of the *Star of the West* to the bottom of the Tallahatchie. Give 'em the blizzards, Johnny!"

Kitchens wasn't certain. He swallowed his glass of Irish whiskey in one gulp.

"Well, that was easy enough," Farris said, patting his friend on the back. "I don't know what you needed me for, but I'm willing to be paid, nonetheless. I'll take a vodka martini this time, bartender."

"It's not the ethical problem that concerns me."

"So what else is new, moneylender to the mob?"

"Oh, please! You know what I mean. Earn your drinks, Richard."

"To call the loan and die or shut your mouth and live, that's the question, eh?"

"I suppose so."

"That's no issue. Call the FBI. They'll dig around, find what they need, lock up the scum bag and incinerate the key. The hoods won't know how they got wise and you'll live to make more questionable loans."

"Based upon a conversation I had with my patron, the loan obligee, which I recorded without his permission? Is that even legal? How could I be certain the FBI would act on my information even if it was? And if they did, would they tell the court they got their information from me? If the tape was legal, maybe the court would let it into evidence and the jig would be up, so to speak. My patron could say that it was all taken out of context. He'd be off the hook and he'd know who ratted him out. Before long, I'd be at the bottom of the Tallahatchie and you wouldn't have anybody to kick around on the golf course anymore."

"Ratted him out? Somebody's been watching the gangster classics on late night TV."

"Not funny, jackass. You're not any help. Pay for your own stinking drinks."

"Why, John! You know I have your best interests foremost in mind. I'm always thinking about you, John. I'm always concerned about your problems. You know I'm your buddy."

"Sure, pal. So what the hell do you think I should do about this?"

"I know precisely what you should do."

"And that is?"

Richard waved his napkin over his head. "Another round here, waiter," he announced. "Now, as I was saying, John, your problem is entirely due to your unremitting failure to consider the effect of your actions upon others."

"What in hell are you talking about?"

"Hell is precisely what I'm talking about."

Kitchens frowned. "I beg your pardon?"

"John, do you want to spend eternity roasting in the outermost circles of Hell? I'm not talking about the deeper hotter regions, where hard-core sinners like your patron, the 'obligee', eventually land. I'm referring to the lukewarm outer circles, reserved for pissant sinners like yourself."

"What in God's name are you babbling about, Richard? I need some advice here and—"

"And I've got your advice, John. Your problem is that you only seek to alleviate a symptom, and make no effort to cure the disease."

"Richard, if this is leading to another discussion of my failings as a human being, please wrap it up as quickly as possible so we can decide what to do about this loan situation."

"As you wish, John," Farris said, taking the martini glass from the waiter and savoring the first sip as if he had been served the nectar of the gods. He turned to face his increasingly impatient friend. "Your failing as a human being, as you put it, is that you're so self-centered that you've once again forgotten what's best for the people who're endangered by your patron and his thugs. This is to say nothing of society as a whole, which suffers dearly as a result of your patron's penchant for violence. It's much like your marriage, where you allowed your overwhelming desire for your secretary to disrupt an otherwise happy home—"

"You advised me to take a lover," Kitchens wailed, pounding his fist on the table in exasperation before noticing that he was drawing attention to himself and reducing his voice to a whisper. "You said adultery was inevitable, after sex within marriage became tedious."

"And so it is, John. But I never advised you to put on a public performance of Office Karma Sutra and send tickets to your wife."

"So she waltzed into the wrong place at the wrong time. What has that got to do with—"

Farris silenced him with a gesture. "Just listen to me, John. Your problem is not adultery. Your adultery is only a symptom. Besides, as a man, I certainly understand your interest in your secretary."

"I appreciate your understanding."

"You haven't quit seeing her, have you?"

"Richard!"

"Sorry. Back to your problem. The fact is, your lack of banking ethics is not precisely the problem, either."

"What do you mean, 'lack of banking ethics'? What could you possibly mean by that, Richard?"

"Excuse me, John. It's my fault, after all. I forgot that bankers don't have a code of ethics like lawyers do. On the other hand, perhaps *you've* forgotten that I'm the one who sent our loan-seeking clients to you, remember? You got the loan business and we closed the loans. Everybody was happy. It's the American way, after all."

"But I refused to offer one of your clients a risky loan and your firm quit sending me the referrals!"

"When you felt independent enough to do so, Mr. New Vice President," Farris grinned, thoroughly enjoying taking a best friend's conversational liberties. "Prior to that, however, we worked our way to the top together, didn't we ole buddy? We sent over the applicants, you made the loans. So what if they crapped out on the bank a few years down the road. We got our money, eh, pardner?"

"My job was to—"

"Your job was to stand up to me from the beginning and not make loans to those of my clients who weren't qualified to have them."

"The decision was ultimately the bank's—"

"Upon your advice. And when those loans defaulted, and every other banker's bogus loans defaulted in 2008, the whole economy deep-sixed and here we are mired in the worst recession since the 1930's. Good work, John."

Kitchens shrugged his shoulders. "I'm not to blame for the recession, Richard."

Farris leaned across the table and tapped his friend on the arm. "As a lawyer, I completely understand your shady dealings with my law firm. I profited by the agreement, myself. But letting yourself get sucked in by evil lawyers isn't the problem. It's only the symptom."

Kitchens rubbed his eyes wearily. "What are you talking about, 'symptom'? I have no idea what you're talking about."

"Why, John, even your cheating at golf is only a symptom of a larger problem."

"Cheating at golf? I don't—"

"Oh, I see you moving the ball around in the rough. Looking up in the trees and swatting the ball off a root with your ever-so-handy foot wedge. And I understand why you do it, my friend. As a competitor and fellow golfer I understand your motives perfectly well. Consequently, I understand your ultimate problem all the better."

"Okay, Richard, okay. You win. If I allow you to tell me what my 'ultimate' problem is, will you tell me what to do about this loan?"

"Certainly."

"Then lay on McDuff. I think I've had enough."

"I know, John. I know. It's difficult to face the truth, and you're taking it like a real trooper—"

"Richard!"

"Sorry. The point being that, with your secretary, your banking *ethics*, and your golf game, you were so caught up in what *you* wanted at the time, you didn't take sufficient precautions to avoid hurting others."

"And what exactly does that mean?"

"It's quite simple, really. Because of your overweening desire to gain carnal knowledge of your secretary you failed to prevent your wife from walking in on your tawdry little office scene. Much to your wife's detriment, I might add. Or, by making bogus loans you helped trash the economy in 2008 and brought about the death or ruin of several innocent lives in 2009. I'd be surprised if Father Flannery would even entertain such a confession should you care to debase yourself to the Pope's minions and purge yourself of this latest abomination."

"He already has! Heard my confession, that is."

"We'll come back to that in a moment. Meanwhile, you're only hurting yourself, John, when you cheat me in golf, robbing yourself of the joy of winning a match by the book, and improving your golfing skills in the bargain. The same goes for your success in business, when it's achieved at the loss of your now-blackened soul. Of course, you're bringing the wrath of the gods on others when you forget about the consequences flowing from your ill-gotten gains. In this case, we're talking about your patron and his ilk killing old ladies, framing honest politicians, running an ethical journalist out of town... And land sakes, John, how many honest politicians and ethical journalists did we have to lose in the first place? All of which was perfectly acceptable to you in the abstract, until you told the mob to shove it and then *your* life was on the line. Suddenly the abstract became a little too personal, too close to home. Or office, as the case may be."

"But—"

"If you fail to stop this career criminal now, you'll be an accomplice to any future crimes or murders he commits. On the other hand, turn him in to the FBI, and you'll be an informer on your very own patron. Whereupon he and his thugs will ultimately discover the betrayal and kill *you*, John. Which is in all likelihood what's really worrying you in the first place. After all, we both know you're not particularly concerned about anyone besides yourself. Tell me if I'm wrong."

"You're wrong, Richard."

"And you continue to have these problems because of your sorely deficient memory."

"My what?"

"Your deficient memory. You persist with this unacceptable behavior because you forget that this behavior is the source of all your problems. Mother nature, the great compensator, is partially to blame for this."

"What in the hell...What are you talking about, now?"

53

"Yes, nature has a way of compensating for its creature's inadequacies, John. And although you've been cheated in the memory department, Mother Nature has amply blessed you with an extraordinary capacity for rationalization."

"Sorry I asked."

"But life will cure you eventually, John. You see, you can rationalize all you want, make recalcitrance your motto if you choose, but sooner or later life will send a maelstrom like this *Godfather* reject your way, whereupon you'll find yourself teetering on the edge of the abyss. And your explanations as to how you came to be there will avail you absolutely naught."

"The abyss?"

"Yes. That's precisely where you are now, John. Leaning over the abyss, with your dick in one hand, a golf club in the other, and Vito Corleone shoving you over the edge from behind."

"I think I may throw up."

"And what you truly need in your arsenal, my friend, is the soul-saving parachute of truth!"

"No Richard, what I need right now is a life-ending cup of hemlock."

"So, now that we've isolated your problem—"

"And *you* don't have the same problem, Richard?"

"What does it matter if I have the same problem? No one's trying to kill me. Besides, I've admitted that I've sold my soul to the devil. I represent banks, businesses and insurance companies, you see. I make my living by ripping off the poor, uneducated blockheads of the world. You'll be glad to know that I do gain them some measure of revenge by padding my bills to our own insurance company and bank clients."

"Give *you* a medal."

"No, John. I neither deserve nor request a medal. For my transgressions, I deserve nothing less than a one way ticket to the outermost circles of Hell. True, my $200,000 a year salary

($350,000 prior to the market crash, thanks very much) with benefits makes my fate a great deal more palatable for the time being, but I'll eventually roast with all the other money-grubbing capitalists. You, however, have a chance to avoid my fate. And because I'm your buddy, I'm going to tell you exactly how to do it."

"Sometime this week, I hope."

Farris rubbed his bushy black beard as he downed another martini. "How's your journal coming?" he asked. "Or haven't you begun one yet?"

"My journal? Why no. I haven't started it yet. Never should have told you about it in the first place. What has that to do with—"

"I knew your idea about writing your own journal *for posterity* was just another means of preserving your solipsistic world view. I've no doubt that, unlike your grandfather and father, both honest men who kept journals that you eventually discovered, you'll utilize a journal as another forum for your numerous rationalizations and ludicrosities; a sounding board of excuses for your adulteries, client betrayals, and other mortal sins. Indubitably, such a journal would serve you in much the same way as confession serves rationalizing Catholics."

"I *am* going to throw up."

"Yes, John, just as confession allows *certain* backsliding Catholics the luxury of flushing their sins down the confessional toilet, so too could you wipe your sins away within the pages of your journal; flushing them down the sewer of your memory, washing them away in a stream of black and blue ink. Not unlike a constipated man voiding his gut with a double dosage of chocolate Ex-Lax— quick, simple, and relatively painless."

"You Episcopalians are jealous of the fact that we Catholics give more credence to sacramental rites than you do. You should try a little confession now and then, Richard. It's good for the... Oh, I forgot, you don't have a soul, do you, Mr. Lawyer."

"Yes, I do," Farris sniffed, "albeit a blackened one. As for confession, Episcopalians and other agnostics need no sacramental rights. Besides, I must object; the issue is irrelevant. You're not really a Catholic. You only joined that church to placate your wife and avoid wearing a suit to church every Sunday."

"That's not—"

"And stop attempting to change the subject or you'll end up stranded in the outermost circles of hell."

"Right. I forgot."

"But of course! Your bad memory rearing its lobotomized head! However, because I'm your pal, John, and because I have less chance of beating you at golf so long as you cheat, I'm going to help you solve your problem. I'm going to provide you with that parachute of truth that will break your fall into the abyss. A proper journal is precisely what you need. Let's call it... *The Book of Sin*! A written record of all your mortal and venal sins, a constant reminder of how short you fall from the ideals taught you in your youth."

"Oh, please!"

"Trust me, John, the *Book of Sin* will prove the panacea for your many problems. Problems, I might add, which will ultimately land you in the outermost circles of hell, where the flames are not so hot, but burn continuously, throughout eternity."

"Why the outer circles of Hell, Richard? Why not the fiery center, if I'm such a poor excuse for a man?"

Farris grinned wickedly as he fingered the dark bristles hanging from the tip of his chin. "Oh, that pitiful memory of yours, John! I've already answered that question, remember? Your sins are not of the magnitude of Mr. Corleone's. You don't murder people, remember? You don't even sell them dilapidated used cars for a living or ghost write celebrity novels. You merely fail to live up to the standards you set for yourself— competent banker, faithful husband, honest man, fair-minded sportsman, and so on. It's my greatest hope that you'll honestly and faithfully record your sins in this new journal I'm going to bequeath you, which is specifically created for that purpose. And while you do so, you may come to see rationalization for the odious escape valve that it is. You'll recognize the error of your ways, take steps to avoid future sins, appease your wrathful God, and avoid spending eternity in the outermost circles of Hell."

"I thought you didn't believe in God or Hell?"

"*I* don't. *You* do."

"I do?"

"Yes. And that's the essential distinction between us. You see, I'm aware of my sins, but have no intention of making contrition. I'm content to earn my two-hundred grand a year, and spend eternity in the outermost circles of Hell. And since I don't really believe in Hell in the first place, I may get off Scott free after all. But not you, John. Your parents taught you to believe that you should rise above the lust, greed, and other evils of the world. Your father was, despite his choice of the legal profession, an honest man. Your grandfather, Eugene the planter/statesman, possibly even more so. So I'm going to give you what you need to accomplish the goals they once set for you— your very own *Book of Sin.*"

"Thanks a lot, *pal*. Now, what about the matter we came here to discuss? This "symptom," as you call it, wherein my 'patron' is threatening to kill me? What about that little problem, Richard?"

"Why, turn the bastard in, of course. Quite obviously, your tragic death at the hands of your 'patron', prior to entrusting your soul to me and my Book of Sin, would land you in—"

"The outermost circles of Hell. I know."

"And you'll be there all alone, John, until I join you in another thirty or forty years."

"What, no chance to save yourself?"

"No, John. Even if lust, greed, sloth, and all the other Seven Deadly Sins aren't enough to land me in Hell, I'll be consigned there because you came to me for guidance and I failed to take the necessary steps to cleanse your blackened soul before you met your ignominious end at the hands of a wanna-be star of the *Godfather* movies. Don't drag me down to hell with you, John. Turn Vito in to the police, give the FBI what they live for, stop the shedding of innocent blood, and utilize the *Book of Sin* to your advantage. And buy me another drink."

"So you're saying I should call the FBI, give them my tape, and blow the whole casino scheme sky high? You believe they'll issue a warrant for him merely on my say so?"

"I believe I've already answered that question, John. Why do we always end up talking about you and your problems? Why, John, why?"

KAFKA IN REVERSE

The first three hearings had come off without a hitch. Brief, to the point and with perfectly acceptable resolutions. I thought another fine day was in the offing. I was wrong, of course, but that's getting ahead of myself and no way to tell this story. Let me tell you the whole story the way it actually happened, and then I'll ask you a question that you, a taxpayer, are amply qualified to answer. Okay?

Why not, eh? It's a fine day here in the Cotton Capital of the World, there's a gentle spring breeze wafting along the Yazoo River, we can smell the Magnolia blossoms blooming on both banks of the river, and our vantage here on Old Keesler Bridge affords us a lovely view of the river, the greenest landscape this side of Ireland, our magnificent old marble courthouse and the lovely turn-of-the-century mansions lining pulchritudinous River Road. So what do you say? A good day for a story you'll never forget?

Fine! Excellent choice. It happened exactly like this...

The first claimant, an elderly black gentleman who couldn't write his name but had labored over forty years pulling a plow then driving a tractor as a sharecropper on a farm just outside of Money, Mississippi, had injured his back wrenching his truck's wheel from the mud. Obviously suffering radicular pain down his left leg during the hearing, his X-rays had shown disk herniation at two levels. Since he was over fifty years old and illiterate he was disabled under Social Security regulations as a matter of law. I issued a bench decision in his favor fifteen minutes into the hearing.

The second claimant, a young Cajun lad, had been shot twice in the leg in a barroom scuffle and fired off his job for failure to show up the next day. Under the auspices of New Orleans' Charity Hospital he made a complete recovery in two months, moved to the Delta and took a job selling used cars. The bottom dropped out of the market and they laid him off. Faced with few prospects for employment he decided to try to cop a free ride at the tax payers' expense. No lawyer would represent him and his case had gone south when our examining doctor found he could lift one hundred pounds without raising a sweat. Then the doc peered through his window after the examination and saw the claimant bouncing across the parking lot and tossing his cane in the back of his Camero while chasing down a passing ice cream truck to buy an ice cream bar. Or so the doc reported. The claimant didn't deny any of this at the hearing and everybody knew where he stood halfway through the hearing. We had a congenial hearing, mostly because I could rarely fathom his Cajun accent, and he was a very good sport about it. Then, at the end, I asked him how he managed to get shot twice in one leg, and he said with a perfectly straight face, "Well, judge, you don't ever go to a gun fight armed with a stick, no."

The third hearing was the easiest of the bunch. The man's psychiatric record indicated diagnoses of schizophrenia and psychosis, and his inability to answer simple questions at the hearing confirmed what our doctors had already determined, that he was incapable of functioning adequately in the workplace. I rendered a favorable bench decision on the spot. His wife cried when she thanked me for my decision, and I don't mind telling you I was feeling pretty good about myself at that moment. Helping the disabled in troubled economic times, while looking out for the taxpayers interests whenever the circumstances required it. Who could ask for a more rewarding job than that, eh?

Well, don't congratulate me yet, my friend. Not 'till you've heard what Paul Harvey always termed 'the rest of the story.'

As I was saying, I'd enjoyed a fine spring morning that should have only gotten better. Four short morning hearings, then lunch at the Crystal Grill, maybe a gumbo appetizer, a broiled Gulf snapper entree, and for dessert, lemon ice box pie with meringue piled on so high you couldn't see the person seated across the table from you.

Only I had forgotten that my clerk had filled the last morning slot with an older case I had been hoping to put off indefinitely. As a consequence of my failure, *she* was coming before me.

Mind you, I can't tell you her name because that would violate our ethical requirement of keeping all personal information confidential. Big problems all around if you violate that one, my friend.

Can't describe her either, in case anyone should make the connection and fathom her identity. You understand my dilemma, I'm sure.

Anyhow, what follows is the story about how I came to be standing here on Old Keesler Bridge, spilling this tale to you, gazing out over the gently rolling Yazoo River meandering its way through downtown Greenwood, wondering whether or not I really want to remain among the living.

That's right. You heard me. But don't let me prejudice you about the story before you've heard it. I want you to give me an unbiased answer to my question after I tell you the story. Okay? Fine.

So anyhow, *she* saunters in…Oh, I forgot to say that I had heard her case twice before, denied her both times, got reversed both times, and she was back before me for the third time. The first decision got reversed because I supposedly didn't fully consider her own doctor's opinions. Opinions I well knew had been purchased by the claimant as were any opinions ever given out by those white-coated charlatans. Everybody around town knows those doctors are bogus, but of course there was nothing in the record to prove that, nor could there ever be short of a federal fraud investigation where somebody in their clinic got nervous and shot off their mouth. That's not going to happen, I assure you. These docs didn't fall off the snap bean truck yesterday and they're far too attached to the yachts, fancy German cars, mansions on Grand Boulevard and good looking nurses jumping their bones to make stupid mistakes like that.

The second reversal occurred largely because the transcript to the hearing didn't transfer properly to the computer, leaving us with no record of the hearing, in which case reversals are mandatory, as they should be. But just my luck, huh?

Now the time had come for round three.

Anyhow, here's how it went the third time around. You've heard the third time's the charm, right? Well, that's as close to reality as anything else I learned in high school, law school, Sunday school or any other school other than the one of hard knocks.

But I digress.

She saunters in, plops down in a chair directly across from my bench, looks me in the eye and licks her lips. That's right, you heard me. Licks her lips! She knows that I've read our examining psychologists' reports about her offering them blow jobs for favorable reports. She's messing with my head, you understand.

I ignore the lip-licking and take one last look at a new exhibit that my clerk had filed in another related case earlier that morning. To my stunned surprise, it was a Report of Contact with this very claimant. It had originally been filed in her brother's case, with whom she lived and who was also filing a separate case for disability, just as their mother, father and three other siblings had already done. The government case worker had phoned their house looking for her brother to get an update on his condition. This claimant, my nemesis, had answered the phone, and when asked how her brother was doing, she said, "Aw, he's doin' great. He's out in the back yard right now humpin' the family dog."

You heard me. Believe-you-me, that's nothing for her. The basic MO for my one-of-a-kind claimant. I didn't know whether to laugh out loud or sob silently, so I just attached the Report of Contact to her record and convened the hearing.

"Let's come to order," I announced. "This is the hearing of _____, Social Security number _____, Title 2 & 16 claims for Social Security benefits. Present today with me and the claimant are the court reporter and the vocational expert. The claimant is unrepresented. I know you know your rights to an attorney by now, Ms. ____." I told her. "Is it your wish to proceed without one or do you desire a continuance?"

Now, you can't blame me for trying, can you? Who knows? If she asked for a continuance one of us could die before the case came back up for hearing.

"That's funny, judge," said the claimant, her voice dripping with sarcasm. "You know no one around here goan' represent me. Them white lawyers is all racists and them nigger lawyers don't know shit."

"Ms.___, please," I admonished. "I'm going to have to ask you to refrain from using that kind of language in my court. If you can't do so, I'll have to conclude the hearing at this point." Not that I wasn't offended by her disrespectful language, but I had an ulterior motive in threatening to end the hearing. I had to make this one last attempt, you understand? God help me, I was desperate and growing more so by the second.

"That's okay, judge," she replied casually. "Don't mind me. I knows how you white folks does. Doin' it's okay, believin' it be fine, but sayin' it out loud jus' won't do. Let's get this done."

"I'll take that as confirmation that we're in agreement about the improper language," I said authoritatively. "Alright, Ms. ____, raise your right hand. Do you swear or affirm to tell the truth, the whole truth, and nothing but the truth, so help you God?"

"Not that you believe me, judge, but I sho' do. In fact, let's just get this over with so I can get on home and get to bed where I belongs."

"Very well. I'll dispense with all the preliminaries. This is your third time before me and I think you know the procedures quite well."

"I sho' do know the pro-ce-dures well," she snorted. "The gub'ment doctors lie like a rug but you buy their line like they wuz the Gospel. You ignores the only doctors who treated me for three years and turn me down faster than George Bush dumped on the folks in New Orleans after Katrina blowed 'em away. And you goes home and has a hot toddy and feels good about yo'sef. I appeals the case and they grants my appeal jus' like before. But the next time I gets me a new judge."

She crossed her arms triumphantly and bared her teeth in a wicked, malevolent grin. "That's right," she crowed. "I knows this the last time I gots to see yo' smilin' face, Mr. high and mighty judge. So let's get on with it, like you say."

She was right of course. The original judge gets three bites at the apple and if the case is reversed a third time, another judge is assigned that claimant's case, and so on, *ad infinitum*, until the claimant gets hit by a bus or a bleeding heart judge pays the claim. And your tax dollars fund that circus my good fellow. How do you feel about that, eh?

Oh, I know we judges help disabled people every day. Like the people who work hard all their lives, hurt themselves on the job and get shafted by their employer. You know, the company doc says there's nothing wrong with them so the Worker's Comp judge denies their claim. Even if they win the amounts are so low in Mississippi that it almost amounts to nothing either way. Or in case of some terrible disease like cancer, AIDS or leukemia, the poor souls can't afford the treatments or surgery or medications and would probably die if not for Social Security and Medicare benefits. But there's a dark side of American charity, my friend. And don't you ever forget it.

But...Back to my story.

"Very well," I said. "What's wrong with you, Ms. _____? What physical or mental impairments...ailments that you suffer, prevent you from working?"

"You knows as well as I do what they is. Why I got to go through all this, all them lying psycho-lo-gists and this joke of a hearing to get my check? That jus' ain't right!"

"I see that you refused to attend the recent consultative examinations with our psychologist and internal medicine physician. Would you care to explain why you didn't attend those exams?"

"Sho' would. They ain't nothin' but a damn lie and I ain't goan' waste my time."

"And you haven't submitted any new medical records since your last hearing. Do you have any new medical records you'd like to submit, Ms. _____?"

"What the hell for?" she asked angrily. "You ain't believed my docs the last time even though they the only ones that seen me for three damn years. So what I'm goan' pay more money for somethin' you ain't even goan' read?"

"I always read every document in the record, Ms. _____. I'd send out another subpoena but *your physicians* haven't responded to any of the previous ones."

"If you pays my doctors the same money as you pays yo' lying gub'ment doctors you'll get anything you want. I ain't got no job, no money and no chance with a judge like you."

"Very well," I blurted, too weary by this point to disguise the disgust in my voice. "What are your impairments, for the record, Ms. _____?"

"My memory ain't worth two cents, judge. I can't remember my own name some days. My back hurts. I got the coppertone, too."

The court reporter cast a uncomprehending glare in my direction. "The what?" she asked. "What did she say?"

"Carpal tunnel syndrome," I explained. "Anything else, Ms. _____?"

"Ain't that enough, judge? I can't walk half a block because of the gouch—"

I saw the court reporter's perplexed expression out of the corner of my eye, turned to her and mouthed, "Gout." She nodded her thanks and continued typing.

"—I can't lift a gallon of milk with my coppertone hands," the claimant continued, "and can't remember where the bathroom beez half the time. I'm depressed, too. You would be, too, yo' 'onry, if you wuz messed up like me."

I'm depressed as hell, I thought, but didn't say it on the record. Why make things worse than they already were?

"I understand some of our doctors believe that your memory problems have to do more with excessive drinking than mental disease, and that you showed up for an examination last year smelling of alcohol, stumbling around and even falling on your face in the doctor's office."

"I always stumbles around 'cause my back be hurtin' me. With my bad memory I forgot where the chair was and busted my butt. I done tole you that the last time you axed me. But my memory be so bad I jus' don't recall for sho'."

"You deny that you drink daily?"

"Hell, yeah I denies it," she growled. "I ran outa' money and the liquor run out, too."

"I thought your brother bought the liquor."

"He disabled now, too. When he run out of money his liquor dried up quicker than mine."

"Didn't you find other ways to get the whiskey?"

She frowned and shook her head testily before she spoke. "I ain't no hooker, if that's what you means. Not no mo'. Not since my back went out. And my memory bad, too. You ever try to do somethin' with somebody and forgot where everything go? That ain't no way to make whoopee. I ain't lyin', judge."

"Thank you for that, Ms. _____. Now..."

"Besides," she added flippantly, "when you lives with a drunk, you gots to drink, 'cuz if you don't, you gots to kill him!"

"I see. What about your activities of daily living? Do you read anything? Books, newspapers, magazines?"

"I reads my Bible."

"Does *your* Bible contain the Ten Commandments?" I asked, my voice bereft of emotion.

"You knows damn well it do."

"Doesn't one of those Commandments condemn bearing false witness?"

"Smart ass judge," she whispered.

"What was that, Ms. _____?"

"Nothin' judge," she replied in her most polite voice. "I wuz just mumblin' is all. I does that a lot since my memory went and I got all depressed. Talks to mysef' every day. Chatterin' on like a fool, and the only thing good about it is that my memory be so bad I forget half the crazy shit I be saying."

"Can you make a telephone call?"

"Ain't got no phone," she nodded. "Phone comp'ny turned it off 'cause I ain't got no money, thanks to you. 'Sides, my mind too messed up to dial a phone right now."

"Do you watch television?"

"Sho' do. Watches them judge shows all day long. They treats folks with respect, unlike some judges I knows. They...Oops..."

My friend, I don't suppose I really need to say it, but at precisely this moment the cell phone in her purse rang out with

67

the shrillest, most obnoxious noise I've ever heard. She continued to stare at me as if nothing had happened.

"Can you silence that phone," I commanded, "or do I need to ask the security guard to take it up?"

She waited for her phone to stop ringing then took it from her purse and appeared to turn it off.

"Thank you," I said taking care not to overplay the sarcasm. "Do you fish or hunt, or engage in any outside activities?"

"I fishes some. If I don't catch nothin' I don't eat. But huntin'?" She laughed at said, "ain't no huntin' goin' on 'round here. These fools callin' theyselves huntin' ain't huntin', they ambushin'. Hidin' behind a tree till a deer come 'round and ambush it with a elephant gun. Huntin' my sweet ass."

"Ahem. What else do you do during the day, Ms. ____?"

"I lays on my couch and waits for my disability check. That's what I be doin' all day, every day. You be doin' it to if you broke down like me. Down in yo' back, mind half gone, hands all crippled up...And flat broke besides."

"Do you smoke?"

"Sho' do. Calms my nerves."

"But you can't afford the liquor?"

"Naw. Jus' beer. Ain't got no money and can't afford to buy vodka no mo'. It's done got high as a'... Wait? What you axe me?"

"Never mind. I'm just wondering how you can't afford your medications, as you've asserted in the past, but nevertheless come up with the funds for smokes and beer."

"Yeah, yeah, yeah," she scowled, "you plenty smart, judge. You ought to be on TV, too. Makin' a poor, sick woman who don't know what day it beez sound like a fool in court. I hope you proud of yo'sef'."

"So what do you do," I said ignoring her remark, "when you're not waiting on your disability check?"

"Can't do nothin' else."

"Very well." Then I turned to the government vocational expert also seated at the witness table. "Thank you, Ms. ____. Now, Mr. Vocational Expert, I've got two questions for you."

"Yes, your honor?"

"If a hypothetical individual with an eighth grade education, age range of 25 to 30 years old, with the same work history as the claimant, could perform a full range of light work, would that individual be able to perform the claimant's past relevant work as a cashier?"

"They would, your honor," the expert replied. "The cashier is a light exertional job with an SVP of 3, semiskilled work."

"Hypothetical number two. If in addition to the limitations given in hypothetical one, suppose that an individual, because of mental impairments, was limited to performing simple repetitive tasks and could not work around the general public more than on an occasional basis, and could perform no high stress production pace work. Would that individual be able to perform the claimant's past relevant work or any other work in the national economy?"

"The past relevant work, no," he replied, "as that requires interaction with the general public on more than an occasional basis. However, that hypothetical individual could perform other jobs in the national economy. These would include a parts and accessories packager, sedentary exertional level and unskilled with an SVP of one, unskilled, with over a million jobs in the national economy and over a thousand in the local economy; and a stringer, that's someone who strings beads or other such items, light exertional level and unskilled with the same SVP, with over 200,000 jobs in the national economy and 500 in the local economy. This is consistent with the information found in the Directory of Occupational Titles."

"Thank you, sir. Ms. ____, do you have any questions for the expert witness?"

"Sho' do, judge," she declared, sitting up straight in her seat, glaring menacingly at the expert. "So tell me, Mr. Expert, you sayin' that someone like me with no schoolin' to speak of and a weak mind that ain't half right can work all day long?"

"The jobs I've cited, yes, ma'am. They exist at the lowest level of unskilled work and require little or no education."

"So what you sayin' is that a trained hyena could do those jobs?"

"Not just any hyena," the expert replied with absolutely no hint of emotion. "It would require a very motivated hyena."

I can tell you, my friend, and for the first time since she had sauntered in, I gave a broad smile at that particular juncture.

"Ahem," I finally managed. "Any *other* questions for the expert, Ms. ____?"

"Yeah. I got one. Is they any chance, mister expert, that you is ever gonna know yo' ass from a hole in the ground?"

"All right," I said firmly. "I think that wraps up the vocational expert part of this hearing. Do you have anything else to offer, Ms. ____?"

"What difference do it make? You ain't goan' pay me a damn thing today no matter what I says. You knows it and I knows it."

"Well, Ms. ____, for one thing, you filed a Title 16 claim with an alleged onset of disability date of April 1, 2002, but didn't file your petition until July 15, 2007, so I can't possibly pay that claim until July 2007, as per our regulations, which clearly state that the earliest date a Title 16 claim may be paid is the date of filing of the application. And as for your Title 2 claim, and the Title 16 as well, you were in prison from 2005 to February 19, 2008, and as you well know, you can't receive benefits while you're in prison, so with your continued refusal to amend your onset date to February 20, 2008, the day after you were released from prison, I couldn't pay you today on either application even if I were inclined to do so."

For the first time during the hearing her face brightened noticeably. "You means to tell me," she said, "that if I amends my onset date to February of last year you goan' pay me today?"

"No," I countered, "that's not what I'm saying. I was merely answering your question about why I can't pay you today in light of current onset date of disability. If there's nothing further, this hearing is adjourned."

And that was that, my friend. Witness excused, hearing ended and record closed.

Except for the seemingly endless stream of expletives she heaped upon me during her rousing exit from my courtroom. Before the day was out I received a call from the home office saying that she had filed a complaint against me for being, and I quote, "a racist, incompetent, prejudiced, smart ass, and a damned lie!"

So now I'll likely be summoned to Washington to answer those charges and fall farther behind with my caseload I already am. With fifty cases set every month and hundreds more claimants filing petitions every day, it never ends, believe you me. Meanwhile, her case will be assigned to another judge from another region outside the Delta who'll read the record, likely accord substantial weight to the opinions of her treating physicians, and pay the claim without giving it another thought.

So here I am standing on the walkway of Old Keesler Bridge, looking out over the Yazoo River, wondering if I ought to jump.

Hell, you're a taxpayer! You're paying the freight for this nonsense. Your opinion ought to count for something. Do *you* think I should jump?"

Without a moment's hesitation, the man who had stood beside the judge on the walkway of Old Kessler Bridge, listening patiently to the judge's sordid story, calmly stepped over the concrete rail on the outermost edge of Old Keesler Bridge, perched himself on the iron beam running just below the old concrete structure's frame, and launched himself into space, plummeting headlong into the swirling muddy waters below. They swallowed him whole before the judge could utter a sound, then rushed silently over him, sweeping away the ripples he had made as if he had never been there at all.

OLD TIMES NOT FORGOTTEN

December 21, 1917— Tucker Henry phones me with news that Mother is dying. Have been busy for several days with soldier boy's Questionnaires. A crowd in office at 12:30 PM when message gotten. Left office, went home, shaved, clothes pressed. Sharecropper Brooks packed grip. Left Leland on horseback at 2 P.M. Reached Greenville at 3 P.M. Caught train to Gloster. Reached Gloster at 9:30 P.M. Found Mother conscious, but very ill with Bright's Disease. She knows me, but too sick to talk. Brother Howard reached her at 8 A.M. when she was first stricken. Dr. Featherston been here twice today. Dear Mother says she is willing to go, if it is God's will, but would like to live longer to be with Papa and the children. We hope and pray God's will may be to spare her. To bed at One P.M. Did not sleep. Mother, oh, Mother, why do you have to suffer so?

CHRISTMAS
Tuesday, December 25th, 1917—
Mother seemed conscious until about 6 A.M. Then breath gets long and she passes away into the Great Beyond "Across the Bar." Just about four hours before death she says "Dear Jesus I am piercing the guilt which all must pierce, and the stars are what we make them. Dear Jesus, I am coming home, not my will but thine."

Mama's death occurs at 9:40 A.M. I went to Summit to get hearse, shroud, and casket. Phoned Bro. Dezell to come and preach funeral. Mother to be buried in white according to her expressed wish. Monday afternoon she told sister Evelyn not to leave her tonight, that it would be her last night on Earth before she crossed over, and to keep her clean.

She was such a good mother. Oh that I had known six weeks ago when I was home that I would never see her alive and well again. Yet I rejoice for all the good things she has said and written me. Would to God that I had kept her letters for the past few months.

Casket arrives and mother dressed and placed in it and placed in front of parlor room. Poor sister Evelyn, it's so hard for her and me, all try to bear up. We give away at times, but try to be brave. When I stop to think of the larger life mother has entered I cannot weep, yet it is so hard when I think I shall never see her again on this Earth.

Wednesday, December 26, 1917—
Mother's funeral held in Mars-Hill Church. Sermon by Rev. Dezell of McComb First Methodist. Read 90th Psalm. 15th Chapter, 1st Corinthians 1 to 20. Subject "If a man die, shall he live again? I am the resurrection and the life." Treated in a scientific, spiritual, and human way, and was best sermon I have ever heard at any funeral.

Songs sung:
1. *What a Friend We Have in Jesus,*
2. *Nearer My God to Thee,*
3. *Asleep in Jesus,* and
4. *In the Sweet Bye and Bye.*

I never saw a prettier corpse, and it seemed so much like she should speak. So white, so clean, so pure, so sweet she looked. Oh, God, help me hereafter to keep my body and life as free from evil as she has always been in life, and grant that her spirit may direct me in all my paths. Lead me, Oh God, through Jesus to the pure life and a home in heaven where I shall never be parted from Mother.

Hard for us all. Sister Evelyn so nervous, but takes it better than yesterday. Church full of folk and every one seems so much concerned and sympathetic. Would love to give up my law practice and just be a farmer back here with them again.

Spent afternoon at mother's home with folk. Evelyn and Howard went home in P.M. Got horse from Jack Criss' stable at 5 P.M., left for train station. Got off at Leland Station at 10:30 P.M. Sent check for funeral expense to E.M.F.- $81.52.

More Army Draft Questionnaires for sharecroppers to fill out. Oh Lord help me to do my duty faithfully and as it should be done. These poor negroes—how sorry I feel for them. They have no conception of what it means. Lots of poor whites here tonight, too. They are as much in the dark as negroes. Much to do this afternoon.

Friday, December 28, 1917 —
George Brooks, one of my sharecroppers, sent to jail without bond for killing Alex Love in alleged gambling dispute. Family hired me to represent him. Went to Greenville in P.M. to see Brooks. Will be difficult case to defend, as two witnesses claim to have seen him with Love immediately prior to shooting. He proclaims innocence, however. Back in office at 3:00. More Army Questionnaires. Oh but how these Q's do make you work. I'm sorry for these people, but wish I could catch up.

Today was the day I always had a letter from Mother, but those letters will come no more forever. My spirit though, can go to her and commune. Oh that I could see her today. Found her letter written in 1910. Mother angry with Theodore Bilbo for slurring my name in Iuka. Bilbo had accused me and other legislators of stealing senatorial election from Gov. Vardaman. Vardaman not worthy of serving in place of Senator Percy, and I had told Bilbo as much to his face. They wanted to prevent negroes from having any education, and eventually succeeded despite all Sen. Percy's efforts to the contrary. Papa angry about Bilbo's slurs and had told Bilbo that if he was found in Tishomingo County after dark, it would be the last time. No other letters found.

Sunday, December 30, 1917—

Went to church with cousin Hattie Davies. Met Miss May Rainey and believe that this was not a coincidence. Miss Rainey reminds me of mother in many ways. So kind of cousin Hattie to think of me at this time. Made date with May to go to the moving pictures Wednesday night. Am looking forward to that evening.

Monday December 31, 1917—

New Chancery Clerk Taylor refused to accept McKinney deed because it did not contain all appurtenances thereto belonging. Thinks he is a lawyer. Knows nothing of law other than requirement of land to convey. Rewrote deed to please smart hillbilly court clerk. Would rather deal with man who knows law or one who doesn't make any pretense of knowing. Taylor is a worse pest than the Army Q's; but guess he is to be excused. Teach me, Oh Lord, to have patience. Am afraid I offended Taylor when I likened him to a monkey in three-piece suit. Also, help me not to be cross with poor negroes and their Questionnaire problems, when they ask me, "What did you say, Boss? What did you say this means?" Etc. Oh Lord! We must educate these people quickly, or our children's children will pay for our shortsightedness.

Posted Brooks' bail and brought him back from Greenville in my car. Brooks very fond of my new Empire automobile. Explained upcoming legal hearings to Brooks, and he seemed to understand. He continues to assert his innocence. Says that one Jethro Jones killed Alex Love. Says Jones has murder weapon, a new Colt .45 of which Jones is quite fond and with which he will never part.

Told Brooks that even if murder weapon still around, we couldn't get sheriff to search Jones's house without proof. Two other poker players say that Brooks was only other player in game which led to shooting. Brooks says they are good friends of Jones, and will not make good liars. Brooks is very convincing, but I am concerned that no jury will believe him.

Tuesday, January 1, 1918—
More Army Draft Questionnaires all day. Planters could help, but send all their sharecroppers to lawyers for help filling out Q's. Nonetheless, I am sorry for these poor, ignorant sharecroppers. Many planters take proceeds from season end crop sales and don't share with their croppers at all. Say "they'll just get drunk and spend it. They don't know the difference anyway." These planters forget that God knows. They remind me of those who argue that slavery was most Christian method of dealing with negroes. I understand planters thinking that poor sharecroppers and I are stupid, but cannot fathom how they expect to take God for a fool who believes their lies.

Did some work. Wrote deed of trust for Billy Saylor. Fee $5.00. Got $50 fee for abstract of title to Paul Sullivan's land. Judges and lawyers at courthouse express sympathy for Mother.

Baptist Deacon Ben Hurd ringleader among those who called a meeting at County Courthouse today to discuss passing local resolutions against lawful liquor sales. I listened to Hurd's lengthy 'sermon' about evils of alcohol, but when he called on me to testify, I said that, although I rarely partake, I understand that others do and whisky is legal product, and I did not see how the trade could be ended even if resolution passed. He got angry with me when I told him a good start to ridding Washington County of liquor would be for him to unload all the contraband whiskey in his hall closet. Don't think he will be asking for my testimony again, or hiring me to close any more loans for First Baptist Church members. Am sorry for that, but cannot take part in such hypocrisy even though I believe whiskey does more harm than good.

Took Miss Rainey to movies and believe I am falling in love with the "Little Teacher." Wouldn't it be romantic if she would allow it?

Wednesday, April 24, 1918—
More Q's all day. This war, like these times in general, is terribly hard on these poor sharecroppers. Herman Moeller cheats his sharecroppers, makes them live in shacks not fit for animals, then sends them to me, complaining about losing them to fight in a war we shouldn't be in. *Shame!* Met him on sidewalk today and he said he wanted to let bygones go. Told him yes, but never do his pro-German talk around me or our Barber Shop scrap of last April would only be a breeze beside the cyclone that would be started. Am glad to have this fool thing off my mind, as I know Moeller to be a cheat and a crank and might have had to hurt him. Must believe the many decent hard-working German families here are as put out with him as I.

Prepared abstract and deed of trust for Mrs. Horton. Fee— $25, two chickens and three of her special pecan pies.

Had a preliminary hearing for Brooks at 1:00 in Greenville. Prosecution has a lead pipe cinch case. Told Brooks to consider entering a plea of guilty. He refused, insisting on his innocence. Says I must find Jones's pistol. Am afraid nothing will save this innocent man from the gallows. To church at night. Prayed for Brooks. He and his family have worked my land for better part of 15 years. Must find some way to spare him punishment for crime he didn't commit, but cause seems hopeless. Miss my letters from Mother which will come no more.

Thursday, April 25, 1918—
No work today. Took May Rainey to pictures. Saw Mary Pickford in *Poor Little Rich Girl.* Made fool of myself making love to May. Took her to Deer Creek in buggy. Horse caught foot in reign and pulled bridle off. Had a time with that!

Friday, April 26, 1918—
In court all day. Represented Italians opposing state's attempts to take their land in south of county with eminent domain proceedings. They are hardest working citizens in the Delta and fine people besides. Will see that they get fair shake, if at all possible.

Went to pictures with May and Miss Hood in PM. War pictures make me want to get into the fray, despite my 37 years. Miss Hood told me I had overplayed with May and made fool of myself. Slept none.

Saturday, April 27, 1918—
Went with Misses Coolie, Hood, and Rainey to the Hood family cabin on Lake Ferguson. Car gave trouble with valve in carburetor and backfired all the way. Reached lake at 7:30 AM. May caught two perch and I caught three bass. We had jolly time and left at 3:00 PM. Tire blew out, and I bought new tube for $7.20. May and I some worn out.

Sunday, April 29, 1918—
Called May at 7 AM and she wanted to sleep more, so went on to breakfast. Took May to West Point on 8:15 train. Caught Southern at 1:45 to Mathiston. Rode with several girls leaving Blue Mountain College. Floyce, the fleshy 17 year old was full of fun. Played ukulele at depot and took collection. Also said she had drunk 9 Cokes. Was funny to watch the girls' excitement as each reached their particular town.

May proved to be different from the other girls, and was asking me not to spend money. I like her pep, her emotion, her deep sense of right, her pure and innocent nature, her fire, her Christian spirit and ideals. A true woman. Am fortunate to be in the running for her hand.

Found a message from Brooks' uncle on door when I returned home. Brooks not doing well in jail. Wants to see me Monday. Brooks has good reason to be concerned. Will talk to him and Uncle Ned tomorrow. Slept little.

Thursday, June 27, 1918—

Argued Koury case before jury in county court and lost. Also lost will be about $200 which I will have to pay for costs of court. Losing this case has made me more determined to win hereafter. Don't want to be like lawyer Brown who never prepares. During murder case in Greenwood, Brown called his first witness, one Hunter Cole, twice, before someone in gallery spoke up and said that Cole was the deceased.

Won James Cade's case against oil works, getting $250 for his loss of arm. This was 10th case disposed of this term, and all won except Koury fire suit. This meant great deal to me in developing self-dependence and self-consciousness.

Back here writing letters at 5 P.M. Went to show at night with May. Saw Mary Pickford in *How Could You, Jean*. Mother dead six months.

Friday, June 28, 1918—

In afternoon, May and I went to Iuka to visit her folks. May was very sweet to me, and candid as all lovers should be. No other girl would have been, and I think so much more of her for being so.

Saturday, June 29, 1918—

May is pretty as a peach and sweet and dear to me. These people are feeding me too high. I like their way of living. May and I discussed asking her father, the doctor, the big question, but I didn't. Back to Leland by 10:00 P.M.

Sunday, June 30, 1918—
Wrote May. To church in A.M. Had interesting visit from Brooks and his Uncle Ned, in afternoon. Uncle says he has seen Jethro Jones with Colt .45 murder weapon while on hunting trip last week. Called Sheriff Odom and went to Jones' house. Pistol not found. Uncle says he keeps it buried under outhouse, but Sheriff not willing to dig there. Sheriff a little angry with me for leading him on wild goose chase.

Uncle and I agreed to meet later to figure out solution to this problem. Case is set in August. Told Uncle that Brooks's case hopeless unless Jones's pistol located. Pistol probably moved or hidden elsewhere, by now. Am deeply concerned about this case. Brooks has wife and three children. But what can be done to avert this travesty?

Monday, July 6, 1918—
Paid for Mama's tomb- $210. While I think the other children might have helped, I am glad to do it in memory of the dearest mother who ever lived. She did so much for me. Help me, Oh Father of the universe, to shape my life in conformity with Thy will and mother's desires. To pictures at night. Letter from May.

Tuesday, July 7, 1918—
Nothing unusual in AM. May got to Leland at 4:00 PM. I was working in garden and she came out to be companionable. I talked to her too rough about getting out of my hoe's way, etc. Made her mad and she took a cry and at supper accused me of being "neither polite nor having common manners." I kept my tongue, but was awfully hurt. Afterwards I came to the conclusion that she was right about what I had said and done. I admire her spirit in speaking out, after all.

Wednesday, July 8, 1918—
Strange day! Brooks stole my Empire automobile from parking lot of Presbyterian Church during evening service. Called Sheriff and reported theft. Spoke to Brooks' wife, who was ashamed and frightened, especially since I had put up the money for her husband's bail. She told the Sheriff that Brooks had probably gone to Minter City, just 15 miles north of Greenwood, where his other uncle lived. Called Lester Shipley, the Greenwood sheriff, who met us at the Brooks place on Wells plantation. My car was parked in shed, and Brooks surrendered after seeing me with Sheriff Shipley.

Refused to press charges against Brooks and convinced authorities in Greenville to once more release him into my custody. Sheriff Odom says I am crazy, but whole thing is my fault for telling Brooks his case is hopeless. Told Brooks that his uncle and I will think of something, but please don't steal my car again. Brooks' wife assured me there would be no more trouble.

Thursday, July 18, 1918—
Won an automobile accident case today that all the other lawyers told me I was bound to lose. Tried Savage vs. Whitehurst case in Greenwood and won out before their jury. Was somewhat afraid of trying it as my client was a negro and theirs was white. They asked for the jury, too. One of the mysteries of the practice is winning when you think you are bound to lose.

Friday, July 19, 1918—
Fire broke out in New Town at 10:00 and burned 16 houses before it could be checked. Had Greenville Fire Wagons over here. I lost two rent houses worth $2000 and had only $800 insurance. Looked like the whole town would burn for a while. Had to spend most of the PM getting places for the negroes made homeless. Red Cross sent $700 to help. One planter

suggested that we split the money to make up our losses. I made a fool of myself remonstrating with him. Must learn to guard my words and deeds better.

Business is a drag since Christmas. Note of $3640 due at bank and nothing to pay it with.

Saturday, July 20, 1918—
Everything went wrong today. Finished my third Saturday filling in for Landrum at the P.O. and decided to quit. Need the money badly but have other worries. May has come down with the flu and is very sick. Neighbors had a 12 year old girl to die with the flu last week and one now affected by St. Vitus Dance. My dear May very weak and had to use Camphor.

Sunday, July 21, 1918—
May still in bed and I did the cooking and dishwashing and couldn't get any help. Some day and experience for me.

Monday, July 22, 1918—
Same as yesterday. Usual chores of housewife for yours truly, as not a sharecropper could be gotten. All have the flu.

Tuesday, July 23, 1918—
Brooks' Uncle Ned came by to see me today. He and Brooks are plenty worried about the upcoming case. Ned asked me why we can't simply force Jones to give up pistol. Explained that the law did not allow it, even though I had tried to put the fear of God in Jones. "He ain't afraid of God," Uncle Ned said. "But I know what he is afraid of." He wouldn't say what this was, but said he'd see me again soon. Long time going to sleep this night.

Thursday, July 25, 1918—
My darling May agreed to marry me today! I am deeper in love all the time and can never show May how happy she has made me today. She is a full fledged chum and sport. I know

now that I have won the love of one of the most wonderful women in the wide world. Time will only add to my love for her and cleanse me thereby from many faults. We left for Iuka at 3 PM to break the news to her father but car stripped gear about a mile from town. May took train, while I stayed behind to see to car. How I will miss her!

Friday, July 26, 1918— Up at 8 a.m. Bought cabin on Lake Ferguson from Fitzhugh for $1500. $300 to be paid on delivery of deed and like amount for five years @ 6%. Cabin worth $2000, but wrote off estate work fee for Fitzhugh in return for reduced price. Also bought a new 4 cylinder Empire car from Marble @ $1100. Had telegram from May to meet her in Memphis and left on train for Greenville.

Saturday, July 27, 1918—
Up at 1 a.m. Reached Memphis at 6:30. Spent evening downtown. Went to pictures. Saw Elsie Ferguson in "A Doll's House." Peabody Hotel is a delight. Saw minstrel show in lobby. May fell in love with lead performer, and I drank Cooks Gold Blume Near Beer. May is joyful traveling companion. I have truly won the cream of the crop.

Sunday, July 28, 1918—
Arrived back in Leland at dusk. May to begin wedding preparations after returning to Iuka. Mother has been dead for seven months but her presence has seemed very real to me this night. How I would love for her to be with May and me, but I feel she sees us in the spirit, and that we shall some day see her in Heaven. I'll never cease loving her.

Monday, July 29, 1918—
This AM May asked me, "Gene, do you still love me as you used to?" After assuring her that I did a thousand times more, she said, "then don't forget to tell me about it." I have thought

that I was making it so plain she could never doubt that I loved her, but will daily tell her the feelings of my heart hereafter.

Car broke down and repaired. New battery put in and went dead! Car sent back to shop. Got beat in pool game with Fitzhugh. He is as much a pool shark as he is a slick lawyer. My own fault for wagering. In office in PM. Still no break in Brooks case. Am wondering what Uncle Ned meant when he said he knew what Jones was afraid of. Am even more concerned I am going to find out.

Thursday August 8, 1918—
Got my draft notice today. I was Class A One. Part of German fleet surrendered today to the English. Our boys will be coming home now. Hurrah for the conquering heroes! Am sorry I can't be with them.

Friday, August 9, 1918—
May feeling better. Teased her about going on her annual trip West with her sister. Told her she could be having a good time with all the boys. She made me feel proud of her by remarking, "No, I believe in living decently and have no patience w/ married women who don't." Don't know how I'll get along when she's gone, but have pretended that it will be an easy matter, as I want her to go, and feel that she needs the trip.

Saturday, August 10, 1918—
Home all day. I know that I can truthfully say that May has been all to me that a wife could be in love and goodness. So much better than I deserve. The greatest good she has done for me has been to make me consider those things I formerly passed up lightly— that the greatest aim in life is the greatest good for all. Even my own mother, were she alive today, could find no fault with May.

Sunday, August 4, 1918—

Brooks' Uncle Ned came by after dinner and we discussed Brooks' case. Uncle is convinced he has solution to problem with Jethro Jones, but his plan may land us both in jail. Even so, I cannot allow an innocent man to die for a crime he didn't commit, and must take whatever steps necessary to save Brooks' life. Hope this does not prevent me from enjoying a happy life with the most wonderful woman in this world, but I have no choice but to do as my conscience dictates. Letter from May. To church at night.

Monday, August 5, 1918—

Met with Uncle Ned and Greenville Sheriff after supper. Assured sheriff that we would not come back from Jethro Jones' house without pistol. Promised sheriff there would be no physical violence. Sheriff drove Ned and I to Jones' house and waited in patrol car while Uncle and I visited with Jones. Ned closed door while I set brief case down on dining room table. Ned, strong as an ox, held Jones in his seat, while I opened briefcase, exposing 'water moccasins' to Jones. Ned had caught several king snakes on fishing trip, and had painted the insides of their mouths white, to resemble deadly cotton mouth snakes. In short order, Jones directed me to location of Colt .45 murder weapon, hidden under loose board beneath deep freeze. Sheriff took Jethro Jones into custody and will recommend Brooks' case be dismissed tomorrow. This has been one unforgettable evening!

Tuesday, August 6, 1918—

Brooks case dismissed by Judge Gerald. Brooks one happy man! I thank God for bringing a just resolution to Brooks' case. I will be happier only when May becomes my bride!

Cyclone hit near Panther Burn, in which Fraser McMasters was killed. We in Leland have much to be thankful for that we escaped. Letter from May. I realize more than ever that I am deeply in love with my May. Life is indeed a pleasure to me now in living. Went to pictures at night. Saw *Unbeliever* at Paramount. Letter from May.

Friday, October 3, 1919—
In office all day. Nothing special done. Good news in Brooks' case, however. Jethro Jones' conviction upheld by State Supreme Court, so Judge Gerald released Jones' Colt .45 from evidence properties, and gave it to me as a "reward" for solving Brooks murder case. May uncomfortable with pistol in house, so will keep this fine, expensive weapon at the cabin.

Read at night and retired at 9:30. May woke me at 10:30 with our little baby on the way. Called Dr. Featherston. He told us to go on to Kings Daughter's Hospital in Greenville. Left Leland at 11:30 and there at 12 PM.

Saturday, October 4, 1919—
May was in a good deal of pain when we first arrived and continued to grow worse all the time. The nurses gave her every attention. Dr. Featherston came as soon as he could. Looked for a while like May would die. Our son, John Eugene Clements, Jr. came into the world at 5:00 AM, and I went back to May at 5:30. Dr. had made me leave but I stayed just outside the door and waited.

I've wept, prayed and now am the happiest man in the world. One who has not stood by one who is dearer than life itself, under these circumstances, does not truly know life, and can not feel what it means to give life to another. Nor can he know the cost to his own life, bringing another into the drama of the world's existence. I can never be good enough to my darling wife, my lovely May, hereafter. There is so much I feel that is too sacred to pen, and no eye will ever know just how I feel. The Great Ruler of Nature and all her laws knows my heart, and I humbly bow at the shrine of Motherhood and pay homage to God and thank Him for carrying us safely through.

Left at 6:30 AM and went to Greenville barber. Back after getting shave and spent an hour with May. Left for Leland. Closed Armstrong deal with Hammett for $3,000. Brooks' wife made booties for baby, and Brooks brought them by after lunch. Left again for Greenville at 3 PM. Found May and the little life doing fine, and stayed with them until 9:30. Drove to Leland and slept all night. Bought small undershirt and hot water bottle for baby.

Thursday, December 30, 1920—
In City Court in Greenville in AM. Defended Davis Negro whom J.B. McLain was prosecuting, and jury acquitted him of carrying concealed weapon. McLain wanted to start fight about me questioning him about whipping and shooting Negroes for getting drunk and shooting up Arcola, Miss. When, Oh Lord, will these planters ever learn?

Home at 3:00. Canceled trip to cabin. Had to look after Gene Jr. Baby is growing and developing so, and is a world of pleasure to both of us. May and I look with wonder on his new development each day. We think he is the most wonderful baby in all of creation. He took his first steps today and is some proud little man of his accomplishment. May went to Greenville to shop, and I made a fool of myself over her staying too late.

Friday, December 31, 1920—
In office all day. Went to church service at night. Visited cemetery. Thought of my dear sainted mother. She was always such a joy at this time of year. It's still hard for me to believe that she's gone from this world forever. Today reminded me of how little we amount to in this world, only one of many atoms that go to make up the whole. And yet our troubles seem as large to us as the planets in the heavens.

Little Gene has touch of whooping cough, and my sweetheart had to postpone her trip to Iuka to visit her mother.

Made up with May for squabble yesterday. Cannot stand to be at odds with finest person I know, and must take great pains to see that there is never any need to be.

This has been a very trying year. Mosquitoes have gotten into the house and given us lots of worry the last few nights. Anthrax is all over the country and worlds of stock are dying, although my mules are still living. To begin with, everything was high, and it was very expensive to live and make a crop. Then it rained and rained in late spring and grass worms got after the cotton. This time, cotton has gone down from $250.00 per bale to $85.00 and less. Fitzhugh Italians owe me, I will be about even on real estate transactions.

Other things all look dark financially. I owe about $2500.00 to be paid before Feb. 1st and don't see where the money is to come from. If I could only stop expenses, but they must go on. I am afraid that I have lung trouble as I have been coughing for past two months. Also have touch of deadly rheumatism. So it seems that the greatest thing I have to be thankful for is a happy home, a loving wife, and a baby whom God has given us and blessed with worlds of life and energy.

While we begin the New Year under a cloud, I look forward with confidence to the future and hope to see all the dark places made bright and my difficulties overcome. If I am given health and energy, I can trust in God to provide a way for me as He has always done in the past. I hope and pray for the Grace to overcome my cross ways and disposition, and make me worthy of all the blessings I enjoy.

AFFAIRE D'HUMOR-1803

The hulking blacksmith wiped his sweaty palms on his shirtsleeve, raised himself to full height and strode from his table to the restaurant doorway, blocking the diminutive Creole's path from restaurant to plank sidewalk beyond. Standing fifteen inches taller than his adversary and sporting arm muscles larger than those of the Creole's thighs, the American stood fast, determined not to allow the smaller man to leave.

"I hear you been calling me out a coward."

The Creole regarded the American with a haughty gaze that said more than his most insulting words ever could. "Face me, blacksmith," he finally said. "That's the only way. An *affair d' honneur!* I demand that you face me like a man. *Show* them that you are not a coward."

The big man shrugged his shoulders. "It was joke, nothing more. I meant no insult to you."

"A cruel 'joke' *at my expense*, my friend. Honor demands satisfaction. Face me. I make the challenge. You choose the terms. That is unwritten law. I am a man. I face you anywhere, anytime."

"But..." the blacksmith sputtered, "you're the best marksman in Louisiana. It's as good as cold-blooded murder."

"Choose swords."

The blacksmith shook his head angrily. "You're the finest fencing master in New Orleans. Go back to your city. Leave Biloxi and return to your home. It's was just a joke, I tell you. How can your honor be offended by a joke?"

"I go home after we duel. Choose your terms."

The blacksmith hesitated.

"Coward."

"That's enough!" The larger man brandished a muscular fist above the Creole's head. "One more word and I'll thrash you within an inch of your life!"

"Gentlemen do not brawl in the street like dogs."

"I'm no *gentleman.*"

The Creole's face was as expressionless as clay. "This much is certain, blacksmith. What everyone in Biloxi wants to know is, are you also not a coward?"

The anger left the blacksmith as quickly as it had overtaken him. The sight of his fellow townsmen lurking behind the Creole, glaring at him with accusing eyes, made him feel like a strip of copper melting in a forge. He gazed up at the cloudless sky and considered his problem. Fight and die or refuse and humiliate himself beyond measure here in front of God, the Creole and his townspeople. There had to be another way.

"Well?" his would-be-dueling opponent demanded.

He kicked at the ground and cleared his throat.

"Well?" the Creole asked again.

The blacksmith's sullen expression suddenly vanished as he turned his gaze from the ground to glare directly into the Creole's eyes. "I accept your challenge," he said.

"Excellent."

"I choose the terms, right?

The Creole gestured dramatically to the crowd gathering in the street. "As I have said. You are the challenged. Honor demands that you choose the terms."

"The weapons and the location?"

"I prefer to face you under the large oak here beside Mrs. Mahony's restaurant. That is the local custom, I understand. But, again, that is entirely your choice."

The blacksmith took a deep breath. "Very well. I choose twenty-pound sledgehammers in six feet of water in the Mississippi Sound."

The Creole's wicked grin dissipated into a mask of stunned amazement. Then, as he felt the Biloxians' eyes burning holes in his back, he wiped the shock from his face and offered a broad, devil-may-care smile. "You know, blacksmith," he laughed, draping his arm across the larger man's waist, "I believe you are right, after all. Who says a gentleman cannot take a good joke now and then?"

THANKS A LOT, JACK

She was down to her last mini-cassette tape and had very little she could use. She decided to ratchet up the interview to another level by broaching a subject she knew was *not* near and dear to the writer's heart.

"So," she asked energetically, startling him with a sudden onslaught of renewed interest, "do you think your book of short stories will sell better than your novels?"

The writer grinned sheepishly. "How could I not? Although the reviewers loved my novels, they didn't sell like my non-fiction books." He regarded her closely as he spoke. If she had intended any sarcasm in her question, she'd covered it well with an innocent expression.

"Then," she said, "if you won't challenge your friend, Jack Weston, in sales, do you expect to your book to garner better reviews than did *his* recent short story collection?"

"Sure," he quipped. "That's how it's always been. I've got the local book critics in my corner and he's got thirty million dollars in the bank."

"I believe," she replied without hesitation, "he's now up to forty million with his latest novel and most recent movie contract."

"Thanks a lot," he retorted, striking a poorly disguised bitter note. "It's bad enough that his books sell better than mine, but he gets the movie contracts, too. Make no mistake, though. The big reviewers in New York haven't trashed any of my books like they slaughtered his last two."

Her nose crinkled, registering mild confusion. "Have they ever reviewed any of your novels?"

"Well, no," he nodded thoughtfully, "now that you mention it. Several of my non-fiction books, yes. The novels, no. But they haven't trashed them is my point."

"Perhaps they'll base a movie on one your non-fiction books."

"Oh, sure," he frowned. "I can see that, now. Just imagine the riveting dialogue... Tom Cruise leads Nicole Kidman onto the porch of a crumbling Delta mansion and says, 'That transom is in the Greek Revival style, my love. And there, underneath that staircase,' he urges passionately with a broad sweep of his hand, 'is where the mistress of the house sewed her daughters' petticoats.' Oh, I can *really* see that happening."

Mark one up for you. "I think Tom and Nicole are divorced, anyway."

"Right. Anyhow, neither Jack's runaway success nor my flagging novel sales are really what bother me."

"What does bother you, then?"

"Well," he shrugged, "several of the critics—while according me excellent reviews, I add with all alacrity—have accused me of imitating Jack by writing Southern thriller novels."

"And now you're worried they'll say the same thing about your new book, since he came out with a book of short stories shortly before you did?"

"What, me worry? I'm done anguishing about that. I was in Lexington, Kentucky, this last October, enjoying a quasi-successful book signing and reading before a crowd of almost fifteen people who were clamoring—yes, clamoring I say—for my latest book, a novel about a fanciful meeting between dashing Confederate cavalrymen John Hunt Morgan and Nathan Bedford Forrest, and just as I told them about the book of short stories I was writing, my wife, Letitia, texted me that the national news announced that Jack Weston had just published a book of short stories. Just like that, without warning and out of the blue, he did it to me again. Now I'll endure reviewers proclaiming that ole- copycat-me has done it again and boldly gone where Jack Weston has already gone before. Well, heck, it's not as if Faulkner or Welty ever wrote a friggin' short story, is it? Why don't they say I'm copying them, huh? Tell me that, why don't you?"

"Because," she pounced, "even Jack doesn't claim to be following in their footsteps, two of the greatest literary authors of the twentieth century. Surely you don't, either."

The writer groaned, rubbing the lines on his forehead with two pale, spindly fingers. "Yeah, well…Jack will be the first to admit he's never attempted anything literary. I've got him on that account, too. He's written no non-fiction books and had no literary output *at all*. That's me two, and Jack zip."

"You wrote a literary book?"

The writer adjusted himself in his seat. "Well, not exactly. It was more a cross-genre effort, like *Cape Fear, Thanatos Syndrome, To Kill a Mockingbird*, and so on."

"What?"

"You know…A Southern thriller but not so formulaic as the typical popular fiction thriller, and brimming with literary devices such as leit-motifs, foreshadowing, metaphor, and gritty, realistic dialogue (as opposed to Hollywood-friendly, politically correct drivel) that make the story something more than the usual pop culture rubbish."

The interviewer screwed up her expression as she considered his words. "You're comparing your first novel to Harper Lee's *To Kill a Mockingbird*?"

"I certainly am. But …To be completely honest, I must admit that Jack's first novel was also in that genre."

"So you're even on that count, to be perfectly honest."

"But," he sputtered, "everyone in law school knew I was

more creative than Jack. Heck, he did, too. When he took a break from law school exams one night to attend a big University Theater production, he and his buddies found me not in the audience with them, but up on stage directing and starring in my own theatrical adaptation of one of William Faulkner's novels. *I* was the creative one, I tell you. He just thought of writing novels first."

"With two bestsellers and a movie deal before you published your first novel."

The writer wrung his hand in frustration. "Look, I'm tired of talking about it," he groused. "Let's talk about something else, shall we?"

"Such as?"

"Real creativity in writing," he declared with a sudden burst of enthusiasm. "Let's chat about that!"

"Sure," she said with an equal lack of enthusiasm. "Be my guest."

"OK," he said, warming to the task by slapping his hands and hanging on the edge of his seat. "Jack Weston based his first novel on a real-life story where three Latino gang members raped and murdered a white girl in Arkansas, but he changed it around and had three rednecks murder a Latino girl. You know...A story about racial reconciliation in the Arkansas Delta. That's all well and good, but he had the KKK marching through downtown El Dorado, for God's sake. What the heck was that? The Klan hadn't marched in downtown El Dorado for three decades. I mean, it was a good enough story, one that would have been groundbreaking thirty years ago. But nothing earth shattering in 1995, now was it?"

"And you?"

"I did something that hadn't been done in the 1990s. I started with an actual case I had defended, where a Native-American psychopath murdered an elderly white woman near a reservation in West Helena, Arkansas. Brained her with a frying pan so he could steal her car to take his girlfriend to a drive-in-movie. To watch *Psycho,* no less! But I made up the rest of the story (we're talking *real* creativity here), where the protagonist lawyer defended the killer and took the case to trial. But I added an intersecting subplot where the lawyer read his grandfather's diary about the wild west days when deputies from a Fort Smith hanging judge's court hunted down renegade Indians and brought them to Fort Smith for trial. In the diary the grandfather defended an innocent Indian falsely charged with murder.

"That book had it all—two plots, one from diary entries, another set in modern times, that contrasted present-day morality with turn-of-the-century mores. I threw in a few philosophical underpinnings for good measure, used various literary devices to heighten the drama, and offered what the critics termed 'gritty dialogue reminiscent of *Cape Fear* but more chilling for offering greater realism.'"

"Wow," she exclaimed. "You memorized that review, did you?"

He cast an icy glare in her direction. "The point is," he harped bitterly, his fingers drumming nervously on his chair arms, "my first novel garnered better reviews than Jack's, *sold a thousand more copies*, and proved in every way the more solid of the two efforts."

"You mean until his second book became a best-seller and *garnered him* a movie contract for his first and second novels, instantly propelling both to runaway best-seller status?"

"Well ... sure, until then."

"So what are you saying?"

"What I'm saying is ..."

"Well?"

"I'll tell you," he said resolutely. "I may not sell as many books as Jack, but at least I can damn sure finish one. Mine don't end suddenly; as if the writer got up to fix a sandwich and forgot to finish the first story before starting another one. With the same formulaic plot and Hollywood dialogue, I might add."

She restrained an urge to laugh out loud. "Which apparently is what everyone in America, and around the world, for that matter, would rather read, judging from the multi-million dollar sales of each of his books."

The writer loosed a deep, anguished whimper. "That's well and good, you know, but we'll see whose short stories the reviewers prefer. I bet they pan his book as bad as they waste those awful celebrity tell-alls and novelizations of *Star Trek* movies."

The interviewer offered a smug expression. "The *New York Times* gave his short stories a good review yesterday."

"Yes," he nodded, "for the most part they did. But the reviewer did say it was a poorly researched effort."

"Is that the same reviewer who commented on the great writers from the Mississippi Delta—including William Faulkner, Eudora Welty, *and* Jack Weston, none of whom hail from the Mississippi Delta? Sounds like that reviewer is nobody to be casting stones about shoddy research, eh? Although *you* seem to be big on research, having pounced on that review as soon as it came out. Has the *Times* reviewed your book of stories yet?"

"Hey," he demanded angrily, "whose side are you on, anyway? I'm the one giving the interview. I bet you won't be interviewing Jack anytime soon."

"I wish!" she gushed. "We couldn't get him this week. He's in Paris promoting the new movie based on his recent novel. That's why we're interviewing *you*."

The writer threw up his hands, shook his head in disgust and glared malevolently at the interviewer. "If you print that, I'll sue you."

"And we'll hire Jack to defend us," she snapped confidently.

"No you won't. He's a plaintiff's lawyer. I'm the defense lawyer."

She paused for a moment, considering. "As I recall, Jack Weston won a big lawsuit against a corporation a few years ago then turned that experience into a bestselling novel the next year. You didn't defend that lawsuit, did you?"

The writer exhaled a long, pained sigh. "Let's talk about something else," he finally moaned, straining his last ounce of self-restraint to the limit. "If we must talk about the competition, why don't we talk about Charlie Hilson, my other writing friend who helped me find a publisher for my first novel. He's a bestselling author, too. And that's a heckuva story, isn't it? One author showing another one the ropes? Why don't we talk about that, for God's sake?"

"Sure," she beamed. "Now that you mention it, I read just the other day that Charlie Hilson is publishing a book of short stories next month with material that wowed the New York critics at a literary festival last fall. What do you say about that?"

The writer cradled his head in his hands. "Thanks a lot, Charlie," he mumbled under his breath.

IT'S REALLY TOUGH TO BE A TEENAGER

July 23
Dear Diary,

I am so happy!! I LOVE LOVE LOVE Luke!!!! I think he loves me too!! Oh if he did I would be content forever!!! I think I don't just love Luke, I think I'm in love with him!!!! I love the air he breathes, his eyes, his kind smile, I love the ground he walks on!! The way we just flow when we talk. The way that when he looks at me I feel like I'm a helpless damsel and he's my prince, but at the same time like I could take on the whole world if I wanted to!! This must be love!!! Is it??? I don't know.... But I'm sure it is. Don't worry, I won't do anything like have sex with him. I'll wait till it's time. But I know that Luke is the one I am meant to be with!! He's the only thing I ever think about!! He's the air I breathe!! When I feel down or angry, if I just talk to him my problems just go away! That song is WRONG!!! It's not hard to be a teenager in love!! It's amazing!!! When I see him or even just think about him I feel like my heart took a vacation to Lover's Land!!! I feel free and wonderful around him!!! And when I look into his eyes I feel like the world is right. And that maybe, just maybe, the world will be whole one day. I love Luke so much!!!

But...Dear Diary...Do you think Luke loves me?

THE ULTIMATE DISGRACE-1872

The young boy fidgeted nervously in his chair, his eyes wandering from the parlor where all his family had gathered, to the dining room door which had remained closed for the past several hours. His father noted his son's nervousness as the boy squirmed in his seat like a worm on a hook.

"What's buggin' you, boy?" he asked.

"Nothin', sir."

"I reckon you done picked up on the fact that yo' folks is a might testy this afternoon. Eh?"

"Uhm, hmm."

"Well, you got to understand, boy, it weren't but ten year ago when them damned Ohioans and Minnesotans came through Hinds County and ate everything they didn't burn and stole everything they ain't stomped. They stole cattle, looted houses and burned barns all up and down the Pearl River. Yo' mamma ain't come from hereabouts, so she don't know nothin' 'bout all that. She wuz from Jones County, where they was so poor the Yankees ain't found nothin' they could steal. What they didn't steal those crazy Jones County renegades that seceded from the Confederacy rounded up as soon as the Yankees left.

"Anyhow, boy, she up and come here to Jackson in '65. That's when I met her. That's why you sittin' here today. What I want to know is, why you acting nervous as a cat? It ain't got nuthin' to do with you, no how."

The boy swallowed hard and asked his father the question he had been hoping to avoid ever since he had realized that his family was gathering in the parlor, a room they had formerly used only for funerals and weddings. Notwithstanding his tender years, he knew that none of his three brothers and sisters were old enough to take a bride or husband.

"Out with it boy," his father growled.

"Did someone in our family die, daddy? Was it Aunt Sue? Or Uncle Jack?"

His father gaped at him in silence for a moment, then burst into a loud, unrestrained guffaw. "Heck no, boy. Ain't nobody dead. But somethin' worse has happened."

"What?" the boy pleaded, crossing his legs tightly enough to avoid wetting his pants.

His father placed a calming hand on his son's shoulder. "Yo' Aunt Sue has done gone and married a Yankee!"

THE NIGHT JIM BOWIE DINED AT LUSCO'S

"Tell the story, Rob. The one about the night you and Jim Bowie dined at Lusco's."

"No thanks, Lee. I hate that story. Nobody believes a word of it. Don't know why I told it in the first place. How'd you hear about it, anyhow?"

"Deb Davis told me. But she wasn't exactly crystal clear on a few details."

"Yeah, most notably the part about her promise to keep it to herself if I told her the story. She apparently wasn't too clear about that."

"Aw, whatcha' worried about, Rob? It sounded like a great story. But I want to hear it straight from the horse's mouth."

"No."

"Tell me and I'll by the drinks."

"No way. Why should I hold myself out to scorn for a few measly drinks?"

"Tell me and I'll by the drinks and then we can mosey on in to the dining room and I'll treat you to Giardina's best fried oysters and asparagus, as well as a piece of their flourless chocolate cake. And the best pinot noir money can buy to flush it all down."

"That's not fair, Lee. You know how I love Giardina's oysters and flourless cake. Nobody can resist chocolate and red wine. That's just not fair."

"Not fair? Giardina's ain't cheap, buddy boy. And it's just a story, after all."

"It's not a *story* at all. It really happened."

"You bet, Rob. A man who died at the Alamo a hundred-and-seventy-five years ago ..."

"A-hundred-and-seventy-three. I looked it up. After having dinner with the guy, why not?"

"Uhh, sure. So this dead guy, his corpse riddled with bullet holes and molderin' in the grave for a *hundred and seventy three* years, ambles into Lusco's ..."

"Not Lusco's. He was sitting over there at the bar, right here in the Alluvian. Drinking all by his lonesome. Somehow we started talking, I bought him a drink, and he eventually told me who he was. One thing led to another, and we wound up at Lusco's for dinner of broiled catfish and filet mignon."

"Why didn't you just dine here, Rob? You too cheap to spring for Giardina's dinner? For a hundred-and-seventy-three-year-old famous dead guy, no less?"

"*No* ... I just thought that, well...With him being a frontiersman and all, he might prefer the more casual dining atmosphere at Lusco's to the more formal decor here at Giardina's. The food's great both ways so why not make the guy comfortable after the long trip?"

"Long trip? I'll say. Long trip from hell, huh?"

"He didn't say anything about hell, Lee. And I haven't forgotten about your offer to buy dinner and the drinks, by the way."

"No problem. Had a banner cotton crop this year. Bartender, two glasses of your best pinot noir right here."

"Thanks, Lee. Okay, you win. You know I can't turn down a free meal at Giardina's. But you gotta' let me tell the story without a lot of hooey about how I'm lying and how it never happened and how it's impossible and all that jazz."

"Okay, Rob. You got a deal. You and I both know the guy was just an actor using a very creative technique to bum drinks and a free meal off you, but hey ... You're doing it to me and you're not even an actor. I'm paying for amateur night and loving it. I said when Deb came out with the story that I had to hear the whole thing from the horse's mouth and my old lady didn't raise a liar. Tell it, Rob. Give me my thirty dollars' worth."

"Thirty dollars? Good try, Lee, but thirty will cover the meal, maybe. We'll drink twice that much in wine."

"No problem, buddy boy. Knock yourself out. Lay it on me, pardner."

"You wanted it, you got it. Like I say, Bowie and I hit it off, so we hopped in my car and booked it over to Lusco's. I must admit that, before we crossed the tracks, I considered talking him into dining at the Crystal Grill, where the food's almost as good as Lusco's but not quite as expensive."

"You're wrong about that, Rob. I think the food's better at the Crystal and just as expensive as Giardina's. But I appreciate your honesty in admitting what a cheap bastard you are. Makes the story more believable. Go ahead, pard."

"I'll let that one pass for the moment, Lee. Anyhow, I decided to stick with Lusco's because I thought it more the type of joint he'd relate to, what with the run-down brick exterior and quasi-illicit atmosphere. On the way there I told Bowie all about the place, how they built that old red brick building during prohibition so Delta luminaries could enjoy toddies during fancy meals in private booths behind drawn curtains. How they pressed a buzzer when they wanted service, and how the black waiters, dressed in full white-coat waiter regalia, arrived at their table singing the menu. How the place sold beer, but patrons could bring their wine or liquor in a brown paper bag. Liquor they'd just purchased right across the street in the state-owned liquor store, which by state law collected an illegal whiskey state tax on every bottle they sold during prohibition. I even told Bowie about how Lusco's patrons liked to take their butter pats and toss them up to the ceiling where they'd stick in place for the rest of the night. You know, Lee...The rich traditions of the place."

"Sure."

"So anyhow, if Bowie was impressed with our local traditions he didn't show it. He was as cool and laconic as you'd expect from the history books. Just like Richard Widmark played him in the Alamo movie. But he was a lot taller than Widmark. And, of course, he was more or less dressed in modern clothing."

"Oh?"

"Sure. Though he could have worn most of it back in his day. Blue jeans, a linsey-woolsey shirt, cowboy boots and a wide-brimmed hat."

"Just like the movie!"

"Not exactly. Well, kinda, I guess. Just taller, like I said. And jet black hair, not sandy-colored like Widmark's."

"He could've dyed it."

"You want to hear this story or not? No making fun or I quit right now."

"Sorry, Rob. Pray, continue."

"Okay. The fact is Bowie was not the type to dye his hair. Nothing metrosexual about him, if you know what I mean."

"A real macho man, huh, Rob?"

"No. I mean, yeah, sure. He killed people in hand-to-hand duels, for God's sake. But he wasn't trying to act macho. That's the way he was. Naturally. Like you'd expect a rugged frontiersman to be. The guy who fought a hundred fights with his bare fists and no small number to the death with his Bowie knife and black powder pistol."

"Like the time he killed a guy in a duel on the sandbar at Natchez?"

"You know about that, Rob?"

"Now *you're* making fun, pardner. I went to college, you know."

"Sorry, Lee. Anyhow ..."

"Weren't you worried he might pull that knife on you and take your wallet?"

"Not at all. Bowie wasn't a common a thief, Lee. He was landed gentry. Owned plantations in Mississippi, Louisiana, and Texas. At least that's what I recall from history class at Ole Miss. And he mentioned the plantations once or twice, I think."

"Big braggart, was he?"

"Heck, no. I asked, that's all. He was very modest. Or at least he wasn't big on talking about himself. Seemed more interested in hearing what I had to say."

"Oh, now you're screwing with me. One of the great legends of all time, hero of the Alamo, no less, is more interested in what a middle-aged accountant in Greenwood, Mississippi, has to say than expounding on his own grand adventures? After over a century of silence, Bowie was more interested in listening to you gab than telling wild tales about the old Southwest to anyone who'd listen? No way I'm buying that."

"Very funny, knucklehead. No, I meant that Bowie was more interested in hearing about modern times, about the people of today, than in hearing himself talk."

"What'd you tell him?"

"Everything I could think of. I told him about all the things that had happened since he ...Well, I mean since the Alamo. A lot of it he already seemed to know, things like the Civil War ..."

"The War for Southern Independence."

"Of course. World Wars I and II, the important stuff. The wars especially. Either he already knew about them or didn't care to know any more. Maybe he was just tired of that sort of thing. I got that distinct impression, at any rate."

"Sure. Rob. Sure. Perfectly understandable, given the circumstances of his demise."

"Of course. At any rate, he didn't seem surprised to hear about the wars. He was more interested in ..."

"What? Spit it out, Rob."

"I don't know, Lee. The social things. Television. Movies. Integration. The moon landing. The women's movement. Civil rights. Welfare. Pop psychology. Woodstock, the Super Bowl, hippies, drugs, fake breasts, abortion, Disney World, all of it."

"I bet he hated all of that, huh? Thought the old USA had gone to hell in a hand basket, am I right?"

"I didn't get that impression, Lee. Oh, he winced when I mentioned partial birth abortions—mothers killing their own babies and all that. As I recall, he lost his daughter and wife shortly before the Alamo, so that was somewhat understandable. He also cringed when I told him tobacco is terribly addictive and causes cancer, and that we know it's killed millions but haven't banned smoking. And, if I'm not mistaken, he gave a pretty stern look when I described American celebrity worship, rock stars, soap operas, million dollar salaries for sports stars, Dr. Phil, and the like."

"I figured Bowie, a slave owner and man of his era, would've been more shocked by civil rights or women's rights—that sort of stuff."

"Not at all, Lee. Not as I could tell. To the contrary, after I told him about all those things, I sensed a bittersweet feeling of loss about him. Like he died too young, missed out on everything that happened after the Alamo. I got the idea that he wished he could make up in our time what he missed in his."

"Wait a minute, Rob. Are you saying that he had to go back?"

"Go back where, Lee?"

"You know ... Back to wherever the hell he came from."

"I don't know where he came from and he absolutely refused to tell me. Only said he had to go back at midnight. That he had the one night in Greenwood and then had to go back."

"I don't believe it."

"It's true. I hung out with him at Lusco's until midnight just to see what he'd do. And sure enough, I got up to go the restroom around 11:45 and when I came back he was gone."

"No not that, Rob. Not the part about his disappearing at midnight. That's not the part I don't believe."

"Then what don't you believe, Lee? That I dined with Jim Bowie at Lusco's? That he didn't rob me? That he only had the one night on Earth?"

"No. None of that. I got no problem buying that Jim Bowie came back from the dead. He's not the first person to make that claim, is he? About half the fundamentalist preachers make that claim and threaten to sue you if you call 'em liars. I can certainly believe that he showed up at the Alluvian. Every other celebrity does, sooner or later. Finest boutique hotel in America and a four-star restaurant to boot."

"Sure."

"And hey, Rob, I don't doubt for a second that you were too cheap to treat him to dinner at Giardina's and took him anywhere else. The fact that you admitted you thought about taking him to the Crystal Grill, even though the food's just as good if not just as expensive, especially if you order drinks rather than brown-bagging at Lusco's. But *you thought* it was a lot cheaper and almost steered him to the Crystal, so, that makes your story all the more believable, at least up to that point."

"Thanks."

"You're welcome, pardner. Tell you the truth, I can even go so far as to believe that given one night on Earth, Jim Bowie chose to dine at Lusco's, because, like the Crystal Grill and Giardina's, it's a one-of-a-kind restaurant that people drive hundreds of miles to enjoy every weekend. No, it's the other part of your tall tale that I find unbelievable. Downright bizarre to tell the truth. So unbelievable, in fact, that I'm gonna' have to call bullshit on the whole story just because of that one part."

"*What part,* Lee? You're telling me you can buy the fact that Jim Bowie came back from the dead, that he showed up in Greenwood, Mississippi, with no explanation about where he'd been for the past hundred and seventy-three years and not a word about where he was headed? You'd buy all of that but some other part of the story is so unbelievable that you'd doubt the word of your very best friend? Your friend who's never lied to you once in your entire life? Tell me, Lee. What part of the story are you talking about? What part is so unbelievable that you doubt the word of your very best friend?"

"Oh don't get me wrong, Rob. I don't think you're lying. Hell, you don't cheat at cards or golf, much less lie. And like you say, you've never lied to me. That's not your style, pardner. If anything, I'd say you got taken in by some actor, if for no other reason because you're so damned gullible. But that's not what I'm saying. I'm saying I was with you all the way on this one, just like I always am with all your cock and bull stories, until you came out with that part I could never believe no matter how many oaths you took."

"What are you talking about, Lee? What part don't you believe?"

"Don't take this the wrong way, Rob, I am your friend and always will be. But no one knows you better than I. And that's why I simply can't buy that ridiculous part of your story."

"What part, *Lee*?"

"The part about how Jim Bowie had one night on Earth after one-hundred-and-seventy-three years of oblivion, that he had to go back to wherever he came from at midnight, and knowing that, nevertheless went to dinner with an accountant from Greenwood, Mississippi, who is so damned dull he makes up stories about dining with long dead frontiersmen to chat up girls like Deb. That's the part I'm not buying. That Jim Bowie spent his one night on Earth gabbing with you, Rob. No siree. I'm not buying it, not one damn word."

"Lee ... I'm hurt on so many levels, I just don't know what to say."

"That's okay, Rob. God loves you and I love you, and by gobs, Jim Bowie had one night on Earth and chose to spend it dining with you at Lusco's. So far as I know, he didn't shoot himself and he certainly didn't shoot you! So the least I can do is treat you to dinner at Giardina's. Come on, buddy, let's put on the feed bag and have us some fried oysters and chocolate cake."

As Lee draped his arm around Rob's shoulders and led him out of the bar and into the restaurant, a man seated at the Alluvian bar, who may have been a mere actor, but bore a striking resemblance to a long dead former U.S. Congressman and bear hunter extraordinaire named David Crockett, eyed them closely from his secluded perch. After they left, the man laid a gold coin on the bar, slid gracefully off his stool and quietly slipped out into the night onto the red brick streets of downtown Greenwood, Mississippi.

YOUR LOVE IS WICKED

She made a point not to stare at him as the crew techs wired him for sound and touched up his curly black hair. She soon realized she needn't have concerned herself; he seemed far less self-conscious than she remembered; far more at ease in his own skin than when she had known him before.

Or maybe it was his well-reported steely determination to succeed that had helped him overcome the self-doubts he harbored since childhood. They had attended elementary school together and fallen in love her senior year at St. Andrews High. Yes, she had been a bus stop on his meteoric ride to the top, a point she'd have resented but for the fact that she had used him, too. After all, her need to become a woman had been just as urgent as his need to become a star. They had both gotten what they needed from that passionate but short-lived affair.

Anyhow, that was ancient history. Fifteen years later she was the rising star in the pantheon of capitol city news anchors, and he was fresh off a successful run on a cable TV series before landing a role in the certain cult classic sci-fi movie of the summer. She had landed the interview in part because of their friendship, but also because he had mysteriously refused to accompany the film's stars on a nationwide promotional tour, taking interviews only by satellite feed from LA, Chicago, and

New York to her Jackson, Mississippi, TV station. When her news director had asked her if she knew Avery Seaton, she had confidently whipped out her cell phone, said, "Watch this," and dialed his cell and set up the interview right there in her boss's office.

The interview would be a major coup for her career, would reconnect him with his hometown fans, and garner them both the biggest market share for any celebrity interview in Mississippi since a fledgling Tupelo station had run an interview with a youthful Elvis Presley back in 1963.

He took the chair directly in front of the camera and she seated herself beside him. He seemed sincerely pleased to see her and they had no difficulty making small talk until Rod the Cameraman said, "OK, ten seconds. And ... four, three, two..."

She smiled at Avery and turned toward the camera. "This is Cindy Speejens with WLBT-TV, bringing you a very special segment of *Focus on Folks* with Jackson native Avery Seaton, whom many of you will recognize as Jim Hunter on the popular cable series, *Do Not Disturb*, which recently ended a very successful four-year run. Avery is currently starring in the hit movie, *Your Love Is Wicked*, which opened to critical acclaim and record-breaking numbers this past weekend. Welcome to the show, Avery."

"Thanks, Cindy," he purred. "It's great to be back here in Jackson, where it all started for me fifteen years ago."

"That would be your first starring role in the New Stage Theater production... What was that show?"

She was being coy; she remembered the show's title. She had seen *The Drunkard* from the front row during his opening night and returned three consecutive nights thereafter. She had dreamed of meeting Avery Seaton every night but never told him so. They'd met after the fourth show in the Green Room with her father, who had bought a ticket solely to meet her new crush. To their surprise, her father had coached Avery in Pony League baseball years earlier.

Avery obviously remembered Cindy five years later when he reintroduced himself at a New Year's Eve party on a houseboat in the Ross Barnett Reservoir. As luck had it, deep into the evening the boat hit a submerged log and sank in ten minutes. A nearby houseboat took everyone on except Cindy, who couldn't' swim and almost drowned in ten feet of water before Avery hauled her on his back forty yards to the rocky shore near the marina. She didn't leave his side for the entire summer.

But if he recalled meeting her backstage that first performance of *The Drunkard* he didn't admit it on the air. "That was *The Drunkard*," he smiled, "the show that hooked me on acting for good."

"You went from there straight to off-Broadway, then Broadway, then Hollywood. What a whirlwind tour, eh, Avery?"

And then the interview took a surprising turn. "But it was more than that for me," he offered with an unexpected surge of emotion. "I met a girl that night in the Green Room at New Stage who I couldn't stop thinking about for the next six months."

She only needed a beat. "Oh, yeah?" she grinned, her dimples aglow, floating in pockets of their own warmth. "What happened to that lucky girl?"

"I hear she's made it big in television," he answered, trying to be kind, she figured. "I'm just doing my best to catch up. I hope she's happy," he said sincerely.

Despite their broad smiles, she sensed something out of place. Something lurking in the backstory she hadn't expected to encounter in this interview. "Are you?" she asked suddenly. "Happy, I mean." What an odd question to ask a movie star she told herself. Odd, yes, but appropriate for a strangely developing interview.

"Yes," he replied, the veritable picture of cool. "Very happy. I never thought it could be like this."

His eyes sparkled, the pallor of his face brightening with each word. And something else, she noted. The dark need in his eyes was gone, she finally realized. But why?

"You mean success as an actor?" she asked. "You never thought it would be this great so soon?"

"As an actor?" he asked, one eyebrow arched as if she had asked him if he enjoyed orbiting Saturn. "Oh," he grinned sheepishly. "No, I didn't mean that. But sure, it's great, as you say. It's what I thought I wanted since age fifteen. "

"Thought you wanted?" she asked, pouncing instinctively on another chance to take the interview down an unexpected corridor. "You're saying there's something more important than your first starring role in *Your Love Is Wicked,* the movie that's taking America by storm? More important than great reviews, million-dollar studio contracts, offers to work with the best directors in Hollywood and New York?"

He looked askance at her like a Chickasaw native gaping at a fifteenth-century Spanish explorer who had just stumbled upon the Mississippi River. *All you seek is gold? With all this land and endless bounty the Father of Waters offers you, you seek only gold?*

Out of the corner of her eye she caught the perplexed expression on the Rod the Cameraman's face as he momentarily peered over his camera before diving back into his appointed task.

"Yes," Avery mumbled, as if finding his own words difficult to fathom. "More important than that," he finally said. "Oh, I suppose I shouldn't underestimate how fantastic a hit movie can be and what it can do for my career. What I could then do for my family."

Family? *Was that what this was all about?* she wondered. Not possible, she told herself. An actor? A celebrity? Well, becoming a celebrity at least. Stop the presses. This was news if anything ever was. "A lot of your lady fans are going to be very disappointed to hear you talk about a wife and family."

"They'll get over it," he laughed bemusedly. "I hear my costar Josh Headly is fresh on the market."

Which way to go, now, she asked herself. The plan had been to do the textbook hometown-boy-turned-celebrity interview. She knew the star personally; he was there in town, and her director loved the idea. But something else was happening, she realized. Whatever it was, she had to dig it out.

"Come on Avery," she prodded, "don't gloss over this family thing. What in the way of family could possibly make you so ... so ..."

"Happy? Contented?" he grinned. "It happens to actors, too, you know."

Not very often, she wanted to say, but didn't. Self-satisfied maybe. But happy? Celebrities were infamous for leaving a trail of betrayed spouses and neglected children, then opining to anyone who would listen about their naïve political views, babbling on incessantly about "learning the craft" or "perfecting the instrument," whatever that meant, as if anyone cared about the opinions of self-absorbed immature jerks. On the lighter side, they habitually peppered interviews with words like "ironic" or "surreal," the meanings of which they had absolutely no clue. Yet, throughout all these egocentric ramblings none of them ever remembered the maxim that "brevity is the soul of wit." And God help the late night television viewer when an actress adopts a "cause" or an actor mistakenly assumes that anyone other than Larry King or Jay Leno cares what he thinks about anything other than memorizing his lines. Vanity, thy name is surely thespian.

But true happiness? That proved an illusory dream for most celebrities. No, something was different here. It had to be. At least that's what her reporter's instincts told her.

"What happens, Avery? What also happens to actors?"

While he considered his answer, she asked herself if this could possibly be the same man who had just played the leading role in the hottest chick since *Love Story;* the biggest sci-fi smash since *Avatar?* The same actor who made every girl in America melt in her seat when he kissed Carmalita Jones on the sands of the French Riviera?

The same man whose eyes had lit up like bonfires when, years earlier, on a sandbar on the Pearl River, he had spoken of his dreams—Broadway, Hollywood, even the Oscars. But whenever she'd mentioned her dreams—news anchor in a major market, maybe even the 5:00 national news—he'd grown distant, a faraway look creeping into the corners of his eyes no matter how hard he tried to disguise it.

It had worked only when they made love. It was then that he had immersed himself in *her* desire like a man stranded in the desert for three days who suddenly stumbled upon an oasis, knowing he may never see another oasis again.

But after, as soon as she had spoken about anything that interested *her*, she had seen that specter of alienation edge across his visage like a dark cloud spreading across a leaden sky. She had seen that interminable restlessness overtake him like quicksand swallowing a wildebeest. Then *she* had known the loneliness of the desert, her thirst sated temporarily, but her soul left completely barren.

"What happened, Avery?" she asked again.

And then he told her.

"I never thought I wanted children, Cindy. Nothing against them—the thought just never occurred to me. Had other things in mind, you know?"

She knew.

"But, when it happened, well, it was a big surprise the first time, let me tell you. Anyhow, when the doctors brought my baby girl to me right after she was born, and I called her name, she recognized my voice from hearing it in the womb! My Lucy stopped crying and clung to me with all her might while I rocked her to sleep in our hospital room. Well, as you say, something happened, alright. I'm not exactly sure what."

She suddenly noticed that everyone on the set was staring... No, gaping at them. Rod the Cameraman rolled his camera toward them, the big lens whirring open and closed as if Rod had suddenly happened upon Neil Armstrong setting foot on the moon for the first time. As always, she followed her instincts.

"Tell me."

He shrugged his shoulders as if he couldn't believe what he was saying, much less during a TV interview. "And then my second child, Mary Adelyn, was born, and it seemed like, to borrow theater parlance, every act was better than the one before."

"What were the best moments, Avery?"

He paused a beat, then said, "Those high-pitched squeals the girls made when I came home from the theater for dinner. They would hear me opening the front door, stop what they were doing and leap into my arms squealing with joy, saying, 'Dada, Dada!' Their first Christmas mornings—that look on their faces when they saw all the presents—" All this is for me?" they asked. Their first theatrical productions in third grade, our first trip to Disney World. All of that was worth more to me than any movie review or offer to play on Broadway.

"But best of all was putting them to sleep every night, one head on my right shoulder, another on my left, singing *"The Itsy Bitsy Spider"* or reading *Good Night Moon*. No matter what I did—making up stories, singing out of key, reciting poetry I didn't understand—they were the perfect audience, the only one that mattered to me anymore."

And *that's* when it had happened for him, she realized with crystal clarity. The restlessness gone, the fear of rejection banished. That's when his career had really taken off.

As if reading her thoughts, he reached out and patted her hand, then said, "And when all I wanted was to be at home with them and didn't care if I got the part in the next film or sitcom casting call, that was when they started offering me those roles. That's life for you, isn't it?"

Sure, she thought. That's life. But it all seemed too perfect, didn't it? And celebrities' lives were never as perfect as they appeared in the tabloid features. She had to know the absolute truth. And she knew how to get it.

"That's wonderful, Avery. But in all that beautiful story, you never once mentioned your wife."

He smiled again, but this time not so broadly. "Sure I did."

"You did?"

"Yes. Holly gave me those girls. She's the one who stood them in the doorway when I got home from the theater. She made their costumes for their elementary school plays. But what she taught me later, well ... That turned the laws of my universe upside down."

A cursory glance out of the corner of her eye told her that not only were they glued in their tracks and staring with jaws agape, but now it seemed that none of her crew even took the time to breathe.

"Tell me, Avery."

"Well, one night, on Christmas Eve, after the girls and I had sung Christmas carols for a long, long time ...They were *not* going to sleep early with Santa on the way and all the other presents under the tree. So, when I finally got into bed, I found Holly crying. I asked her why. She said because she was so happy that her daughters had something that she had never known."

"What was that?"

"A happy song, a funny story, a long snuggle with her daddy every night. He had died young, you see, just as mine had, but we'd never really discussed that for some reason. Just took it for granted that we had one more thing in common. But she had missed out on all that, you see. The songs, the stories...All of it. Had good times with her mother, you know, but that's only half the picture, isn't it? Well, anyhow, after she told me that, whenever I'd put my girls to bed and we'd be singing our little songs, '*Twinkle, Twinkle, Little Star,*' '*Silent Night,*' you know ..."

She didn't. But now, more than ever, she would, someday.

"I snuggled my girls," he continued giddily, "just like before—heaven on earth every night. But, in a way I don't fully understand, I could sense what Holly was feeling in the next room, listening to us singing out of key. And for the first time in my life, I realized that the old saying, supposedly one of the great verities of the universe, was far, far from true."

"What are you saying?"

"That you can never improve upon perfection."

THE PITCH

"Thanks, J.B., for allowing me to pitch this story to you today. This is a young author with a bold new voice and I think you're really going to …"

"Cut the horsepucky, Jacobs, and give it to me straight, no chaser. I haven't got all day to ass around with agents, you know."

"Sure, J.B. Sure. Like you said. But we can really be the first ones on this guy, a big launch, book signings in Times Square, the *Today Show,* maybe even Oprah if…"

"*Jacobs!!!!*"

"Sorry, J.B. Right as always, J.B. Boy, I do go on, don't I? But it's just that I feel so strongly this time, I can't help but …"

"Two minutes, Jacobs. You got two minutes left. You want to spend it babbling nonsense, be my guest."

"Right. You're right, J.B." The young agent cleared his throat, straightened his tie and dove right in. "So here it is. It's set in 2525 A.D. The future, you see. There, the …"

"I know 2525 A.D. is in the future, jackass. Where? Where's it set? You always lead with the setting. Didn't they teach you that in agent school?"

"I'm coming to that, J.B. Geez, you think I don't know how to do this? Geez."

"I once thought you knew how to do this, Jacobs, but now I'm not so sure. You've got a minute and a half left. Get on with it."

"Sure. I'm just so excited, J.B. OK, OK, don't say it, please. Ahem. The Martians have just conquered Earth. So...On Mars. The novel's set on Mars."

"This oughta' be great."

"Don't think I don't recognize sarcasm when I hear it, J.B. But hold on to your seat. When Obama took the White House I went straight to my cabinet and dug this manuscript out. Timely manuscript if I know the meaning of the word."

As the publisher leaned back in his large, comfortable leather chair, the agent wiped his sweaty palms on his shirt sleeves, planted his feet solidly apart, straightened himself to full height, and spilled his guts on the publisher's plush carpet and tiger skin rug.

"After the conquest," the agent began, "the Martians ship millions of Americans as slaves to Mars, forcing them to 'assist' the Martians with their two-hundred-year Canal Renovation Project. They ..."

"Why just the Americans? Why not the Europeans, Asians, Africans?"

The agent hesitated, brushing a lone lock of hair out of his face and back onto his oblong-shaped head.

"I don't know, J.B., it doesn't matter. Uh, the Martians had other uses for them on Earth, maybe. Who cares? I've only got two minutes so I'm going straight to the heart of the thing."

"One minute. Proceed."

"Sure, but this is backstory, OK? Two hundred years pass, and a civil war breaks out on Mars, resulting in the full emancipation of the American bondspeople. Over the next two hundred years the Ameri-Martians either hire out as sharediggers in the southern regions or get shuffled off into the Northern region's regrettos. They're kept largely ignorant of the highly advanced Martian civilization that functions almost entirely upon mathematical language, virtual reality computers, and bizarre, unfathomable customs."

"Like what?"

"I don't know. Maybe they marry their sisters or eat red dirt on weekends. Worship the gods on Jupiter. Anyhow ..."

"What's so bizarre about all that? My uncle married his sister in New Hampshire or Vermont, somewhere they can marry their sisters. Hell, you ever been to Alabama? I hear poor people down there munch dirt for afternoon snacks."

"Do you mind, J.B.? With respect, may I continue?"

"Be my guest."

"So, the Americans are demoralized, see? They use Martian drugs, are sexually promiscuous compared to the prudish, almost Victorian Martians, believe in ancient, superstitious religions, and double the crime rate every other year. So this is where we pick up the story."

"Great. Finally."

"Can I have another minute and a half?"

"You get two. I'm, intrigued."

"Really, J.B.?"

"Yes, really. I never knew a pitch could be so ridiculous. This may be a new record. Go on, Jacobs. I'm riveted."

With that the publisher stuffed a cigar in his mouth, lit it with a lighter shaped like an Oscar, and leaned back in his chair to a three-quarters position, his eyes fixed at a point on his wall several feet above the agent's head.

"OK," the agent exclaimed with mixed exuberance and relief. "We're rolling now, J.B. I can feel it."

"Say it, don't feel it."

"Gotcha. J.B. Loud and clear. So some of the Americans overcome these difficulties, but the Martians still refer to them as American'ts and give them few chances for advancement."

"I thought we were done with backstory."

"We are, J.B. This part comes out in the dialogue and action."

"I see. Proceed."

"OK. One day, a good Martian with great vision, in league with a courageous American with a righteous dream, demands equal rights for all Americans. They get caught up in a movement whose time has finally come, and this American gets elected president of the Northern Region. Americans assimilate themselves into the culture and things get better all around. But in the Southern Region, especially in a southern flatland in the most backward province nicknamed the Hell-ta, and of course in a few Northern Region regrettos, Americans still scrape the bottom of the barrel. But the Northern President works out a deal with the Southern President ..."

"Let me guess. The Southern President is a hot babe with brains, like Sigourney Weaver, say, or Sharon Stone, and that's where the love story comes in. You gotta' have a love story, eh, Jacobs?"

"Uhhh, sure, J.B. Absolutely right! That's the love story. Hot stuff. Women readers will love it. The guys go for the sci-fi premise, and the girls love the romance, huh? That's what I'm talking about!"

"I'm with you. Go on."

"OK. So with the New Deal banged out, the Martians provide the Americans with adequate housing, competent health care, proper nourishment, essential educational facilities, and gainful employment for all Americans. They even take the money they were wasting on wars with Venus and Saturn and invest it in the new social programs."

"I see. Now you got the liberals slathering at the mouth. Dancing in the streets, right?"

"Right, J.B., they're loving it. But I got the other side on board, too."

"How's that? The Republicans will boycott this book."

"Wait for it, J.B. Wait for it."

"Oh, yeah?"

"Yeah. This is the best part. After reaping the benefits of the New Martian Deal, the Americans respond by forgiving the

Martians for past injustices perpetrated by their forebears, accepting responsibility for themselves and their problems, welcoming the burdens that go hand-in-hand with equality, and refusing to take advantage of naïve, guilt-ridden, pseudo-liberal Martians with their offers of special privileges and politically correct agendas."

"Wow!" the publisher exclaimed, chomping his cigar and banging his hand on his table. "You weren't kidding, Jacobs. Something for everybody. That's brilliant, is what that is. So tell me, what screws it all up? An earthquake? Dust storm? Volcanic eruption? I know they've got some big volcanoes on Mars. Or hey, what about an asteroid, huh? Just like Rod Serling would have done on the *Twilight Zone*. Like that, umm, *To Serve Man* episode, huh? 'It's not a policy book, it's a cookbook,' right, Jacobs? What have you got for me, there? Slay me, baby! Slay me."

The agent, whose face had slowly morphed from sheer elation to stunned disappointment during the publisher's rant, tried vainly to shake it off and recover.

"Uhhh, no, J.B. Nothing happens. Nothing bad, that is. Everything works out well, and the Martians and Americans live happily ever after." Gaining momentum as he spoke, the agent pressed gamely forward. "It's a happy ending, J.B., something everybody wants! Are you with me on this one, J.B.?"

The publisher bolted upright in his chair and smashed his cigar into an ashtray. "Are you crazy? A story with race and politics where everything works out OK? Are you kidding me, Jacobs? Hell, I can buy the Mars thing; anything like that goes after *Star Wars, Aliens,* and *Avatar,* you understand. But you gotta' be outa' your mind to fob off this mamby-pamby pablum on me. Everyone living happily ever after on Mars, my

"But J.B., I ... It's such a ... a happy ending ..."

"Get out of my office, Jacobs," the publisher barked with a dismissive wave of his hand. "Get the writer to change the ending or quit wasting my time."

"Right, J.B. I'll talk to him. Who knows, maybe he'll ..."

"SCAT!"

The agent scurried about like an ant under foot before gaining some measure of self-control and stumbling out the door. The publisher leaned back in his chair shaking his head in bewilderment. "Happy ending, my sweet ass," he muttered. "Who would ever believe a story like that? Even the American public's not gullible enough to swallow anything that far out."

HISTORY LESSON

John Clements shuddered and blinked his eyes in rapid succession as the shotgun barrel edged through the slight opening in the front door and halted several inches from the tip of his nose. Drops of sweat sprouted across his forehead despite the chilly breeze wafting across the shotgun house's screened-in porch. Clements struggled to remain calm, hands at his sides, eyes staring straight ahead.

Charles Ezell peered through the opening, cleared his throat, and mumbled, "What you want wif' me? Git da' hell off my porch!"

Clements choked down the lump rising steadily in his throat. "Ch...Charles? It's John Clements. Your lawyer. Your friend. Y-you don't want to shoot me, do you?"

"Lawyer Clements? Well, urruh, not 'less I has to."

Clements gazed past the looming gun barrel at the whites of two severely bloodshot eyes and the short grey hairs on Ezell's temple that stuck out like shortened porcupine spines. The sight of those grey hairs and the unmistakable ring of kindness evident in the old man's terrified voice helped ease Clements' mind. They were the first positive signs he'd encountered since he'd talked his way onto the porch and Ezell had greeted him with the business end of a double barreled twelve-gauge shotgun.

This is just a scared old man, Clements reminded himself. But a *good* man, if ever there was one. Even so, he had to say something. "You won't have to use that shotgun, Charles, I promise you."

"So you say."

"May I come in?"

"Where you is be just fine, right now."

"That's fine with me, too," Clements agreed, standing purposefully still. During their ten-year professional and personal relationship, Charles Ezell had never committed one lawless act, much less a crime of violence. He had killed in Germany during World War II, of course, but that had been different. Or so Clements now hoped. He waited patiently for Ezell to make the next move.

"What you want 'round here, lawyer?"

"You safe, Charles, nothing more. Why don't you put down the gun and let me come in?"

"Why don't you get on out from here and let me handle this by myse'f. This ain't no bird hunt today. You ain't got no business 'round here."

"These people don't want to hurt you, Charles," Clements said, gesturing across Ezell's front yard toward the F.B.I agents and sheriff's deputies crouching behind cruisers and unmarked government vehicles lining the street in front of Ezell's shotgun house.

"They goan' kill me soon as I steps off this here porch."

"The F.B.I. is going to kill you? Surely you don't believe that?"

"No suh."

"Sheriff Carter, then? Surely not Joe Carter...."

"Naw."

"Then what are you talking about, Charles? Who's going to kill you?"

"Same ones that got Levester, next door."

Clements had seen the photographs. Levester Riley had died of the Melanin-X plague, just as had thousands of

Washington County citizens in recent weeks. But unlike the rest, who had died slowly and agonizingly when the sun's rays had fried their skin off their bones, Levester had taken the hit *from inside his body*. The plague had somehow begun in his abdomen and eaten its way *out*. Riley had succumbed in a matter of seconds. Or so the F.B.I. experts had postulated.

"Levester died of the plague, Charles. At least that's what these agents told me."

"They was right. He flew the plane and they killed him. Now they goan' get me, too."

Clements' jaw dropped as he stared at his old friend in disbelief. "What plane, Charles? Do you mean the crop duster I saw flying over Leland the night before the plague began? Is that how this damn thing got started? Somebody paid Levester to dump the virus on the town from a goddamned crop duster?"

Suddenly, and without warning, Charles Ezell, a former army sergeant and 30 year construction foreman, sobbed like a ten-year old child.

"What's wrong, Charles?" Clements asked helplessly. He glanced back over his shoulder toward the myriad of law enforcement officers staring at them with guns drawn, some aimed in their direction. This was not the time, he reminded himself, to solve the mystery of Riley's death, or how it related to the sudden arrival of plague in Washington County. He had more immediate pressing concerns. "I'm sorry about Levester," he said, reaching through the doorway and placing a consoling hand on Ezell's shoulder. "You were good friends, I know."

Ezell blew his nose into an old, yellowed handkerchief. "He the lucky one, lawyer Clements. He ain't got to face it no more, like you and me. He gone now, jus' like a lotta' yo' folks 'round here. And I know who done the killin'."

Clements conciliatory expression vanished. "W-what?" he finally managed. "Who killed—"

"And they goan' get me too," Ezell interrupted frantically, "cause they knows I know. Jus' like Levester."

"What *do* you know, Charles? Let me help you. Please!"

"Ain't no help for you nor me. No help, now. No suh."

Clements pointed to the cars lining the street in front of Ezell's house, where local sheriff's deputies and F.B.I. agents crouched silently, awaiting the unfolding of events on Charles Ezell's porch. "They can help you, Charles, believe me. They're the F.B.I., for God's sake. And Sheriff Carter. You've known him all his life! Let me work it out for you, Charles. I've never let you down before, have I?"

Ezell grew silent except for measured, heavy breathing. "I knows you a good man, lawyer," he muttered, his voice ringing with a deep sadness that shook Clements to the core. "I knows that for sho'. You represented me fo' three years when I ain't had nothin' to pay 'cept some scraggly old chickens and all the birds you could shoot. But..."

"But what?"

Ezell breathed in deeply, exhaled slowly, then lowered the shotgun, opened the door, and stepped onto the sunlit porch.

"Thank you Charles," Clements said, gently lifting the shotgun in the air so everyone could see the danger had passed. "I want you to know that—"

Ezell suddenly placed a hand on Clements's shoulder. "You ever read yo' Bible, lawyer?"

The question took Clements by surprise. He tightened his grip on the shotgun. "What—"

"Book of Revelations, I mean."

Revelation, Clements started instinctively to say, but didn't. A common mistake, he realized, but not one that needed correcting just now. "Uh, no, Charles. Not for a long time."

Clements slowly raised his weaponed hand to halt the steadily advancing officers. The last thing he needed right now was for Charles to see heavily armed men advancing toward his porch and panic.

But the old man didn't panic. To the contrary, he seemed the very picture of serenity as he gazed calmly (resignedly?) into Clements's eyes.

"You ought to read yo' Bible, son. The last book tells how it all goan' end."

"What's going to end, Charles?"

"You knows what I'm talkin' 'bout."

Clements didn't. "Let's go talk to these agents and—"

Ezell began to speak, only to stumble backward in a shower of blood and bone fragments. He collapsed in a bloody heap onto the porch.

"Oh, God," Clements sputtered, staring down at the remains of Charles Ezell's head. He had seen photos of murder victims—big, 8 x 10 photos of heads bashed in, throats slashed ear to ear, and other typical murder case horrors. But none of it had prepared him for what he had just seen on his old friend's porch. He stumbled backwards until he fell off the porch and landed hard on a concrete sidewalk.

Before he could move, he felt the weight of another person on top of him. Clements looked up and saw Agent Bill Rhodes shielding him with his body as he barked orders to his men.

"That way," Rhodes shouted, pointing toward an abandoned house across the street. "It came from over there!"

Feeling an oddly warm sensation on his scalp, Clements ran his fingers along the crown of the back of his head. He struggled to see his hand. It was covered in a dark, red wetness. The world began to spin, and the last thing Clements heard before slipping into unconsciousness was the sound of automatic pistols and high-powered rifles popping all around him like a surreal July Fourth fireworks display on the outskirts of Hell.

TWO DAYS LATER

On Wednesday morning, after a brief, crosstown trip in Sheriff Joe Carter's cruiser from his temporary 'residence' in the Leland Psychotherapy and Recovery Center to his forthcoming sanity hearing at the Washington County Courthouse, John Clements sat impassively in the small, informal courtroom in the marbled building's cramped basement. The main upstairs courtroom hosted all the jury trials and this recently converted office space offered barely enough room for two counsel tables, a few extra chairs, and an unimpressive judge's bench which was nothing more than a hastily requisitioned modular-style lawyer's desk. The court personnel consisted of the judge, bailiff, two attorneys, a court reporter and two witnesses named Carter and Levine.

Seated at a counsel table beside his attorney, Clements ignored his psychiatrist, Dr. Allison Levine, as she testified about his mental state and opined that he suffered from extreme situational depression, subject to alternating fits of dangerous rage and sullen quietude. This had been brought on, she asserted, by the deaths of his fellow townspeople occasioned by the Melanin-X plague, which had reserved its most devastating effects for the lighter-skinned citizens of Washington County, including Clements' relatives and friends. His condition had been exacerbated, she continued dispassionately, by the death of Charles Ezell, another friend, who had been gunned down in front of him by an unknown assassin. Anyone would be challenged from a psychological standpoint by such harrowing circumstances, Levine assured the judge.

When she expressed concern that, in his current state of mind, he might harm himself or others, Clements appeared not to notice, much less care. Even her testimony regarding his bizarre conspiracy theory and cover up of the Melanin-X plague was met with stone-faced nonchalance by the respondent. But her testimony did have a noticeable effect on Judge Audrey Scott.

"Thank you, Dr. Levine," the judge said, peering balefully over her bifocals at an obviously disinterested Clements. She turned to the young prosecuting attorney. "Do you have any other witnesses, Mr. Hardy?"

"Yes, your honor," replied the short, mustachioed black man. "I call Mr. Clements, as an adverse witness."

"Very well. The witness will take the stand."

Clements complied with the nonchalance of a banker rejecting a homeless gypsy's loan application.

"I'll waive the oath," Judge Scott declared. "Mr Clements remains a member of the bar in good standing."

The youthful prosecutor wasted no time with preliminary inquiries. "So, Mr. Clements," he began, exuding the confidence of a lion tracking a baboon on barren terrain, "is it still your contention that local African Americans devised the Melanin-X plague to eradicate the white citizens of Washington County, and that the President's task force, including Nobel Laureate scientist Henry Roberts, the esteemed Dr. Levine, here, who, I note for the record, is Jewish and not African-American, oft-decorated F.B.I. Agent William Rhodes, and others presumably, are involved in a cover-up of this heinous act?"

Clements gave a wan smile. "I never said the original perpetrators were local. But yes, that's the general idea in a nutshell."

"Do you have any facts whatsoever upon which to base this curious claim?"

"Not really, no. It's just a theory."

Hardy approached the judge's bench, made fleeting eye contact with Judge Scott, turned back toward the witness and continued, "You're a lawyer, Mr. Clements. Surely you must know how preposterous this sounds to all of us, the court personnel? Conspiracies, racial genocide, and so on?'

"Is that a statement or a question, counselor?"

"A question," Hardy cooly replied.

"I suppose it makes me look paranoid. Rather like Caesar's wife on the Ides of March. Or, more to the point, like Socrates during his conspiracy trial. "

Hardy grinned. "Very good analogies, Mr. Clements. I'll grant you that. But, be honest with me, now. Isn't your theory more than just a *little* paranoid? Racial genocide, Presidential cover-ups, and all? Doesn't it sound more like an Oliver Stone movie than real life in Washington County?"

"Possibly. On the other hand, Mr. Hardy, I note that all the court personnel here are African American. Her honor, yourself, Sheriff Carter, even my own court-appointed counsel, the honorable Jesse Blackmon. The court reporter and the bailiff as well, I might add. I'm immersed, it seems, in a sea of distinguished black faces. Looks more like the cast of a Spike Lee movie than one of Oliver Stone's."

"And is it your contention," Hardy asked, gamely masking his astonishment that the witness seemed so intent upon incriminating himself, "that we, the court personnel, are also involved in this conspiracy and cover up?"

Clements smiled. "Not the conspiracy. Just the cover up."

"I see."

"However unwitting your participation may be."

"And as a good American citizen, are you prepared to do what ever becomes necessary to expose this conspiracy and avenge the murders of your fellow Mississippians?"

"I most certainly am prepared, to paraphrase the great Malcolm X, to do so by any means necessary."

"Even if it becomes necessary to use violence?"

"I have no doubt that violence *will* become necessary. You may recall that the Nazis, the Klan, and other such criminals in power never surrendered their authority simply because someone said, 'please'."

Hardy returned to his seat. "No more questions, your honor. I rest my case."

"Mr. Clements?"

"Yes, your honor?"

"Is it your contention that *I* am involved in some subterfuge of justice, designed specifically to silence yourself and, I suppose, others as well?"

"I don't know, Judge. As I said, it's only a theory. Not a contention at all."

"Even so, Mr. Clements, you must realize how this theory must sound to all of us."

"Yes, your honor. And I as I recall my father's telling of it, when your uncle was on trial in the 1960's for glaring at a white woman on the sidewalk—I believe 'Reckless Eyeballing' was the charge—don't you suppose your uncle experienced more than a little paranoia throughout those proceedings?"

Judge Scott's hand slid off her chin and thumped loudly as it landed on the bench. Before the noticeably stunned judge could frame a reply, the prosecutor cleared his throat.

"Neither paranoia nor emotional distress are the issues here today, your honor. Lord knows, the prosecution deeply sympathizes with Mr. Clements. Between the horrors of the recent plague and the experience he suffered with his friend, Mr. Ezell... To say nothing of the recent passing of his wife—"

"That's right," Clements growled, "say nothing about that. My wife died at the hands of a drunk driver before the plague arrived and she's got nothing to do with this!"

"Order in the court," boomed Judge Scott. "Please restrain yourself, Mr. Clements. And, Mr. Hardy, please make your point as quickly as possible."

"Yes ma'am. As I was about to say, the sole issue today is whether or not Mr. Clements represents a danger to himself or the community while in his current state of mind. Dr. Levine has answered that question in the affirmative. He is obviously prone to sudden angry outbursts, in addition to the recently attested delusional aspect of implicating all of the court personnel in a conspiracy to commit mass murder, to which he testified today. The man is dangerously depressed, your honor. The state requests remand to the appropriate psychiatric facility."

The judge cast a weary glance toward Clements's attorney. "What say you, Mr. Blackmon?"

Jesse Blackmon, the quintessential Philadelphia lawyer in his three-piece suit and distinguished touch of gray around the temples, rose to address the court. "Mr. Clements makes a good point, your honor. A very sane one, in my opinion, considering recent events and the prevailing court personnel."

Judge Scott lowered her head into her hands. "Not you, too, Mr. Blackmon," she finally said. "Do you find any credence whatsoever in this 'theory' about a governmental conspiracy, particularly as it involves Drs. Roberts and Levine, to say nothing of the members of this court?"

Blackmon merely shrugged his shoulders. "What can I say, your honor?"

"Good come back, Jesse," Clements mumbled sardonically.

"As Mr. Hardy has ably pointed out," Judge Scott declared, "the issue is one of danger to himself or to others. You've heard Dr. Levine's testimony in that regard. What has the defense to say to that?"

"Your honor, as far as this Court is aware, Mr. Clements has never done himself nor anyone else any physical harm. He fully cooperated with Agent Rhodes in an attempt to provide information on the perpetrators of the Melanin-X plague, in the course of which he witnessed the death of his friend, Mr. Charles Ezell. This is surely not an open and shut case. Furthermore, Dr. Levine is not his treating physician, and—"

"You're familiar with the additional authority given her by the federal Delta Emergency Relief Act, aren't you, Mr. Blackmon? The act rammed through Congress by the

President after the Melanin-X plague took the lives of thousands of residents of Washington County?"

"Of course, your honor. She has the right to act as his treating physician for purposes of this hearing. I don't object to her authority; I'm merely pointing out the lack of longitudinal care of my client by Dr. Levine. That goes to the weight of her testimony, not its admissibility. Furthermore, there's still no proof against my client beyond Dr. Levine's opinion based upon several privileged conversations between the two of them, during which my client neither threatened nor perpetrated any violence against himself, Dr. Levine, or anyone else."

"Good point, Mr. Blackmon. It would appear that you, at least, are not a part of Mr. Clements's conspiracy."

"Maybe not, your honor" Clements interjected. "And many Leland whites opposed the KKK in the 1940's. But that didn't stop the Klan from getting away with murder. No more than it stopped somebody from killing half our townspeople with the Melanin-X plague on New Year's Day."

"I rest *my* case," Blackmon said.

"Well," Judge Scott frowned, "this is getting us nowhere fast."

"May I make a suggestion, your honor?"

"Yes, Dr. Levine?"

The psychiatrist rose from her seat, adjusted her eyeglasses, straightened her herringbone jacket and approached Judge Scott's bench. "I neither ask for a full commitment nor believe that one is necessary under the circumstances."

"Then why, Doctor, have you burdened this court with your Petition?"

"The Emergency Relief Act," Levine said softly, "grants you the authority to give me supervisory status of Mr. Clements for 48 hours. That should give me all the time I'll need to determine the necessity of further intervention in his case."

"Sounds reasonable to me," Judge Scott declared, then banged her gavel loudly on her desk. "That will be the ruling of this Court. Prepare me an order, Mr. Hardy, and I'll see everybody back here in two days. Wednesday morning at 9:00 A.M. Sheriff Carter, escort Mr. Clements back to the Leland Psychotherapy and Recovery Center, where he'll remain under Dr. Levine's supervision for the next 48 hours."

Sheriff Carter led a brooding John Clements and pensive Allison Levine through an otherwise empty parking lot to his cruiser for a short ride back to the newly erected mental facility. As they cruised slowly down North Deer Creek Drive Clements gazed silently out the rear passenger seat window while Levine eyed him in the rear view mirror. She scanned his face for telltale signs of depression or ill will.

"John," she began, tentatively, "I hope you understand that what I did today I did solely in your best interests."

"No sweat, doc," he replied matter-of-factly.

Clements knew all he needed to do was bide his time for the next two days. After all he'd recently been through, two days of interpreting ink blots seemed like a springtime holiday in Paris. He pointed to the graceful, moss-laden oaks that towered over the lazy flowing dark brown waters of tiny Deer Creek.

"Look at all those black-birds, doctor. Did you know that before the plague gave us something else to worry about, we'd been trying to run them out of town since the late 1980's?"

"No," said Levine, glad to hear the upbeat tone of his voice. "I didn't."

"We sure did," Sheriff Carter added. "They'd show up here every other year or so, usually in the thousands. We tried everything from firecrackers to shotguns to run them off. But nothing ever worked."

"Be careful, Joe," Clements dead panned, "or somebody around here will accuse you of pinning a conspiracy and cover-up on our fine, feathered friends."

Carter frowned uneasily as he steered the cruiser north onto the Recovery Center's driveway.

Levine's smile evaporated. Forty-eight hours could be a very long time, she mused as she viewed a wickedly grinning John Clements in the cruiser's rear view mirror.

TWO MORE DAYS LATER

"Come in Mr. Clements."

Although he couldn't see anyone inside the darkened doorway, Clements obeyed the incorporeal voice without hesitation. He had nothing to lose, after all, having recently lost everyone he loved to the Melanin-X plague and having only gained his release from the Leland Psychotherapy and Recovery Center by such subterfuge as had become necessary to relieve himself of the emotional burdens forced upon him by a presumptuous psychiatrist and an overreaching judge. More significantly, he sensed that something remarkable was awaiting him across the threshold of the antebellum mansion looming before him.

The oversized, double panel oak doors opened wide onto a central dog-trot hallway from which a singular staircase rose along a side wall, then turned away from the supporting wall and made an unsupported half turn as it ascended to the second story. A great foyer divided the mansion into north and south wings, furnished in grand antebellum style with hardwood pine flooring, a Tussie Mussie courting couch and windows treated with velvet tapestry. But despite the mansion's grandeur, Clements' eyes were inescapably drawn to a tall, silver-bearded white man standing by himself on wide cypress steps halfway up the flying wing staircase.

"My name is Carl Sykes. Welcome to my home."

Clements frowned. "This is your home? I though this was now commercial property."

Sykes pointed to the second story. "Above us, yes. But the first floor is reserved for social occasions. And I presume that yours is a social call. Won't you join me in the parlor?"

The what? Clements almost said aloud before Sykes led him into a large living room that opened onto the north wing.

"Have a seat," Sykes entreated, gesturing toward two large, velvet-cushioned chairs sitting before a massive, marble-trimmed fireplace. "Drink?"

"No thanks."

"Very well. You may leave us, Linton."

Clements hadn't seen the younger, powerfully built black man lurking behind him; hadn't heard him close the front door or seen him standing rigidly in the hallway. The enormous gold-trimmed mirror over the fireplace afforded Clements a good view of Linton as the young man turned on his heels and silently exited the parlor.

Clements seated himself beside Sykes and found that he couldn't help staring at the imposing, older man. No less impressive off his feet, Sykes properly attired could have passed for a 19th Century Confederate general on leave from the front with his charcoal-grey suit, thin black string tie, well-groomed grey beard, full head of silver-edged black hair, and wide, powerful shoulders.

But even those aspects of Sykes' appearance, impressive though they were, paled by comparison to his piercing, coal-black eyes.

"Mr. Clements?"

"What? Uhmm... Yes?"

"Welcome to Three Oaks."

"Why did you send for me, Mr. Sykes?"

"Curiosity, perhaps."

"You were curious about me?"

"No, Mr. Clements," Sykes replied, leveling a muscled finger at his guest, "*you* were wondering about *me.*"

"I was?"

"Of course you were," Sykes said, his deep, sonorous voice assuming a barely discernable derisive tone. "You and everyone else in this town. But isn't that to be expected, after all? A new owner ensconces himself in the largest antebellum mansion in the county and cruises around town in a long, white, limousine? Hmpf. Yes, Mr. Clements, we both know how small town minds react to news like that."

"So you say, Sykes."

Clements searched the man's face for the slightest reaction to his own casual, bordering-on-disrespectful use of Sykes's last name. Seeing none, he tried another approach. "As it turns out, some of us small town yokels even go so far as to take a spin by the county courthouse and find out who owns that impressive mansion and costly limousine. It seems that Sykes Enterprises is quite the growing concern."

"Very good," Sykes replied confidently, maintaining relentless eye contact with Clements. "I like a man who comes prepared. And I want you to know that I took it as a compliment when my man in the courthouse phoned and informed me of the diligent title search you ran before accepting my invitation to Three Oaks."

Clements nodded cordially, mentally conceding round one to the increasingly mysterious Carl Sykes. *So they've been watching me since I left the Recovery Center,* he realized. *I won't underestimate the man again.*

"And what else did you discover, counselor?"

Clements crossed his legs and settled back into the chair. "That if your land grabbing continues at the present rate we'll be renaming Leland as 'Sykesland'."

"Hardly, Mr. Clements. Mere egotism drives lesser men than you and I."

"Greed, then. Or power."

"Mundane, Mr. Clements. Mundane. What is it the young people say? Been there, done that?"

"What then, if I may be so bold?"

"I doubt you'd believe me if I told you."

"I'll take that chance."

"But *I* won't," declared Sykes, rising from the chair. "At least not yet. Won't you join me in my second floor study?"

"Do I have a choice?" Clements asked, cautiously watching Linton in the mantle mirror as the young man entered the room and took his place at Sykes's side.

"No, Mr. Clements. You don't."

Sykes guided Clements up the mansion's winding staircase. Linton thrust open a door at the top of the stairs and Clements stood gaping in the doorway.

Sykes' "study" had little in common with the stately first floor rooms of his antebellum manor. Row after row of computers and surveillance monitors filled the room, each of them manned by young, professional-looking black men. Powerfully built, grim-visaged, armed-to-the-teeth henchmen, both black and white, stood guard at all the entrances. The east-facing window, Clements observed, offered a spectacular view of the hardwood forest surrounding the mansion.

Before Sykes led Clements out of the room, the latter realized that the machines were not personal computers at all, but a network of virtual reality terminals operated by each user's hand signals and voice control. Bereft of conventional keyboards and PCs, Sykes's was a first class operation, the type only millionaires and high level government agencies could afford or operate.

"Reserved for social occasions, you say?" Clements offered dryly.

Sykes ignored the remark. "What do you think of my planning room, Mr. Clements?"

"Planning room? What do you plan in there?"

"The future, of course. What else is there? Now, if you'll join me in my basement parlor?"

Sykes gestured toward another stairway, which led directly to the basement. In striking contrast to the upstairs room, with its futuristic terminals and heavily armed, Gucci-shoed, Armani suit-wearing guards, Sykes' basement parlor, like the first floor, was laid out in authentic antebellum decor.

"Have a seat," Sykes commanded.

Clements seated himself on a velvet-covered love seat beside a massive 1876 centennial grand piano.

"Drink? Cigar?"

"No thanks."

"Fine. To business, then."

"Good. What do you want from me, Sykes?"

Sykes produced a long, thin black cigar from a rolltop desk drawer, lit it with a jewel-encrusted, sterling silver lighter, leaned back in his chair, and fixed his gaze upon an increasingly restless Clements.

"Call me "Carl," please."

Clements shrugged his shoulders. "What may I do for you, *Carl?*"

"Do for me?"

"Why am I here? Why'd you invite me here? What do you *want*, Sykes?"

"You, Mr. Clements. I want you."

"I beg your pardon?"

"Our mutual friend, a Miss Megga Coxwell, the lady who extended my invitation to you this morning, informs me that you were once an exceptional trial lawyer. Very well connected, I understand."

"I guess you could say that I've been pretty well disconnected since New Year's Eve."

Sykes smiled briefly, then pointedly met Clements's baleful glare. "Things have a way of changing all too suddenly, don't they, my friend? That's why it's so important to be associated with the right organization."

Clements avoided the larger man's penetrating gaze. "So you say, Sykes. So you say."

Even though he'd refused to look in Sykes's direction when he had spoken, he still felt Sykes's eyes burning holes through the side of his face. *What is it about those eyes*, Clements wondered. Pools of the darkest light imaginable. Easy to get lost in, and well nigh impossible to escape. And the voice was even worse. Terrifying, and consequently, all the more alluring. Clements began to understand how Megga could have fallen under Carl Sykes's spell. He only hoped that she hadn't—

Sykes cleared his throat. "Opportunities abound here in my organization, Mr. Clements. You only need to seize them."

"And what kind of opportunities might those be?"

"Just now, I'm in need of a good general counsel for my employees. You know, the day-to-day legal problems of—"

"Youthful psychopaths?"

Sykes' mirthless laughter struck a sore spot deep in Clements's soul. "Hardly, Mr. Clements, hardly. You must have faith in the young. This is their century, you see. 'Out with the old in with the new' as they say. But more to the point, I was thinking about the civil law; real estate transactions, business mergers, incorporations, and such. You take my meaning?"

"Sure," Clements replied grudgingly. "You need help with your land-grabbing and power brokering. I believe I understand you perfectly well."

"Excellent. Then you're precisely what I need!"

"You're offering me a job?"

"Precisely. Surprised?"

"Well, I didn't expect—"

"Always expect the unexpected, Mr. Clements. That's how you stay ahead in the game."

"Ahead," Clements asked pointedly, "or alive?"

A barely perceptible yet unmistakably sinister smile spread slowly across Sykes's lips. "These are perilous times, Mr. Clements. Or may I call you John?"

Clements shrugged his shoulders with studied nonchalance. "Offhand, I'd say you're more in the market for computer specialists than lawyers."

"Oh?"

"Well, apart from the wall to wall virtual reality terminals upstairs, there's your recent purchase of the Stoneville Agricultural Research Station land."

"Excellent," Sykes boomed. "A good lawyer covers all the bases. I see I was not misled about your capabilities."

"As you so accurately pointed out, this is a small town, Sykes. Even courthouse clerks talk out of hand."

"Yes," Sykes mused, "a small town indeed. Somewhat smaller as of late, I'm afraid."

"Yes," Clements replied icily. "I don't suppose you have any idea how this recent decrease in the local population came about?"

"How should I?"

"Let's just call it a hunch."

Sykes rose and crossed to an elegant oaken cabinet which he opened to reveal an antique crystal decanter beside a set of Waterford crystal glasses. He retrieved a bottle of Gentleman Jack Reserve bourbon. "Won't you join me," he asked, pouring himself a glass.

Clements nodded 'yes'. If ever he needed a drink...

"Very good."

The two men sipped their bourbon in silence. Clements wondered if Sykes had acquired his taste in whiskey from their mutual friend, Megga. He hoped not with all his heart. Sykes didn't deserve a woman like Megga. Not in a million years.

Sykes cleared his throat again. "I'm glad to see that you appreciate good bourbon whiskey, John. I'm also impressed with the way you speak your mind. An up front man is always to be treasured."

Clements made no effort to disguise the contempt in both his expression and his voice. "Well, *Carl*, since you're so fond of my forthrightness, try this one for size—I'm not for sale. Not interested in becoming one of your... minions."

"Minions?" Sykes roared gleefully. "You make me sound like the Devil, himself, Mr. Clements. Hmpf. Minions, indeed."

Sykes took a long draw on his cigar and exhaled the smoke through his nose. "Well, perhaps another approach will interest you. Why don't we, to borrow a local colloquialism, shell the corn, Mr. Clements."

"By all means, Sykes. You first, if you don't mind."

"Very well," agreed Sykes. "Let's suppose that I'm as well informed about current events as you suspect."

"Cataclysmic current events, you mean? Those pertaining to the Melanin-X plague that recently claimed the lives of the majority of white citizens in Washington County?"

"Precisely."

"I'm listening."

"I only discuss those matters with my friends, John. Are you interested in being my friend?"

"No, but as a concerned citizen and an officer of the court I'm wondering why you haven't turned over any such information you have to the F.B.I. or local authorities. I'm sure *they'd* be interested in making new friends."

"Many of the local authorities already *are* my friends," Sykes said in a chillingly monotonous tone. "They know everything I know. Or almost everything."

"How many 'local authorities' do you own?"

"Just enough to convince those I don't own to concern themselves only with matters that pertain to them."

"Such as?"

"Staying alive."

"I see."

"Do you?"

"I don't know, Sykes. Do I? Lately, all I've been seeing is black, but my psychiatrist tells me I should be color blind. What do you think about that?"

"Ah, yes. The estimable Dr. Allison Levine. *She* turned me down, too. I suppose I'm just going to have to learn to deal with this sudden wave of rejection."

Clements' self-assured demeanor evaporated like a teardrop on the sun. "You tried to hire Allison, too?"

"Yes. Just this morning. There's always room at Sykes Enterprises for a woman of her considerable abilities."

"Plenty of employees with deep-seated psychological problems, no doubt."

"Guilty consciences, you mean to say?"

"To the contrary, Sykes, I believe the word is 'psychopathic.' As in free of a guilty conscience, but never free of guilt."

"I'm afraid," Sykes said, pouring them both another drink, "that we seem to be understanding each other a little too well."

Clements finished off his glass.

"I understand how you feel, John, believe me."

"Is that so?"

"Oh, yes. My extraordinary appreciation of history gives me a deeper understanding of human nature than you might expect."

"What are you talking about...'History'?"

"Local history."

Clements managed a puzzled expression.

"It's simple, really," Sykes continued. "This great land was settled by your ancestors, John. Brave souls who traveled humble sailboats across a vast tempestuous ocean seeking their long sought Promised Land. But just as God's Chosen People found their Promised Land to be already inhabited by the Canaanites, so too, did your ancestors find this great land inhabited by another race of people. In this particular region— Choctaws, Chickasaws, and a tribe called the Yazoo, if I'm not greatly mistaken."

Clements nodded.

"But, your ancestors, John, much like God's Chosen People before them, had a better use to make of the new land that destiny had afforded them. So they asked God's blessing and appropriated it for themselves and their posterity, using such means as they found necessary to do so."

"What's your point?"

"Patience, my young friend. Patience. Now, the new chosen people, your ancestors and mine, felt no malice toward the previous owners, the Native Americans, who had lived here for untold millennia. Our ancestors simply acted in accordance with the fulfillment of their manifest destiny. After all, it's only human to take what you need. Don't you agree?"

"Go on."

"Meanwhile, the new owners found this land exceedingly fertile but somewhat temperate for their Northern European tastes. They needed someone more accustomed to these warmer climes to till the soil and reap its harvests. So they reached back across the Atlantic and took for themselves yet another race of people who had the stamina to reclaim this land from its innumerable bayous and swamps in less than a single century."

"This new race of people," Clements said sarcastically, "must have really welcomed the opportunity to enjoy a hard day's work for a hard night's whipping."

"As you say," Sykes replied perfunctorily. "The workers were forced to labor without pay, were required to be content with a meal or two a day, enjoyed the most Spartan housing arrangements imaginable, and suffered a good whipping now and again just to keep things interesting."

"Sounds like the new chosen people really knew how to keep their workers entertained," Clements quipped.

"Indeed they did. Not that the new chosen people had anything against the new workers, any more than they had harbored any ill will against the original inhabitants of these lands. They simply required the workers' services and did what was necessary to secure them. And with their workers' aid and the blessing of their Christian God they built the greatest nation this world has ever known."

"We're all so very proud."

"As well you should be, John. For you are the epitome of everything the new chosen people sought to become.

Handsome, well educated, successful, enjoying the fruits of your labors to the fullest extent."

"Until those fruits turned sour over the Christmas holiday."

"How true," Sykes agreed before returning unceremoniously to his seat, the history lesson apparently over.

"Just tell me one thing, Sykes, if you will."

"By all means."

"I'm wondering about the meaning behind your little story."

"Yes?"

"Is it an allegory, with a little foreshadowing thrown in for good measure?"

Sykes smiled approvingly. "You are an excellent student, Mr. Clements. I applaud you. But you are mistaken about one little thing."

"Oh?"

"I believe we've seen more than just a little hint of things to come. The future, my friend, is already upon us."

"What do you mean?" Clements asked apprehensively.

"As you have apparently surmised, recent 'cataclysmic events' are little more than a foreshadowing of far greater things to come."

Clements's eyebrow arched as he snapped to attention and gripped the chair's arm rests tightly with both hands. "You're saying that whoever's responsible for what's happened around here won't be satisfied with one little self-contained plague? He'll be expanding operations throughout Mississippi?"

"Mississippi?" Sykes bellowed, his eyes sparkling with amusement. "Why, surely someone capable of engineering such a feat as this so-called "Melanin-X virus" would think on a larger scale than just one insignificant southern state. The Promised Land of the new millennium must include more than just one state, or even one region! Mississippi, Virginia, Illinois, New York, California... Nothing short of this entire nation would suffice. Or as much of it as this new age's Chosen People desired to claim.

"All the former bastions of racial injustice we know collectively as the United States of America must fall," Sykes said curtly, scorn having suddenly replaced magnanimity as his basic mode. "Land of the privileged, home of the slaves–this must be replaced by be the New Promised Land, Mr. Clements. The new Chosen People, once slaves to the old regime, will rise to prominence as—"

"You're out of your mind," Clements interrupted, his voice brimming with disgust. "You can't be serious. Can you?"

"Oh, Mr. Clements," said Sykes, wagging a finger as if he were a parent admonishing a child, "you may be certain that I am quite serious. Hypothetically speaking, of course," he added, grinning wickedly as he leaned back in his seat.

"How could you...How could *anyone* hope to get away with such a thing? You must realize that..."

Clements' voice trailed off as he considered the possibilities of Sykes's grandiose scheme. A belt of rising panic tightened around his chest.

"Realize what?" Sykes asked contemptuously. "That someone might wish to stop it? Who will stop it? No one stopped manifest destiny. No one saved the Canaanites from Joshua's blaring trumpets and his followers' flashing swords. Oh, no, Mr. Clements, the success of this recent cataclysmic event, as you call it, has insured that the advent of the new manifest destiny is at hand. No one will stop it. They won't even *suspect* it until their time has run out."

"But why, Sykes? What possible interest have you got in a crazy scheme like that?"

"Let's just say that, like my illustrious great, great grandfather—"

"Your great, great grandfather? What are you babbling about, Sykes?"

"Why, John Brown, Mr. Clements. My great-great grandfather was none other than the infamous Kansas abolitionist John Brown."

"J-John Brown?" Clements stuttered.

"Yes. The man your forefathers hung for mounting a slave insurrection at Harper's Ferry in 1859. You may not recall all the anecdotal aspects of your Civil War-era history, but my estimable forebear fathered twenty children, leaving behind a considerable progeny of which I am the most outstanding descendant."

An uncomfortable silence hung over the room like an early morning fog blanketing a mud-flecked back country roadway.

"John Brown was as insane as you are," Clements finally offered. "You may have forgotten your basic psychiatry, Sykes, but insanity runs in the family."

"I'm as sane as you are, Mr. Clements," Sykes replied calmly. "Like my great, great grandfather, I'm merely a man who cares deeply about bringing justice to this godforsaken nation."

"Justice!" howled Clements. "My God, Sykes! Being politically correct is one thing, but don't you think you're taking this black power thing a little too far?"

"The point is, Mr. Clements, *whoever* is responsible for bringing plague to Washington County should be immanently capable of introducing it wherever else he so chooses."

"But you can't..." Clements began, his voice trailing off as he realized how easily Sykes could make good his threat. He could just as easily inject an air-bourn virus into other communities across the nation as he had already done in Leland. Crop duster planes would do the trick as they apparently had done here. Once the cold weather disappeared in late spring, every city in North America would be vulnerable to an unstoppable, unquenchable plague!

"We can't...*I* won't let you do this, Sykes," Clements cried as he leapt to his feet. "I won't, I tell you!"

"Is that so," Sykes scoffed, calmly crossing his legs and steepling his fingers. "And just how do you propose to stop me?"

A powerful sense of aloneness, of an all-too-keenly realized vulnerability, suddenly descended upon Clements as he stared into the teeth of the four basement walls enclosing him in Three Oaks mansion. He glanced nervously around the room. Although he and Sykes were alone, their conversation was surely being monitored by Sykes's thugs on the high-powered surveillance equipment he had seen in Sykes's 'study.' And he was stranded in the basement of a well-guarded mansion, bounded by a lake on one side, acres of cotton fields on two more, and a dense forest encircling the entire property.

He was entirely at Carl Sykes's mercy.

Lost in thought, oblivious to his surroundings, Clements was startled by the unexpected presence of a powerful but surprisingly gentle hand on his shoulder. He felt helpless to resist as Sykes guided him back down into his chair.

"Have another drink," Sykes murmured warmly as he filled Clements's glass with bourbon. "You appear to have seen a ghost."

"I see them every day," Clements mumbled.

"Yes, John, I know. The ways of Fate are inscrutable. An unfortunate certainty of human existence. But we must never lose sight of the future. And the limitless opportunities it affords those with the courage and vision to seize them."

"Opportunities?" Clements mumbled listlessly.

"Yes, my friend. Opportunities. Won't you join me, after all?" Sykes entreated, rising imperiously from his chair.

Wholly defeated, unable even to make a plausible *show* of resistance, Clements followed Sykes to the study's far doorway. Sykes flung open the door, revealing the most un-antebellum room yet. Clements gaped at what could only be a saunatorium with a large, free-standing marble hot tub mounted on a wooden deck, flanked by a large glass-walled shower and wet bar. But it hadn't been the hardware that had taken away his breath.

Megga Coxwell, Clements' friend and former lover, stood completely nude, waist deep in the hot tub, beside a younger, equally lovely nude black woman whom Clements recognized as one of his Recovery Center nurses. They beckoned for Clements to join them.

"Come on, John-boy," Megga coaxed in her sensually-charged husky voice. The hot steam assaulted Clements' face just as Sykes' whiskey warmed his insides and took the edge off his frazzled nerves.

"You see, John," Sykes urged enthusiastically, "the future has so much to offer the man of vision and courage. Life becomes a paradise for those who wisely abandon the old, archaic ways for the righteous path of justice in a new world order."

Sykes's voice snapped Clements out of his trance-like state. The time had come, he realized with unwelcome certainty, to give Sykes the answer he demanded.

But how, Clements asked himself, could he side with the man who'd destroyed everything and almost everyone he had ever cared about? A man who would keep on destroying people's lives until somebody put an end to his god-forsaken Melanin-X nightmare.

But I can't stop him, Clements anguished, *and if I refuse him now he'll kill me. Just like Charles Ezell and the others.*

Clements felt on the verge of panic when his mind's eye inexplicably caught sight of the face of his dead wife, Susan. With the two women beckoning to him from the hot tub and Sykes standing so close he could feel the man's breath on the back of his neck, all Clements could see was the vision of the woman he once loved, and the child they had conceived but never known thanks to an intoxicated socialite who had crossed a yellow highway line and claimed his wife's and unborn son's lives.

While Sykes stood waiting for his answer; while Megga and her 'friend' embraced in Sykes's hot tub, John Clements simply closed his eyes and dreamed of what might have been.

"I'll have your answer, Mr. Clements."

I don't know why you were taken from me...
"Mr. Clements?"
"But I know what you'd say right now."
"What's that?" Sykes demanded. "What *who* would say now? You're running out of time Mr. Clem—"
"Can it Sykes," Clements announced with a confidence that surprised himself even more than Sykes. "Do what you want with me, but I'll be damned if I'll join you and betray the memory of those you murdered with your unholy plague."

Sykes pressed against Clements, towering over the smaller man, his eyes ablaze with anger.

A person could get lost in those eyes, Clements thought, *but I'm sure as hell not going to be one of them.*

"Don't take it personally, Sykes," he said, backing slowly away from the larger man. "I'd say the same thing to any other psychopath in the same situation."

To Clements's surprise, Sykes merely nodded, his eyes turning as cold and empty as a glass in the moonlight. He closed the door to the sauna room and politely gestured for Linton, standing nearby in the parlor doorway, to join them.

"As you wish, Mr. Clements. Linton, please see our guest to his car, won't you?"
"Yes, sir."
"Just one thing, Sykes."
"Yes?"

"Assuming that you really do believe in what you're doing, that you're really just crazy instead of supremely evil, how do you rationalize murdering millions of innocent people to attain your goal, however justified your acts may appear to be by virtue of past wrongs and institutions?"

Sykes smiled. "The same way your forebears rationalized the eradication of the native tribes and the enslavement of West Africans. It's what's best for those I care about. For those who've suffered in this country all their lives. Whose forebears suffered untold horrors for the past four hundred years. It's as simple as that, Mr. Clements. "

"But the judgment of history is that my forebears acted wrongly when they practiced genocide and enslavement. Hell, Sykes, yours is the same rationalization the Germans used to start WWII. The rationale Julius Caesar used to slaughter a million Gauls in Rome's greatest 'defensive' war."

"Very good, Mr. Clements. You've hit upon the most appropriate examples of all—Adolph Hitler and Julius Caesar. With Alexander, Napoleon, Lenin, Stalin and Mao, they alone cast aside the prevailing hypocritical morality of their day and changed the entire course of human history."

"You're linking yourself with Stalin... *and Hitler?* And smiling about it?"

"No, Mr. Clements, I'm no Hitler or Stalin. The people I'm aiding aren't Nazis or Communists, and the ones I'm replacing are hardly innocent victims, as you yourself have acknowledged."

"But *mass murder,* Sykes... How can a man of your intelligence ever believe
that—"

Sykes silenced him with a gesture. "I'll put it to you, Mr. Clements. If I fail to take this step, how long will it take these people—these descendants of slaves and heirs to several hundred years of racial injustice–how long will it take them to pick themselves up by their own bootstraps and take their rightful place as equal partners in this nation?"

"If you're referring to African Americans, Sykes, they're doing just fine without your help. Good God, man, they owned half the businesses in this town before you ever showed up. We had a black mayor, sheriff, and half a city council before you came down here with your goddamned plague. What the hell more do you want?"

"I want justice, Mr. Clements. *Today,* not tomorrow. Do you expect me to believe that a people downtrodden for four hundred years can erase that past in time to save all the precious children's lives that will be lost in the next few decades for lack of action by an uncaring white upper class?"

"But we were doing just fine without your help, Sykes. People were learning to get along, to live together as friends—"

"Doing just fine? With all of their great leaders like Malcolm X, Dr. King, and Medgar Evers destroyed by your white society, leaving such lesser lights as Farrakhan, Jesse Jackson, and Al Sharpton to lead them? How far can they hope to go in the next fifty or a hundred years? With TV talk show hosts to teach them morality, white drug dealers to keep them entertained, and a useless public school system to educate them, how far do you think they will rise in the next ten or twenty years?"

"But *you* know what's best for them, eh, Sykes?"

"I, the superior man, not only know what's best for them, but am capable of doing that which they themselves would never do, despite all the injustices you and your forebears have perpetrated upon them. I alone am willing to do what must be done.

"To end the shame of children living in ramshackle houses with rats as their constant companions, bereft of hope for advancement for the balance of their lives. While you, Mr. Clements, you and your kind, drive your expensive foreign cars from your white-columned mansions to your beachfront condominiums and your country club balls, and sit in your lily-white, sanctified churches every Sunday morning, with *never a thought* for your less fortunate brothers and sisters! And you have the temerity to accuse me of rationalization!

"No, Mr. Clements. Not another century, not another decade, not another year!" Sykes loomed menacingly over Clements. "Not another day!"

Clements glared silently at Sykes, his heart thumping wildly in his chest. "Well," he finally said, "I suppose you do have a point, Sykes. Why should they limit themselves to their own duly elected leaders when you, a murderer of thousands of innocent men, women and children, are willing to lead them. How lucky for you that Saddam Hussein and Idi Amin are no longer around to offer another option. "

"Goodbye, Mr. Clements," Sykes said in a detached, perfunctory manner.

Linton took Clements by the arm, guided him up the basement stairs, through the front foyer, and out the massive double doors of Three Oaks plantation house.

Clements started his rental car and drove out the mansion's driveway onto the dirt road that connected Sykes's house to the paved road leading toward downtown Leland. Despite his unfamiliarity with the dirt road Clements kept his eyes focused on the rear-view mirror and the fleet of black sedans lining Sykes' circular driveway as he sped down the gravel road toward exceedingly doubtful safe haven in downtown Leland.

MOTHER OF THE CRIME

David Pang took the free time afforded him by a prospective divorce client's cancellation to visit the mother of Roosevelt Dixon, a court-appointed client charged with capital murder. The Dixons had no phone so he took an early lunch and drove across town to the address his client had given him during their jailhouse interview the day before.

Bertha Dixon lived in a rough neighborhood known as Baptisttown in south Greenwood, its tarnished landscape dotted with row after row of dilapidated shotgun houses. Abandoned, broken down car hulks decorated many front yards; few mail boxes remained where their original owners had planted them decades earlier. Her one-story, wood frame shotgun house, so named because shotgun pellets fired through the front door would pass unimpeded out the back, stood on Avenue G two blocks from Lusco's restaurant and just across the street from Booker's Place, a shotgun house-style juke joint whose former owner, Booker Wright, had actually been shotgunned to death by gang members during the past year's neighborhood celebration of Martin Luther King's birthday.

The stout, big-boned woman greeted the lawyer on her shade porch. Pang found the native intelligence shining in her eyes incongruous with her exceedingly humble neighborhood and abode. But to his complete surprise, he discovered that, though her tiny shack was a shambles on the outside, its interior was spotlessly clean and well kept. He also noted that she showed no indication of surprise or disdain that her son's appointed lawyer was Korean. And he'd seen that look enough to know it when it reared its ugly head.

She handed him a glass of iced tea then seated him on an ancient but pristine living room couch.

"Thanks for the tea, Mrs. Dixon."

"You's welcome, lawyer. How my son Roosevelt doin' in that jail?"

"He's fine Ms. Dixon. Saw him earlier today. I felt it would be best to meet you today and see if you could help me help Roosevelt with his case."

"Anything I can do, lawyer," she said with an innocent sincerity that evoked a degree of pity in Pang that he had to struggle to conceal.

"Of course," he finally managed with studied, professional non-chalance. "Thank you. Now…How long have you been living here?"

"Me and my brother lef' our home 'bout twenty-five years ago and come here to Greenwood. I reckon I been livin' in this house for twenty-three years. My Roosevelt wuz born in this house."

"Where did you live before?"

"Leland, another Delta town right out from—"

"Greenville. I grew up in Greenville, myself. Still have a fishing cabin just up the road on Lake Ferguson."

"Well, ain't that somethin'," she said.

"It sure is," Pang lied. This was no social visit; his client was charged with capital murder he desperately needed Bertha Dixon's assistance. "Why did the two of you move here? Looking for better jobs?"

"Reckon so. My brother Willie been fired from his job and the finance company evicted us out my mama's old house."

"Willie Robinson, now a Greenwood policeman?"

"My brother, yeah. He and I wuz teenagers lookin' for work and somewhere to stay. We had folks here in Babtisttown."

"Are you married, Mrs. Dixon?"

"Naw suh. Not no mo'. I still goes by his last name, tho'. My common-law husband Jessee Dixon wasn't nothin' but an old shade tree mechanic. Worked about.... well, to tell the truth," she laughed good-naturedly, her face glowing with a surprising healthiness, "whenever he felt up to it. He run off a coup'la years ago. Don't come round here no mo'. Actually, I run him off after he wuz too rough on my Roosevelt. Used to pistol whip my boy 'till Roosevelt wuz so scared of guns that he ain't never touched one since. All Jessee Dixon lef' us wuz some doctor bills to pay and his last name for me and my son."

"I see. How far did Roosevelt go in school?"

"'Leven years."

"A Junior?"

The woman's eyes knitted questioningly.

"Was he one year from graduating?"

"Aw, no. He got held back twice. Don't know why. He can read and write as good as anyone come out'n that school."

"Does he have any prior criminal record?"

"Jus' in youth court. He ain't never been in the big house befo'. He jus' twenty-three."

"Good. Then he can testify at the guilt phase of his trial, if need be. Was Roosevelt employed when he was arrested?"

"Naw suh. He worked in the shop with Jesse for a time. Then nothin'. Jobs 'round here been tight the last few years."

Pang shook his head. Not good. Juries were not overly fond of unemployed alleged killers.

"Mrs. Dixon," he continued stiffly, "I need to ask you a few questions regarding bail. In the event I can obtain bail for your son, that is. Do you understand?"

"Sho' do."

"Do you have any money to put up for bail?"

"Look around you, lawyer," she said, her gap-toothed grin widening, "do it look like I got money to put up for bail? Shoot, wouldn't have no food neither if it wasn't for the stamps."

"Do you own any property?"

She chuckled as she waved her arm in a circular gesture. "Oh yeah. I owns all a' dis."

"Is your house paid for? Can you borrow any money on it?"

"I done tried to do that befo', but the bank won't give me the time of day. Now the finance company is mo' than willin' to hep' out, but they done already took my car the last time, so I ain't messin' with them no mo'."

"What about Roosevelt's father?"

Her pleasant smile suddenly vanished. "What you know 'bout Roosevelt's father?"

"Nothing. Nothing except what you've told me. Why do you ask?"

She watched his puzzled expression for a moment, until a wan smile creased her face. "Never mind 'bout his father," she finally said. "He goan' do what he goan' do, and it still goan' be up to me, like it been up to me every day of Roosevelt's life." After a slight pause she added, "And up to you now, lawyer."

Pang nodded. "Yes, Mrs. Dixon. I'm going to do everything I can for your son."

"You goan' be able to get him outa 'dat jail, or is he goan be there for a long, l-o-n-g while?"

"He'll remain in jail until the trial unless I can....Unless you can come up with the bail money."

She settled back into her chair and breathed what to Pang seemed almost a sigh of relief. "Yessuh. I 'spose so. Lord knows I tried to raise that boy right, lawyer Pang. But he ain't had no chance to get no education like his uncle Willie. They was just too much happnin' in this neighborhood. Those hoodlums used to beat him up all the time. And they did some things to my baby that wuz worse than jus' a beatin'. And then, later on, there wuz jus' too much easy money on them streets for a po' boy like my Roosevelt to pass up."

"Drug money, you mean?"

She closed her eyes, bobbing her chin up and down. "I sho' tried, lawyer Pang. But they's only so much one po' old woman can do. White folks ain't never come 'round here offering hep outa' the goodness of they hearts. Black folks don't care neither. They got they own problems, I 'spose."

"I understand, Mrs. Dixon," he lied again. How could he, a second generation American and a trial lawyer making more money in a year then she had probably seen in her life, understand anything of Bertha Dixon's experiences or those of her forebears? Him, having every possible advantage, and her, saddled with every conceivable barrier life could erect. No, he didn't understand what Bertha Dixon had been through, and was damned thankful for his ignorant good fortune.

"Do you think you can get a ride to the courthouse this afternoon," he asked, "for the three o'clock preliminary hearing? If not I can—"

"I be there. Melbertha 'cross the screet be home by two thirty. She'll brang me."

"Good. You won't need to testify, but I'm sure you'd like to be there. You know... For moral support."

"Yes, suh, I sho' would."

"Well, I suppose I should be going," he said rising. "Thanks for the tea and—"

Moving faster than he would have thought possible, Bertha Dixon blocked Pang's path to the front doorway. "My baby," she said, "he got off on the wrong track somehow. I knows that. He prob'ly done what they say he done. He go crazy when he get on that crack. But he's all I got, lawyer Pang. No matter what he done, he still my baby boy. You goan' do all you can for him, ain't you?"

"Uh...yes, ma'am. I promise you I'll do everything I can. There may even be a chance that I can work some kind of deal to put him on the street, today, should the hearing bring out anything favorable to our case."

Bertha Dixon shook her head. "That ain't what I means, lawyer. I didn't say that puttin' my Roosevelt on the street is the best thing for him. What I means is... Is you goan' try to save his life?"

"I'm going to do my best, Mrs. Dixon. I promise you that."

She watched the lawyer's eyes closely as he spoke, until, confidant of his sincerity, she turned slowly away, granting him permission to leave.

Pang supposed that experience had taught her to discern when people were lying to her face. He hoped she had seen that he was not.

He had no doubt about what he had seen in *her* face, though. It was a look he had seen in many mothers' faces when they'd asked him to save their sons' lives—deep, hollowed-out shadows under frightened, mist-shrouded eyes. Those eyes provided considerably more motivation than Judge Markham's' $60 per-hour-court-appointed-wages ever could.

"Don't you worry, Mrs. Dixon," he said. "I've never lost a client before."

"Jus' don't make my baby be the first," Bertha Dixon urged as Pang stepped off her porch onto the front walkway.

As he headed toward his car Pang remembered his father's words when he, at the tender age of eight, had asked his dad why poor people committed so many crimes. His father, a first generation American and self-made man, had given him a stern expression and said, "You don't worry about that. You just be thankful you not one of them."

Pang shuffled down the cracked concrete pathway leading to the driveway, noticing for the first time how hollow his feet sounded as he walked. He glanced back onto the porch as he backed his car out of Bertha Dixon's rut-pocked, gravel driveway. The haunted look he saw in her eyes remained foremost on his mind as he drove his shiny black eight-thousand dollar Mercedes along the pothole-plagued Martin Luther King Drive toward his more fashionable side of town.

AFTER THE STORM

"Stevie," said Drew Stone, taking his son gently by the arm, "why don't you give Father Noonan a hand with the folks in the food line. And get yourself something to eat while you're at it."

"Sure thing, Dad."

"Your mother and I are going to take a look around."

The boy hurried to comply with his father's command, tugging on the priest's shirtsleeve and offering to help with the food line.

As Drew and Carole Stone made their way through the throng of shell-shocked survivors huddled together in the sanctuary-turned-helter, they recognized a familiar face moving towards them through the crowd.

"Dr. Serio!"

"Hello, Captain Stone," replied the doctor warmly. "How's that head?"

Stone turned to Carole and explained. "He patched me up last night while you were asleep. From the flying board that cracked me on the head."

"Of course," she said. "Everyone okay at the hospital, doctor?"

"Just fine, thanks," Serio replied. "We were far enough away from the beach to sustain nothing more than a little wind and water damage."

"What happened to the delivery you were in such a hurry to make?" Stone asked.

"Went just fine, thanks. She had a beautiful baby girl. Six pounds and eight ounces."

"What did they name her," Carole wanted to know.

The doctor's fuzzy white eyebrow quivered for a moment. "Why, Katrina, of course."

The doctor moved further into the bowels of the shelter as the Stones exited the building and moved slowly down the broken sidewalk toward Beach Boulevard. Then they headed east toward downtown Bay St. Louis, or rather, what was left of their shattered hometown. The storm had buckled and wiped away large sections of the concrete boulevard, so they had no choice but to watch where they stepped as they cautiously shifted through the debris.

They turned left onto Main Street, which intersected the boulevard at the beach then ran due north through what had once been the downtown shopping area. Although not as badly wrecked as Beach Boulevard, Main Street lay littered with boards of every size, upside down cars, and every conceivable manner of trash. Mud covered much of the debris and the stench of death made every breath an ordeal. Fish, dogs, cats, even one mangled brown and white cow lay entwined among the remains of their once-proud home-town. They consciously avoided looking closer into the rubble for fear of what else they might see hidden among the ruins.

The National Guard, state police, local sheriff's deputies and Civil Defense workers had earlier removed what they could find of human remains, but in such chaos as this, Stone mused, anything could turn up wherever you least expected it. At first light that morning, as part of a search and rescue team in the public library, Stone had uncovered a beagle crushed under a fallen book rack near the shelf marked, "Dogs We Love."

The sound of buzzing chainsaws serenaded them as they weaved their way through shattered boards with protruding nails, fallen electric wires and flaky slabs of broken up sidewalks. Down the street a local grocer served a long line of people from the remains of his tattered stock. Farther north and across the street a hand painted sign hanging off the largely intact steel and concrete structure of a gas station read, "Gasoline at regular prices."

"Maybe," Carole said hopefully, "Father Noonan was right about the small miracles we'll see on this walk."

The only other downtown buildings in fairly good condition, from outside appearances at least, were those constructed of granite—the stately Hancock Bank and the hundred-year-old Neo-Classical Revival style county court-house.

"Why are you smiling?" Carole asked, glad to see him smile for the first time since their harrowing ordeal had begun twenty-three hours ago. When they had climbed through their roof to avoid drowning in the rising floodwaters in their attic and the hundred and fifty-miles-per-hour winds had blown Drew and Stevie off their roof, she had feared that none of them would ever smile again.

"Even a hurricane is no match for a bank and a courthouse," Stone groused good naturedly. "Some things never change, I reckon."

"Drew?"

He hadn't noticed it at first, but as he followed her gaze he saw that several letters were missing from the HANCOCK BANK sign. The storm had left only the letters, "___COCK BAN_."

The simple act of enjoying a laugh together raised their spirits considerably. A mere eight hours earlier they had been stranded in the heart of ground zero struggling for their lives against two-hundred miles-per-hour gusts, a deadly thirty-five foot-tall tidal surge, tornadoes touching down all around them and snakes writhing in the waters engulfing them. Their survival had been as miraculous as many of their neighbors' deaths had been horrific.

But even this laughter proved short-lived. As they turned down a side street and slogged back toward the shelter, the weight of the losses they and their fellow coast residents had suffered courtesy of the storm of the century suddenly came home with a terrible, all-encompassing vengeance.

"Look, Drew," Carole breathed, pointing to a man and woman balancing precariously atop the pile of rubble that had once been their home.

Stone immediately recognized them as the Fourcades, the parents of one of their son's best friends, eight-year old Shelly Fourcade. The man cradled his wife in his arms as she wept inconsolably, her face buried in his chest. In one of his bear-like hands the man grasped a yellow teddy bear, the one Shelly had always slept with according to Stevie, and that she had carried with her whenever the two of them had walked or biked downtown for ice cream or popcorn. The bear slipped from the man's grasp and tumbled into the rubble as he pressed his tear-streaked wife's face against his chest.

"Oh, God," Carole sighed, "how can we bear all of this?" Tears flooded her eyes as she comfort in her husband's arms.

"I don't know," he whispered softly. "But we will endure it, I promise you. This is not going to beat us, Carole. I swear it. It didn't beat our parents in 1969, and it won't beat us now. They rebuilt a better coast, and so will...."

The words died in his throat. He feared he hadn't sounded as certain as he had wished. They both knew the people of the coast had rebuilt after hurricanes almost every generation since the coast's founding by French settlers three hundred ago. But they could find little comfort in the past while faced with such a devastating present. All they had endured the night before and the overwhelming sense of loss they felt this morning had shaken them to the core. What other horrors were yet to be revealed?

Then, as he peered over Carole's shoulder out into the gulf, Drew spied the remains of a structure that had once served as a bustling beachfront department store. The storm had shattered it almost beyond recognition, but he saw something shimmering in front of the vanished store's foundation that pulled him back from the brink of despair.

Protruding from a mangled mass of aluminum, steel and concrete stood an American flag, flying at half mast. Attached to its makeshift iron pole was a five-by-five piece of plyboard on which six words were scrawled in bold, red letters: "THE GULF COAST SHALL RISE AGAIN!"

"Carole...Look there."

Peering beyond the flag out across the horizon the Stones saw gently rolling waves lapping against the shore and an unusually calm sea all the way to the horizon. Sea gulls floated effortlessly across a cloudless light blue sky. Drew and Carole held each other silently, taking it all in. What, after all, could mere words add to a vision of the dawning of a new world, rising ineffably from the ashes of all they had ever known.

MY ANGER'S OUT OF CONTROL

My anger had been slipping out of control for some time before my wife pointed it out to me last night in no uncertain terms. "It's out of control," she harped for what seemed like the fiftieth time. I guess I can add that to the list of things doesn't like about me.

Did I say, 'like'? 'Things that she hates about me' would more accurately sum it up. And that's just how *she* sums it up at least once a week.

Forget about the financial support, without which she'd be flipping waffles at the IHOP; the roof over her head (which never suited her despite the fact that she got a half interest in it for saying 'I do'), the car she's driving (another marital freebe), a wardrobe full of suits, shoes, dresses and pants (also gratis) and the cell phone I bought her with which she slanders me to her friends. The food she eats, the wine she drinks, hell, everything except the air she breaths, I provide her. But, admittedly, not in the manner to which she'd like to become accustomed.

But I'm lucky to have her, according to her. For example, on the rare occasions when we do have sex, say…every other month, the solstice (winter only), her birthday (never on mine) and our anniversary (after she's bombed), she gets off two or three times to my one, and then reminds me how lucky I am to have her. Sure! Makes as much sense as anything else about our marriage.

But if you think she's rough you oughta' see my boss. This guy's a real peach, let me tell you. His ego is the only thing bigger than his butt; his brain the only thing smaller than his patience. And unless I'm greatly mistaken, his dick is the only thing smaller than my paycheck.

I can hear him now: 'Get me this, dumb ass,' 'get me that, NOW, moron!' And my hands down favorite, 'if you don't like the heat get the hell out of the kitchen!'

And then there's that worthless canine of mine that destroys my newspaper, craps in my den, barks at me when I leave in the morning and again when I schlep home at night. And worst of all, he quaffs any beer and woofs down any food I leave sitting on the breakfast table, coffee table or even the kitchen counter now he's learned how to climb up the frigging chairs.

I could go on about my sordid life, but why bother? Nobody gives a fat rat's ass. So it should come as no surprise to anyone but my analyst that my anger went on a world class rampage.

"You should control it," my analyst says, as if he were instructing me on how to flush a commode. "Like a mature man, you should." For that I pay him two-fifty a session.

Well, like the clown who fell in elephant shit at the circus, the first laugh was on him.

Yep. It happened during one of our sessions. Let the boys in the psych ward figure this one out, but my anger sprang out of my body and crushed my analyst's skull with his own paperweight. I'd be in jail right now except his receptionist heard her boss screaming and stumbled into the office just in time to see my anger strike the fatal blow and leap out the window.

Needless to say, I told the cops somebody came in through the window and attacked him for no reason. They bought it, and here I am trying to track my anger down and beg it to murder my wife. It already got my boss. Shoved a No. 2 pencil in the jackass's ear.

Three witnesses to that, thank God. One of them got a good look at my anger and described it pretty much as a larger, redder-faced version of me. Fortunately, I had a perfect alibi. I was having a beer at Webster's Bar and Grill at the precise time that killing occurred. Everybody there backed up my alibi. Talk about a major league change in luck! I never had it so good!

But my anger's still on the loose, and I suppose I ought to do something about it before innocent people get hurt. I can't help but wonder—could it have forgotten where I live? God knows I've tried to lure it back, but it doesn't seem to be affected by conscious thought. Operates entirely on the subconscious level, or so it seems. But if that were so, why is my wife still alive?

Doesn't it know where to find my favorite couch? That's where my wife will be. All one-hundred-and-eighty-pounds of her. Eating Reese's Pieces and glued to the wide screen TV, a sixty-inch marvel large enough to accommodate Oprah, Dr. Phil *and* their egos.

Yep. My anger's out of control. But me? I'm starting to feel a whole lot better. Which is what worries me, to tell you the truth. If this keeps up, and my anger does get around to dispatching my wife (and while it's at it, the damn dog, too) I'm afraid I have a pretty good idea what will happen next.

My analyst planted the thought just before my anger took him out. "Once all the sources of your anger are gone," he told me, "your anger won't have any more reasons to go out of control." Unfortunately, or so my recently deceased analyst opined, that would leave me to deal with another problem. An emotion my analyst said was more dangerous than my anger.

In light of what's happened so far, don't you think I oughta' be worried about what's gonna' happen if my self-loathing runs amuck?

HEAL THYSELF

A spent Jessica Shexnayder rested silently atop her lover for several minutes before either of them spoke. "The third time's definitely the charm," she purred, leaning forward and loosening the leather straps that bound his wrists to her king-sized brass bed posts.

Jon Laboda rubbed his wrists then removed his blindfold. "When you're 25, it may be the charm," he offered, shielding his eyes as they adjusted to the surprisingly bright light from the dozens of candles flickering in her bedroom, "but when you're closing in on 50, you're lucky it's not a killer."

Shexnayder rolled off him, stretching and preening like a feline fresh from a kill. Then her mood shifted as swiftly as would a cat's when another predator happened upon the scene. She regarded him for a moment. "Do you still love your wife?" she asked, her lively jet black pupils turning to flat, lifeless discs.

Laboda stirred restlessly. "What? Where the hell did that come from? How did we go from bondage to confession in one fell swoop?"

"You heard me."

"Are you sure you want to discuss this?"

"I asked you, didn't I?"

"Now?" he asked, mopping beads of perspiration from his brow.

"Why not now?"

The closeness of her skin, the scent of her body, and his reluctance to discuss his marriage drove him to bury his head in her chest, kissing everything that smelled of Shexnayder.

She swatted the crown of his balding head. "Stop that. After."

"Why do you insist upon discussing this now?" he frowned.

"Why does it bother you so much to discuss it? What's your problem, Jonathan? Worried I might be getting too serious about our relationship?" She laughed out loud.

"The thought had crossed my mind," he lied, hoping to change the subject.

"Well put your mind at rest, lover boy. I certainly wouldn't marry *you*!"

"Why not?"

"A man who cheats on his wife? Get serious."

"Thanks a lot, ye who contrived to seduce me."

"Oh, don't get your panties in a wad, Jon-boy. Didn't your mother ever tell you that adultery was a sin?"

"What is all this adultery bullshit?" he growled, uncertain as to whether he should avoid the conversation entirely or attempt to win the argument. He made what he felt was a bad decision at the time he made it. "I wouldn't have thought," he quipped, "that *you'd* find adultery objectionable."

"For me, no. In a husband, definitely. Like my mama always said, if you don't love her anymore, fellah, divorce her."

A scowl clouded Laboda's face. "That's so easy for you, a woman, to say. A woman never risks anything in a divorce. A man, on the other hand, stands to lose his children, his home, half his property and income—"

"You don't have any children," she chided playfully, "and your wife left *you* in control of the family abode. She moved out the day she caught us going at it in your pool."

"Well, maybe Rebecca's different from most women."

"Sure," Shexnayder said icily. "She's a saint. So why screw around behind her back?"

"It's obvious that you've never been married," he sniffed. "Besides, I don't suppose you ever cheated on anyone?"

Shexnayder laughed even louder than before. "Sure. And there's nothing that makes me lose respect for a man quicker than when he's so stupid as to let me cheat on him and not have the sense to figure out what's going on."

"That's sick."

"So you say, because a woman's doing it. Why is it wrong for a woman to get a little nookie on the side, but it's okay for a man to have a mistress? I'd say anyone who makes *that* distinction is sick. Or doesn't understand women very well."

Laboda shook his head in disgust, then consciously softened his voice before responding. "You wouldn't marry me because I enjoy making love to you?"

"You enjoy *fucking* me," she corrected. "What do you need with another wife, anyway? I'm sure you enjoyed '*making love*' to her at one time."

"I don't want another wife. And I can't believe what I'm hearing from my lover."

"What, that I'd never marry you?"

"Yes. Give me one good reason why you wouldn't marry me. And, adultery, which *you* precipitated, doesn't count."

Shexnayder grimaced. "Do you really want to discuss this, now?"

"Absolutely."

"Promise not to take your toy and go home if you don't like what you hear?"

"You can hold on it for safe keeping, if you like."

"Thanks," she said, accepting his offer. "I will. Now, I'll be glad to answer your silly little question. Another reason I wouldn't marry you, Jon-boy, is because you're a hopelessly sexist pig."

He gave a confused blink. "Who says so?"

"I do.

Laboda sat up beside her. "What do you know about sexism apart from what you read in the tabloid magazines? Hell, if you married a rich man we wouldn't hear another word from you about sexism, feminism or any other such foolishness."

"That's true. But at least I don't claim to be broad minded!"

"Up yours, Jessica," he said curtly, staring into the bowels of her pastel-colored bedroom wallpaper. "And Gloria Steinem's too."

"Oink, oink."

"Oh, please."

She grinned mercilessly. "The truth hurts a little bit, eh, Jon-boy? Looks like somebody's struck a nerve."

"Oh, sure. I get it," he announced, keenly aware that he was skating on the edge of a very risky conversation. "To say something bad about a woman is taboo in this insane, politically correct world, no matter the truth of the assertion. But to insult a man is proper, regardless of how far off base?"

"Needless to say," she murmured, pulling him back down on the bed, "if you weren't such a sexist, you'd already be clued in to that."

"I see."

"And in addition to being sexist," she flashed, her mood chilling as swiftly as it had warmed only seconds earlier, "you're one of the most selfish men I've ever known."

"I beg your pardon?"

"But not in bed, of course."

"I'm so relieved."

"And incredibly self-righteous."

"Now, wait a minute, Jessica," he said, intently fixing his gaze upon hers. "I know I'm a little selfish, but you've got to explain that last little comment. I've never claimed to be a saint."

"A Jewish saint? That's a laugh. You don't believe in saints."

"It's just an expression."

175

"No, Dr. Jon, Not a saint. Just a little bit better than others."

"How so?"

"Aren't you always complaining about incompetent hospital administrators?"

"Yes. Who in my profession does not?"

"And aren't you always asking me to lie to other doctors, and to your patients, about where you are and what you're doing at the time?"

"That's what a nurse is for! To cover for her doctor. Besides, little white lies never hurt anyone."

"And I do so much more for you than that," she said, proving it with a flick of her wrist.

"Indeed. You're everything a doctor could ask for in a nurse. And," he winked, "you're a decent health care provider as well."

"And you're a very clever doctor, but not so clever as to completely sidetrack me with flattery. I still want to know if you love your wife."

"Forget it," he huffed. "Drop it, will you?"

"Tell me."

"Now?"

"Yes, now. Do you still love your wife?"

He shrugged his shoulders in surrender. "I suppose so, yes. In a manner of speaking."

"You're not sure?"

"No."

"Do you still make love to her?"

"We're separated, as you damn well know. That's not something you do over the phone."

"Speak for yourself. Do you ever tell your wife that you love her?"

"I don't remember. Sometimes, maybe. I don't know."

"Do you remember, now," she asked, her grip slowly tightening upon a sensitive area.

"It's illegal to obtain evidence by the use of threats and violence. Especially to private parts."

"Ahh, now you're a lawyer, too? Then do you know whether or not it's legal to obtain evidence by the use of promises of reward?" she asked, her lips glistening seductively as she moved into position to receive his evidence.

He resisted the urge to ask her if she had been staying up nights watching old *Law and Order* episodes. No point in winning the battle if it meant that you lost the oral sex. "No, but we'll make an exception on this one occasion."

"Then talk, big boy, and I'll make it worth your while."

"What was the question?"

"Do you love your wife?"

"Yes. But not in a romantic way."

"Do you take her out on dates?"

"No."

"Why not?"

"*We're* dating, remember."

"We're *fucking*! Do you go to temple with her?"

"No."

"Why not? You joined her synagogue when you moved here and married her, didn't you?"

"Yes."

"Well, what's happened? Decided to give 'em both up at the same time?"

"Yes."

"Why?"

"I don't know," he muttered, realizing for the first time that he truly didn't know. "It…. Just didn't seem right, I suppose. Sitting there, looking the rabbi in the eye, knowing that I was an adulterer. I just couldn't play that game. So I quit going, I guess."

"My daddy always said that church was where the adulterers most needed to be."

"Hmpf. To say nothing of liars, crooks, and newspaper reporters. But for me…to keep up the charade when I no longer lived according to the rules... Well, that's bad faith. And I don't do bad faith."

"Why not?"

"Bad faith makes me nauseous."

"Bad faith," she considered, pensively drumming her fingers on his chest. "What do you mean by that?"

"When people run their mouths about loving their neighbor on the Sabbath, and those same people screw their neighbor, business partner or complete strangers on Monday. That's bad faith."

"You mean saying one thing and then doing something else?"

"Precisely."

"Like swearing to be faithful to your wife and then cheating on her with your nurse? Wouldn't you say that qualifies as bad faith, Jon-boy?"

"I wouldn't have *said it*, no."

"Sorry. Didn't plan on shriveling your desire. Besides, I thought you told me *practicing medicine* made you nauseous."

"No, practicing medicine is worse. It gives me diarrhea."

Shexnayder laid her head on his chest. "I'm sorry I asked."

"I warned you."

"I didn't realize you disliked medicine so much."

"I really don't. The practice is a gas. Quite entertaining, actually. Even very profitable, as you well know. It's dealing with other doctors that's so disparaging. It's the worthless hospital administrators, the sleezy plastic surgeons. It's treating a supposedly injured patient and then finding out it's nothing but a scam to get rich in a lawsuit on behalf of some shyster lawyer, or watching my colleagues killing people through gross negligence then evading responsibility in court and walking around in the community with their noses stuck up in the air as if they're God's gift to humanity. And those pestering drug reps.... God knows it doesn't get any more sickening than that."

"What about the truly sick patients? I thought they were what being a healer was all about."

"Some of them are. Some of them are a real pain in the ass. A great deal more painful than you know."

Shexnayder raised her head, looked him in the eye. "What does that mean?"

Laboda shrugged his shoulders.

She tightened her grip. "Jon?"

"Okay, okay," he winced. "It's like this. A few years ago, before you moved here, I had an affair with a drug rep."

"Shame on you," she whispered playfully, caressing his chest.

He shoved her hand away. "Thing was, she was hawking this new drug that supposedly lowered the bad cholesterol, raised the good, and lowered blood pressure in the bargain. With absolutely no side effects. You could even have a few glasses of wine while taking it with no negative impact on your liver."

"Just what everybody here in Greenwood wanted. A drug safe to take with booze. Sounds too good to be true."

"Not at first. We got excellent results the first few months."

"I'll bet you did. Coming like rabbits, the two of you, no doubt."

"That's not...Oh, forget it."

"No, I'm sorry," she urged. "Go ahead, Jon." The look in her eyes convinced him to continue.

"If you insist," he said. "Anyhow, three years later, the patients who'd used her new drug started fainting in their tracks."

"Dead?"

"No. Not most of them. But every single one of them developed pancreatitis, some of them pancreatic cancer."

"Just like that?"

"More or less. No high blood pressure, excellent cholesterol tests. Nothing showed up on our tests because we weren't specifically looking at the pancreas. We were checking their hearts and livers every week, but... Well, not long after we began suspecting a link, an Asian study came out of the woodwork proclaiming the dangers of the new drug and made us all look like fools."

Shexnayder sensed the welt rising upon his conscience. "You put your patients at risk," she scolded mercilessly, "without sufficient studies in support of a new drug. I see."

"Do you?"

"But how'd it get past the FDA?"

"Guess."

"Money."

"What else? Besides, we only prescribed it for the worst cases anyhow; only the ones where the government gave approval. But..."

"But what?"

"I had never taken the government's word for it, before. I'd always done my homework and made my own decisions based upon my own gut instincts. I'd never taken chances like that before," he groaned, pressing his palm into his forehead as if stemming the flow of blood.

"You'd never thought with your small brain before, either Jon-boy. Like you're doing right now. Mmmm."

"Stop that. Aren't you sickened by what I've told you?"

"Are you kidding? That story makes me hot."

"My God! I don't know what to say to that."

"Say nothing," she said, re-positioning her body. "I certainly won't. My mamma taught me not to talk with my mouth full."

Laboda watched her for a moment, then, as the heat rose in his loins and rushed up his spine, he leaned forward and brushed his fingers across her nipple. Then he held it between his thumb and forefinger and squeezed until she moaned. He rolled her over on her side and placed one finger inside her while pressing his thumb against her, moving his hand in a circular motion that sent waves of pleasure coursing through her body. She came seconds later. He laid her on her back and mounted her gently, but entered her with such force she gasped as if in pain. She tightened her thighs around his and met his thrusts with equal force.

"Feeling better, now," she whispered, her eyes half open, her breath warm on the side of his face.

His eyes opened onto hers. "Yes."

"Still angry at that drug rep?"

"Fuck her," he mumbled.

"Fuck who?" she breathed.

—

"What?"

"I—"

She pressed her fingernails into the small of his back. "Forget about the drug rep."

"Who?"

A SECOND MONKEY TRIAL

"I object," howled the defense lawyer. "This is a preliminary hearing in an arson and conspiracy-to-murder trial in Lee County Circuit Court, not a philosophical debate at Millsaps College. He's wandering very far afield, Your Honor."

"Mr. District Attorney?"

"Your Honor," the prosecuting attorney replied, "In order to demonstrate the defendant's guilt, to prove that he did send members of his church to burn down the victim's business, resulting, however unexpectedly, in the victim's death, I need to delve not only into his sermon delivered the night of the crime, but also into his particular religious beliefs, to show how radically different his views were from the victim's. Furthermore, this would be relevant on the issue of motive, and additionally, to demonstrate this defendant's state of mind at the time the crime was committed. I don't believe the jury can understand the context of this case without this line of inquiry. Besides, you've already admitted the victim's book in which he attacked not only the defendant personally, but also *his* particular religious beliefs. As that door has already been opened, I'd like to explore those matters at greater length. Furthermore, this line of inquiry would be relevant to their defense—that the defendant is a deeply spiritual man, not a charlatan, and not the type to promote arson or any other kind of violence."

The judge nodded thoughtfully. "I'm persuaded by your argument, Counselor. You may proceed. But I warn you, do keep it relevant."

"I will, Your Honor. Thank you. Now," said the D.A., striding purposefully toward the witness box and the sharply dressed defendant. "I'll ask again, do *you* interpret the Bible literally?"

"Yes. I do," the preacher replied earnestly. "I most certainly do. It is the divinely inspired Word of God. And the Word is the Word, requiring no fancy interpretation from me or anyone else. I wouldn't presume to edit my Creator's Word."

"It is possible, preacher, that the Word, or at least certain aspects of the first few books of it, was written about spiritual truth as opposed to scientific or historical truth?"

"It's all about *truth* truth, Mr. Lawyer, and that's the truth."

The ripple of laughter rising from the gallery reserved for reporters ended as quickly as it had begun under the judge's baleful glare.

The prosecutor resumed his cross-examination. "Even though many of its books are filled with countless historical contradictions, which in turn contradict other Biblical books, to say nothing of other historical texts, recent archeological finds, and a wealth of scientific discovery that proves beyond a shadow of a doubt that, for example, the Earth is billions of years old and was created over a period of billions of years, and not in a mere six days?"

"So you say. I'm not buying any of it, not for one minute."

"I see. But isn't it possible that some of those verses were not intended as history, but that, through the use of parable, myth, allegory, and symbolism, the Bible's authors intended to make an impression on readers' hearts, not to educate them on the specifics of ancient world history and geology? Didn't Jesus teach by means of parable and allegory?"

"The Lord moves in mysterious ways, but the Word is the Word. And that's good enough for me."

"But don't you mislead your flock, preacher? Don't you yourself miss the whole point of the Old Testament by your literal interpretation? An interpretation, I might add, that the authors, the Jews themselves, disdain today. For instance, don't you mistakenly interpret the story of the Tower of Babel as the source of the origination of the various ancient world languages, which it clearly could not be, since people of different races, such as the Africans and Asians, were not present there in the Fertile Crescent three thousand years ago, and since their languages are so radically different as to have nothing in common with those in Egypt, Greece, Arabia, or Israel? Isn't that story actually a well-told myth that exemplifies the finitude of man's wisdom and the overabundance of his pretension and hubris?"

"What are you talking about?"

"Or this business about the resurrection of the body. Do you believe that you will physically rise from the grave, like Dracula or the ghouls from *Night of the Living Dead*?"

"Objection, Your Honor."

"Sustained."

"That is to say, reverend, do you believe that you will rise from the grave in your physical body, years, perhaps even centuries, after your demise? After being embalmed, buried, perhaps cremated? Or could this part of the Creed be a figurative expression of the fulfillment of life beyond the possibilities of a temporal existence?"

"Let me put it this way, young man. I'll be buried, not cremated, in my best suit."

The judge cast a wary eye in the direction of the gallery, but he needn't have concerned himself. The reporters were too busy writing to utter the slightest chuckle.

"Then if you insist on interpreting *these* parts of the Bible literally, why do you offer grape juice during communion rather than wine, which Jesus consumed at every meal he took, including the Last Supper?"

The preacher gave a thoughtful smile."Well, although perfect in the sense of being free of sin, Jesus, like others of his day, was unaware of the dangers of alcohol that your blessed science has demonstrated to us without doubt in the past few decades."

"So, the Son of God, the scion of the creator of the universe, was unaware that wine could destroy his liver or saddle him with addiction?"

"I'd imagine," the preacher allowed with an exceedingly smug look on his face, "that he knew enough about it not to drink to excess. Perhaps he knew he had no chance of becoming an alcoholic. But I can't afford to take that chance with my flock. Those with lips that never touch alcohol will never end up lying in the gutter with harlots and dogs."

"Did you learn that one in seminary, preacher?"

"Ahem. I didn't attend any seminary, counselor. I received my call directly from God and took up my labors forthwith. With my present church, of course."

"So, what you're saying is that you adhere to Christ's teachings and example when they suit you and abandon them when they don't?"

"His Holy teachings always suit me, Mr. Persecutor."

"Is that so? Well, as I recall, Jesus often spoke on the concept of universal brotherhood. On loving Gentiles as well as Jews, Samaritans as well as Egyptians, even the Romans who enslaved his people and crucified Him. Isn't that so, reverend?"

"That is indeed so, sir."

"Then why is your church the most segregated institution in town, despite God's call for universal membership in His house of worship?"

"I,,, uhh ..."

"Objection, Your Honor," barked defense counsel.

The judge regarded the preacher's lawyer as he would a cockroach wandering across his bench. "On what grounds do you object?"

"What's the relevance of the question, Your Honor?"

"Mr. District Attorney?"

"I'll get to it, Your Honor, if you'll grant me a little leeway."

"Granted. But don't try my patience."

"Yes, your honor. Thank you. Now, where were we? Oh, yes. Isn't it true, preacher, that Jesus criticized the Pharisees for dressing in their finest clothes to make an impression on the people?"

"Well, yes. I suppose that's so. Sin of pride was the issue, as I recall."

"Then why do you and your flock dress in your finest suits for Sunday services, when Jesus expressly forbids overly concerning ourselves with apparel?"

"Oh, we're not trying to impress each other, sir. We're showing respect for our Heavenly Father."

"You're trying to impress the creator of the universe by wearing your best suit?"

The defense lawyer sprang to his feet. "Your Honor!"

"Overruled. Let's move on."

"So tell me, preacher," the D.A. continued with his habitual aplomb. "Since you didn't attend seminary, did you by any chance make up for your lack of knowledge about religious history and philosophy by reading the works of Christendom's greatest thinkers and philosophers?"

"To whom are you referring?"

"Why, Augustine, Aquinas, à Kempis, Anselm, Luther, Calvin, Kierkegaard, Pascal, Merton, Jaspers, Niebuhr, Tillich, or even C.S. Lewis?"

The preacher flashed a wide grin. "Why, no, I haven't. I rely on prayer and the Lord's guidance in preparation of my sermons. Now that you mention it, Mr. Lawyer, I did have an uncle named Luther who sold cars for a living, and he came down the aisle and knelt at my altar and pledged his soul to the Lord just last year. That's the kind of experience I care about, not burying myself in some dusty, old, outdated library book. Real life is my school, Mr. Lawyer. Something I'm confident you know little about."

"But can't we learn a lot from books, preacher? By reading them, that is, not burning them?"

"Nobody burns books anymore, sir."

"Or reads them, so it seems. But perhaps if you had done a little more reading, *sir*, you may have learned the usefulness of myth, parable, and symbolism, as opposed to interpreting everything literally. For example," the prosecutor began, casting a quick glance at the judge and meeting his eyes for a half a second as if to say, "I'm getting on with it *now*, or more accurately, here it comes. "Concerning the walls of Jericho that Joshua supposedly brought down with the blowing of his soldiers' horns ..."

"Yes? I'm intimately familiar with that story. I preached about it in recent months, as I recall."

"Yes, you did. At your church in Saltillo. You condemned the victim for leading the charge to legalize Sunday beer sales in Lee County. The Sunday before the night the victim's business burned in downtown Tupelo, with him in it. Consigned to the flames by members of your 'flock.'"

"I had no knowledge of that incident until the Tupelo police questioned me the next week, sir."

"Of course. But what I'm asking is, don't you think it's possible that the book's author was using symbolism to tell a larger story? That the horns didn't literally bring the walls down, which would, of course, defy all scientific possibility; that the horns actually served as a diversion, with the soldiers marching around the city's walls blowing their horns and drawing the city's defenders' attention on themselves, while Joshua's shock troops climbed the rope let down the city's wall by the prostitute who lived in the wall? The very same woman who had earlier given two of those same troops insider information on the city's defenses in return for a promise to spare her life in the event of a Jewish conquest?"

"No, sir," the preacher corrected, waving a plump index finger in the prosecutor's face. "She let that rope down, a red rope to be specific, so the Israelite solders would see it and know to spare the people living in her room inside the city's walls. That is the Word of God."

"A red rope hanging on the outside of the wall is going to help conquering soldiers who've fought their way over the walls to identify the woman living inside the wall? How, exactly, would that be possible?"

"Well, I'm sure I don't know, sir. I wasn't there, after all."

"But doesn't it make more sense that the walls came tumbling down, figuratively speaking, after Joshua's troops climbed up the rope and let his army into the city, where they slaughtered every living soul and fulfilled God's promise to give the land of Canaan to the Israelites?"

"As I said before, Mr. Persecutor, I believe the Word as it was written, precisely as it was written, without surrendering to the temptation to blaspheme and make up my own interpretation. I leave such machinations to popes and scholars and try to do as the Good Lord commands and obediently guide my flock."

"And do you believe that God's Word should be followed as literally as you believe it was written?"

"You know very well that I do."

"So, you believe that Joshua did the right thing by killing every man, woman, and child, even all the animals, in Jericho, in fulfillment of the prophecy? Even though those people did nothing to deserve their fates other than being in the wrong place at the wrong time?"

"They were heathens, sir. Non-believers in God's Word. Joshua did God's work that day. Woe unto all who defy His Holy ..."

Realizing what he had just implied, the preacher looked first at his lawyer, then glanced sideways at the judge.

"Objection!" shouted his attorney.

"That's all right, Your Honor," the prosecutor announced. "I'm done here. I've heard all I needed to hear."

"But ..." the preacher blurted. "You tricked me just now. I knew nothing about what was going to happen to that man."

The judge sat up straight in his tall, black leather chair. "Going to happen? Is that what you said, reverend? 'Going to happen'?"

"I—I ... That's not ..."

"Objection, Your Honor. Move to strike!"

The district attorney took his seat at the prosecutor's table. He turned and looked the preacher directly in the eye, smiled curtly, then leaned to his right, tapped his assistant on the shoulder, and said, "You want to get some lunch? This sort of thing really makes me hungry."

CANCEL MY REQUEST

Abe Huffstickler hated water travel, especially during spring rain storms when the rivers surged and the lakes churned so violently that his stomach turned to mush after a few seconds in his canoe.

He had come to Leflore County in 1840 when the Delta was little more than malaria-infested swampland, and his neighbors thought it strange that he voluntarily chose to live in a swamp with his irrational fear of water. But swamps, he could have told them, were different from rivers, lakes or oceans. Swamps meant land always within reach, and land meant hope. If things went bad on the river or in the middle of a lake, hope came at a very high premium.

The ubiquitous bears, snakes, cougars and alligators in Huffstickler's swamps didn't bother him at all. That's why he carried pistols and Bowie knives. But the very idea of traversing the surrounding rivers and lakes in dugout canoes turned his stomach long before he dipped the first paddle into the foreboding muddy waters. Knowing Huffstickler and his extreme distaste for water travel, his neighbors had marveled at his decision to give up cotton farming and launch his very own logging business.

Every winter, Huffstickler hacked down hundreds of trees by hand, braving the elements, the swamp, every sort of wild animal and even runaway criminals to collect acres of hardwood. But when rising floodwaters announced the arrival of spring, Huffstickler carved a dugout canoe and floated his logs across the flooded swamps to the Yazoo River three miles south of Williams Landing. Once there, he paddled himself and his logs downstream to Vicksburg where the Yazoo poured into the surging Mississippi River.

But traversing a storm tossed Yazoo River was not the most frightening part of the trip, Huffstickler told his neighbors. Over a river-bound canoe, he declared, he retained at least a semblance of control, even if that meant nothing more than paddling toward shore at the first sign of sucking whirlpools or white water rapids. No, the steamboat ride back home from Vicksburg to Williams Landing was what twisted his stomach into knots. And, he had explained, it wasn't merely the rough ride during bad weather that mangled his guts. The worst was the fact, made abundantly clear to him and everyone else living in the river country year after year, that steamboats exploded, burned and sank on the Yazoo River with a frightening regularity.

This ever threatening prospect, the thunderstorm and raging torrents that had recently transformed the Yazoo to the rampaging stream of his worst nightmares, and the shenanigans of the passenger seated next to him on his third annual steamboat return home had made his 1843 voyage the worst he had ever experienced.

Him or me, the stoical Huffstickler told himself after enduring an hour of the rascal's panicked jabbering and clamoring for salvation from on high. *Him or me, but one of us has got to go!*

The other man, well known to Huffstickler and everyone else in Leflore County as a liar and a cheat, had grown increasingly more agitated with every nautical mile they had covered since they had steamed out of Vicksburg early that April morning. Apparently unable to swim and undoubtedly suffering from a bad conscience, the man finally fell to his knees and prayed aloud, if bellowing like a wounded cow could be counted as prayer, for heavenly deliverance though the storm.

Huffstickler, never in favor of rudeness to strangers despite his hard-bitten choice of professions, finally reached the outer limits of his patience. "Be silent," he barked. "If the Lord finds out you're on board, He'll surely take us under!"

THE APOLOGY

"Damn you, Richard," John Kitchens grumbled as he drove his new F-150 north on Grand Boulevard toward the big Baptist church dominating the entire 500 block. "Why'd you have to run for City Council this year?"

The source of Kitchen's vexation, his friend Richard Farris, had not only announced his candidacy for Greenwood City Council in next spring's elections, he had done so in large part thanks to money Kitchens had raised that fall. In itself, that wasn't a problem. But when Kitchens publicly opposed further Baptist encroachment on property fronting the historic Grand Boulevard, the fat hit the fire.

Kitchens had not merely opposed the Baptists' land grab; he had thrown kerosene on the fire by telling a WABG-TV reporter that the Baptists and other fundamentalists were more pagans than Christians, since the tenets of their sects had little to do with those of actual Christianity, so they were already receiving property tax benefits they had no right to claim.

"This," Farris had demanded, "warranted an apology to the deacons and elders of the church." Not that the Baptists, Pentecostals and other fundamentalists were as potent a political force in the Delta as they were in Mississippi's hills or piney woods regions, or that Farris, an educated man, cared a whit for the opinions of intellectual terrorists. But he was running for public office and had been inexorably linked to his major contributor and fund raiser, John Kitchens, and those circumstances dictated that he demand the apology. And as Farris' best friend, Kitchens had little choice but to offer it.

Kitchens, whose fondness for Southern architecture was exceeded only by his penchant for shooting off his mouth (a habit common to many prominent moneylenders), tried to distract himself from the onerous task at hand by perusing the white-columned Colonial Revival and Neo-Classical Revival mansions lining Greenwood's most famous avenue. To Kitchens, they appeared even lovelier than usual for being draped in their seasonal decoration of large green wreaths, red satin ribbons, glittering trees, and glowing lights. The majestic oaks lining Grand Boulevard usually heightened his mood whenever he passed beneath their ancient boughs, but neither their ageless beauty nor the exquisite symmetry of the classically designed houses beside them lightened his mood this day. He was bound to make peace with the Baptists or doom his best friend's first foray into local Delta politics.

He patted his shirt pocket to make certain the sheet of paper was still tucked safely inside it. He frowned in earnest when the scenery changed radically from finely appointed red brick, white-columned homes and towering oaks to a massive concrete structure covering the southbound boulevard's entire 500 block.

He had often enjoyed himself at the Baptists' expense by likening the church's faux-Greek Revival façade to that of a bank's, with its triangular pediment, massive entablature, and ashen grey columns. But this was no occasion for mirth. He faced the ultimate humiliation, debasing himself before the deacons and elders that awaited him in the concrete structure's cavernous sanctuary.

He approached the church's large double doors in a mildly agitated state, but his heart lodged itself in his throat when he flung open the doors and found half the congregation assembled in pews to savor his humiliation.

But he couldn't back out now. To anger them further by reneging on Farris's promise might arouse them sufficiently to swing the election away from Farris; no mean feat since the only other candidate in the race was a Catholic of Italian descent who owned the most successful beer joint in Greenwood.

The Baptist minister, the man who had publicly called for Kitchens' apology, met him just inside the doors with a 'gotcha' smile. The deacons and elders, grinning like jackals, extended greetings so lacking in the milk of human kindness Kitchens wondered if friendship justified this degree of suffering.

At that moment he made a decision he knew he would probably regret. But as with Caesar at the Rubicon, he knew the die was cast. He politely greeted the deacons and elders and nodded to the congregation as he ascended the pulpit.

"Ladies and gentlemen," he began, his voice louder with the pulpit microphone than he (or his audience) had expected, "thank you for having me here today. I understand that your minister has called for an apology for my remarks to the press last week, and I am here to answer that call.

"However, before I begin my apologies, I want to confirm that this is really what you want. As I understand it, you stand aggrieved at my suggestion that you are, quote, 'misguided fundamentalists more pagan than Christian.' Well, as to who is the pagan and who is the Christian, I must admit that I lack a divinity degree and should not have presumed to offer an opinion on a subject that I knew nothing about. To paraphrase the pagan sage Socrates, anyone claiming to know the precise nature of God is either lying or insane, so I henceforth agree to leave such matters to priests and preachers with the aforementioned degree."

A glance at the reddening face of the Baptist minister told Kitchens that his hunch was correct; the man's education had not included divinity school.

"Furthermore, to paraphrase the Christian author William Faulkner, no one can know the inner workings of any human heart other than his own, if he could even know that." Kitchens had no idea if Faulkner had spoken those words, but they *sounded* like something he could have uttered. In any event, Kitchens was damned certain that no one in this assemblage knew any more about the matter than he. "So I will forgo any such presumption in the future."

He took a deep breath as he surveyed the solemn faces in the congregation. "However," he continued, "if you desire an apology for my denigration of religious fundamentalism, and I assume all of you admit to being fundamentalists ..."

Several "amens" rang out in the audience, none louder than the one spewed by the minister seated to his immediate right.

"Very well. But if you seek an apology for my stand against fundamentalism, you're going to have to get in line. For if I apologize to you, I must also apologize to all the other fundamentalists I intended to paint with the very same brush. For example, the Catholics were in their fundamentalist phase when they imprisoned Galileo, burned Jews, Protestants and atheists at the stake, invaded the Holy Land during the crusades and hacked Muslims to bits, and rendered the Mass in Latin for fifteen hundred years. I don't suppose you want me to apologize to the Papists, do you?"

At least two tentative "no's" rose from the audience, until an elderly man near the back sounded a seething "Hell no!"

"And the Jews were surely in their fundamentalist phase," Kitchens thundered, "when they slaughtered every man, woman, child and animal in the city of Jericho under the auspices of their leader Joshua, when they stoned Saint Stephen and when persecuting early Christians both by themselves and in league with such Roman emperors as Tiberius and Caligula. Surely you don't want me to apologize to the Hebrews for that!"

The crowd roared in agreement, much to the consternation of their minister. Despite his resentment over his flock agreeing with anything Kitchens said, he had little choice but to agree very loudly with what his congregation had to say.

"And I know," Kitchens continued, his voice quivering with emotion, "that you wouldn't have me apologize to Muslim fundamentalists like Osama bin Laden and the al-Qaeda terrorists who bombed our soldiers, flew hijacked planes into the Twin Towers and Pentagon, and continue to persecute Christians around the world as they have done for the past thirteen hundred years!"

A wave of thunderous applause washed over Kitchens like a tsunami smashing against a coast.

"Thank you, brothers and sisters," he regaled the crowd, working them no less than their minister had during last week's Sunday morning TV service. "But don't think for one minute that I don't know that my words to the press were fueled by the sin of pride, and that I'm unaware that the sin of pride can drag me down to hell at the end of my days. We are all subject to going to hell, you just as well as I."

Fervent "amens" shook the building's massive concrete walls.

"Even that preacher, there," Kitchens said, gesturing toward the minister seated beside him, "can certainly go to hell."

As the brethren and sistren shouted their agreement, the minister smiled in terse agreement, the veins in his neck throbbing as if about to explode.

"But I want to express my sincerest apologies for my prideful comments, and by way of making heartfelt amends to read a few words I wrote last night, words apropos for the Christmas season; words I hope will move you sufficiently to find forgiveness in your hearts for this contrite old sinner standing humbly before you today."

A woman on the front row sprang to her feet and shouted, "Read it, brother. Read it!"

He drew the crumpled sheet of paper from his shirt pocket and cleared his throat.

> You and I could fuss and fight
>   like grownups often do,
> and ruin this Christmas holiday,
>   ruin it for me and you.
>
> But what if you and I, this year, really listened
>   to our children pray,
> And remembered why we take
>   the time to celebrate Christmas Day?
>
> For the thing that about this Holy Day that
>   gives it so much worth
> Is the chance that it affords us all to
>   celebrate Jesus' birth.
>
> And the best way we can do that is to
>   hold our loved ones dear,
> And love our neighbor every day throughout
>   the coming year.
>
> So let's have a Merry Christmas & fill our
>   stockings up with care,
> And never forget the reason that the
>   stockings and tree are there.
>
> So I hope your Christmastime this year,
>   all my Baptist friends,
> Brings each and every one of you a
>   joy that never ends.
> And that during this holiday

season every one of us will take,
Some holiday advice from a poet
I love by the name of William Blake.

And truly love our neighbor,
'whether heathen, Turk or Jew,
where mercy, love and pity dwell,
there God is dwelling too.'"

Kitchens promptly descended the pulpit, strode toward the minister, took the man's hand, shook it vigorously, and nodded to the vociferous woman on the front row. With a wave of his hand to the still applauding congregation, he exited the sanctuary doors as fast as his feet could carry him.

Later that night, Kitchens received a phone call from his friend Richard Farris. "That's the last time," Farris quipped, "that I'll ask you to apologize to anyone on ths Earth."

"What?" Kitchens feigned surprise. "They didn't care for my apology?"

"Oh, sure, John. I got twenty calls within an hour of your speech, all of them affirming their support of my candidacy."

"Then what's the problem, Richard?"

"I heard from the minister an hour later."

"Oh. Sorry."

"No, John. Don't even use the word around me. Not even on the phone."

"Have a merry Christmas, Richard."

"And also to you, you unmitigated ass."

"Richard, I'm shocked at your attitude. I debased myself and apologized to the Baptists. If that doesn't prove my loyalty to you, I don't know what would."

"John, if I get one Baptist vote by the time that preacher finishes with his flock, I'll kiss your lily white ass."

"And also to you, Richard. You'll not only get their votes, you'll win in a landslide. I guarantee it."

And just as Kitchens predicted, Farris won the election by several thousand votes.

Some months later, during a post-election party wherein Farris treated several of his major contributors to drinks at the Alluvian Bar, Kitchens told the assemblage about his "apology" to the Baptists. "And to my everlasting discredit," Kitchens said, "Farris not only won the election, he also carried the west Grand Boulevard ballot box, where the Baptist congregation voted, by a margin of at least ten to one."

To which Richard Farris replied, "Shut up, John. I liked you much better as a renegade Catholic than a hard charging Baptist minister."

"Don't worry, Richard. I'll pray for your everlasting soul tonight. I'll pray that you don't allow the sin of politics to drag you down to hell. Not to the hotter regions in the center, but the cooler outer circles, where your suffering is eternal, but not so bad as that endured by so many of your fellow barristers languishing in the fiery center of hell."

Farris shook his head in disgust, choked down the rest of the bourbon in his glass, and ordered another round for everyone.

UNINTELLIGENT DESIGN

So far as he knew, the scientists had never agreed on anything before, much less found accord when mired in such an agitated state. And this hastily assembled conclave had lent even more credence to the notion that strong emotions did not suit a gathering of scientists and science professors.

"I don't understand your reaction at all," declared poet-scientist Lovelock. "You weren't this upset when Professor Richter announced his theory that raptor dinosaurs had feathers and took to the air for short spaces while chasing their prey."

"But don't you understand," argued lead scientist Ward with all the vehemence he could muster, and to the accompaniment of equally vehement huzzahs uttered in unison by the scientists and professors in the group, "there's no way those monkeys could have designed Ape City in the heart of the African rain forest. Our consensus holds that a lost tribe of aborigines designed it. No simian mind could conceive of such a complicated design. The architecture, the symmetry, the mathematical precision.... Simply inconceivable."

"Nevertheless," the poet-scientist countered, "since the day I discovered the Bobolono apes, including the one here that you have so hard-heartedly consigned to a laboratory cage," he said, gesturing toward the black-haired, five-foot-tall ape named Daisy languishing behind a wall of iron bars, "you have found not one shred of proof than any human ever set foot in the vicinity of Ape City, much less designed and constructed it. Nor have you discovered any tribesmen within one hundred and fifty square miles of that area with any conception of complicated architecture, symmetry or mathematics."

"We are not here," the lead scientist asserted angrily, "to offer any proofs. You are the one offering this absurd theory that will make us the laughingstock of the academic and scientific communities."

"Here, here, Dr. Ward" barked university president Dawkins between puffs on his long metal pipe. His long flannel nightshirt had clung awkwardly to his spindly legs as he had rushed to the lab in answer to the lead scientist's early morning summons, and he had arrived at the poet-scientist's lab in no mood to entertain another of the latter's outlandish theories.

"Here, here, President Dawkins" repeated the university grant writer, whose name the poet-scientist could not recall, dressed in bright red long johns with large chartreuse spots. The university president had rousted him en route to the lab and compelled his attendance at this emergency meeting of the university professors and area scientists.

"That's correct," poet-scientist Lovelock agreed. "I'm offering a *theory*. Not for universal assent, but for debate. Since when has the mere request for debate among the scientific or university community become a clarion call to burn the theory's proponent at the stake?"

"We resent that remark," the lead scientist huffed. "Religion burns people at the stake. Science merely withholds tenure from professors who cannot be compelled to see reason."

"Here, here," squeaked the dean of the department in a blood-curdling high-pitched voice that made the poet-scientist cringe. "Who do you think you are, anyhow?"

"Just a seeker of the truth," the poet-scientist replied in earnest.

"They why," the lead scientist demanded, his voice assuming an even haughtier tone than usual, "were you seeking the truth in the jungles of Africa? To what ancient and barbaric gods were you praying during your excursion?"

"I was meditating under the stars," interrupted the poet-scientist as inoffensively as possible, "when the Bobolono happened upon me in search of food. It was as though they recognized a fellow worshiper of..."

"Stop!" howled lead scientist Ward in abject horror. University president Dawkins covered his ears with his hands while the dean of the science department, whose name none of them could recall, cowered behind her, too terrified to open his eyes. The other professors in attendance stomped their feet, slapped their foreheads in anguish and marched lockstep out of the room.

"You see," grunted lead scientist Ward, "what happens when you suggest that these apes are intelligent and capable of designing their own city? Then its back to praying to non-existent gods, substituting them for nature, and before you know it, the proponents of this theory are burning scientists at the stake as witches."

"Actually," poet-scientist Lovelock corrected humbly, "the medieval religious burned witches and placed scientists like Galileo on house arrest. It took science to burn thousands in the wink of an eye at Hiroshima and Nagasaki. Besides, your argument is fallacious on numerous grounds."

"How dare you?"

"In the name of science and intellectual curiosity, I dare. This is not the first time you've been wrong, Dr. Ward. Do you remember opposing debate on the Gaia theory that proposed that living organisms were able to control features of the Earth and keep it habitable? You argued then that the theory was anti-Darwinian heresy, only to be embarrassed when a

Darwinian scientist and a renowned mathematician joined together to prove that the theory does not contradict Darwin?"

"Well...I.."

"And now you oppose my new theory as Darwinian heresy, contending that the concept of intelligent design of Ape City by the Bobolono will lead to an outcry by the religious fundamentalists to teach Ape Creationism of Cities in the public schools. The gist of your argument is, as I understand it, that the fundamentalists are for it, so we are against it. Well, if that's your position, I remind you that the fundamentalists are for instituting tough measures against crime. Would you likewise propose the elimination of police?"

"That is beside the point," Ward carped angrily. "You have convinced no one of the accuracy of your theory with your specious arguments and patent ludicrosities masquerading as scientific theories."

Lovelock determinedly held his ground in the face of all opposition. "Have *you* ever convinced anyone that apes were incapable of intelligently designing their city, Dr. Ward? How would you ever hope to prove what apes think? Or for that matter, that the religious are wrong and there is no God? I can't imagine the intellectual depravity of the mind that would claim to prove atheism as a matter of scientific fact and then scoff at the thought processes of apes!"

"*Wwwe* are not here to prove anything," the university president stammered, straightening his nightgown with one hand and gesturing wildly in the air with the other. "It is you who offers these controversial theories... At the potential expense of the loss of university funding, I hasten to add."

"I haven't sought to prove anything" the poet-scientist countered. "I merely seek to entertain debate on these issues. Isn't that the heart of the scientific method? Debating theories and may the one with the best supporting facts prevail?"

The university president and the department dean groaned in unison, wrung their hands, turned on their heels and stormed out of the room without further comment.

"You will regret those words, sir," lead scientist Ward growled quite menacingly despite his comical appearance in chartreuse silk pajamas, mauve fluffy slippers and shiny pink rayon robe. "This very night I shall speak with President Malarky's university contact. You will be lucky to escape this mess with your life. If I read the dean accurately your job is already forfeit. You were always more the poet than scientist, anyhow," he said as he shuffled angrily our of the poet-scientist's lab.

"Thank you, sir," Lovelock said warmly. Later that day, however, he worried that he had gone too far with the lead scientist and university president.

As it turned, out he was right.

Tameka Malarky had ascended to the presidency of the United States three years earlier after running on a platform her critics jokingly referred to as the "PC ticket." Unfortunately for them her campaign had proven more than a bad joke. Her landslide victory in 2016 had heralded Congress's passage of landmark legislation designed to salvage an America mired in a decade long recession, enduring the humiliation of military defeat in a two-year "conflict" with the Korean/Iranian Coalition and suffering New York City's destruction by a Category Five hurricane. American pride had been further dented by rampant crime, out-of-control inflation and thousands of deaths precipitated by the first airborne flu virus back in 2011. Or at least, Malarky and her administration had hoped, the new legislation would at least distract the people from their troubles long enough for Malarky to consolidate her power.

She seized the opportunity with both hands. She proposed laws such as the Anti-Terrorist and Hate Crimes Act and the Anti-American Way Act, and their passage had met with almost universal acclaim from a public demanding an end to congressional gridlock and the implementation of radical new approaches to longstanding problems. With full support from congress and her appointees on the Supreme Court, Malarky accomplished a great deal in a very short time. And as far as the majority of Americans had been concerned, it all began innocently enough.

Admitted Islamic terrorists and convicted serial killers were executed in public places, their remains unceremoniously dumped in mass graves in the Mohave Desert. Next, Ku Kluxers, white supremacists, Neo-Nazis, street gang hooligans, drug dealers, convicted rapists and alleged child sex abusers were rounded up and placed on boats bound for a deserted volcanic island in the Pacific.

Not long after, Malarky took the country all the way down the slippery slope she had at first only tenuously trod. Tobacco executives who had lied to Congress about the addictive qualities of their products were dragged from their offices and interred in underground smokehouses where they suffocated on tobacco smoke pumped in through air vents. Corporate executives who had taken bail-out money from the government in 2009 and awarded themselves million dollar bonuses were taken to secluded Alaskan outposts where molten gold was poured down their throats. Would-be war-mongering generals were strapped to nuclear warheads and blasted into space. Televangelists profiting from claims of having been raised from the dead were given an opportunity to win over their skeptics

Drunk with near universal acclaim, President Malarky further revealed herself by assaulting the politically incorrect heroes of our history books, erasing all reference to such august figures as Robert E. Lee, Thomas Jefferson and Andrew Jackson in public school history books. She then subjected Jehovah and Jesus Christ to the same treatment, eventually adding Mohammed, Buddha and Billy Graham to the proscribed list. As Lovelock knew all too well, the scientists, university presidents, professors and scholars seized upon this moment to pronounce their wholehearted support of

President Malarky's policies. They had, after all, taught and otherwise proclaimed atheism, anti-patriotism and the denigration of the aforesaid politically incorrect figures for the past several decades. Their enthusiasm waned significantly, however, when President Malarky began striking politically incorrect philosophers such as Nietzsche, Plato, Socrates and Voltaire from college curricula, but in a typical show of academic intestinal fortitude, they maintained a respectful silence in the face of Malarky's secret police-backed edicts.

These matters weighed heavily upon Lovelock's mind for the next few days until his worst fears were realized and President Malarky issued his death warrant just as Dr. Ward had implied she would. After his beheading, Lovelock's brain was encased in a glass jar and placed on display in the very lab in which he had made his final stand against the lead scientist and university president.

But Lovelock ultimately had the last laugh in a most extraordinary way. When the Chinese conquered the United States a few months later, the first people they executed were opposing intellectuals such as university presidents, professors, scientists and all their minions. In a fitting irony, their bodies were sold to science and largely utilized for experimentation in university labs, including the one where the poet-scientist had made his final stand.

The Chinese, who by 2016 already owned two-thirds of the United States after calling in trillions of dollars of defaulted loans, had been deeply offended by President Malarky's banning of Confucius's teachings in American universities. She had done this not because the Chinese sage's teachings were overtly politically correct, but because she and her staff didn't understand them and assumed they must be politically incorrect since they did not plainly support her PC political views. The Chinese seized upon this insult to their national pride as an excuse to invade the United States and take control of the national government.

Unlike those of lead scientist Ward and university president Dawkins, Lovelock's remains did not languish in his former laboratory for long. Daisy the imprisoned Bobolono ape stole the key from an unsuspecting Chinese guard and escaped her cage, purloined the jar containing the poet-scientists' brain, stowed away on a ship bound for Africa, and buried Lovelock's brain under the stars in the land he had come to love during his earlier sojourn with the Bobolono.

Daisy enjoyed her fifteen minutes of fame upon her return to her African homeland. "You won't believe what idiots exist in the land humans call America," she told her fellow simians upon her return to Ape City, a city the apes had indeed designed and built themselves in honor of their god, Mogantubolono. "Fortunately," she concluded, "they were conquered by a superior race of humans who worship a god named Confucius, and who follow his precepts at least once or twice a year."

Daisy's fellow Bobolono thanked her for her report and promptly erected a statute to the revered Chinese god, Confucius.

Just in case.

APOLOGIES TO THE BARD

The reporter stormed into the business editor's office, slammed the door behind him, and stood seething with anger before his editor's desk, waving a copy of the morning edition in the startled man's face. "This just won't do," he declared, his face flushed with rage.

The editor had seen this kind of display before. He stretched out his arms and yawned, deliberately taking his time to respond, allowing his youthful charge a moment to cool down.

But this only increased the reporter's anger. "Did you hear me, Jack?" he demanded.

"How could I not, Robertson? What have you got there?"

"You know damn well what it is. This damned op ed column you allowed that funeral parlor director to write. In rebuttal of my column exposing how their funeral parlor was ripping off the public! How could you allow this, Jack? This is the worst example of yellow journalism since the Nazis turned the German press into propaganda rags."

"Wow, what a metaphor," the editor exclaimed in a mock congratulatory tone. "Why don't you write like that in *your* weekly columns?"

The editor immediately realized he had gone to far. "Okay, okay," he said apologetically. "Don't have a stroke here in my office, Robertson. They bought three ads. Is that what you wanted to hear? How many times have you written columns about some newly established business because you knew the owners and sold them an ad so you would write a column in support of their new venture? Eh? That's how it works nowadays with business journals, what with the advertising dollars gone to hell with the economy. Anyway, you can't compare them to Nazis. They're a funeral parlor, for God's sake. They bury people who died in accidents or of natural causes. They don't herd them into gas chambers."

"But this column is different! I don't care how many ads they bought. It's just different, I tell you."

"How so?"

"Yeah, well…Sure, I wrote columns favoring companies that bought ads with our journal. But I picked and chose those as I saw fit. The ones I wrote about were offering services that I believed benefited the public."

"For example?"

"Well, there was that new woman doctor, a native of India, who graduated med school at eighteen. A prodigy, no less. She needed a little jump start because of the woman thing, the foreign thing, and the youth thing. I helped her launch her practice and she's been a major boon to our community."

"So true."

"But this funeral home is ripping people off and lying to them besides. It's a whole different ballgame, Jack. Why did you do this to me? Why not just send me back over there to the funeral parlor with a note on my forehead saying, 'bend me over a casket but be a gentleman and use the same KY Jelly with which you grease your clientele before you shove it up their ass?'"

The business editor laughed, glided around his desk and came face to face with his star reporter. "I know, I know. Journalism sucks today. It rips the moral fabric, steals the soul and destroys the ozone layer. So what else is new? If you don't like it, do something about it."

Robertson, caught entirely by surprise, blinked a few times before finding the voice to respond. "Like what?" he finally managed.

The taller man looked up at the ceiling, paused long enough to make the reporter wait for it, placed his hands on the younger man's shoulders, looked him in the eye, and whispered, "Do it. Write your own rebuttal to their column."

The reporter's face brightened. "You mean it?"

"Absolutely," said the other as he wheeled about and lifed the day's latest copy off his desk. "But," he said, looking up from the copy, pointing an accusatory finger at the reporter with that certain air of authority claimed by newspaper editors across the globe, "not the usual rant and rave, Robertson. Give me something unique apropos for this special occasion."

"What special occasion?"

"The one where we exposed these guys for ripping off their clientele, took their money and ran their response, then greased *them* up and nailed 'em one more time."

"Can we get in trouble for that?"

"Hell no," roared the editor indignantly, as if the report had flung dog shit on his shoes. "We've got a constitutional amendment on our side. We have an obligation to the public to expose this sort of racket. Who forgot to tell this joker that you don't get into a war of words with the folks who own fifty thousand gallons of ink?"

"Now you're talking!"

"But make it good and to the point," the editor shouted as the reporter flew out of his office. "Remember what Shakespeare said, 'Brevity is the soul of wit!' Do you hear me, Robertson?"

The next day, the following article appeared under the reporter's byline:

"'Death Care' Conglomerates Bury all Sense of Decency.

"If you may recall, I recently penned an article condemning the practices of Garrott and Amos, the formerly locally-owned funeral parlor bought out by a large foreign-based corporation which promptly tripled burial prices to help pay for the costly purchase and consolidation of numerous funeral homes around the country. I noted then that our local incarnation of the new funeral parlor conglomerate retained its old name, Garrott and Amos, in order to continue passing itself off as a friendly, locally-owned concern. Last week that company's spokesperson submitted a guest Op Ed column offering as an explanation for their exorbitant price hikes that "government regulations" wrought by the Federal Trade Commission (hereinafter referred to as the "F.T.C.") "forced" them to drastically increase their prices.

"With apologies to the Bard, (specifically his *Julius Caesar*, Act III, sc. 2), I come not to praise the FTC but to bury it. The evil that government agencies do lives on, while the good is oft interred at mega-conglomerate funeral parlor businesses like Garrott and Amos (and at an extravagant cost to the public, I hasten to add).

"So let it be with the FTC. Noble spokesmen for the conglomerate have told you that the FTC is overweening and ambitious for requiring funeral parlor directors to make honest and open disclosure of the prices and services to the public. If this were so, it was a grievous fault, and grievously has the public answered it, paying as they do double and triple what they once paid for funeral services a year ago, here under leave of Garrott and Amos and the rest. The FTC has been my friend, faithful and just to me, but the conglomerate spokesman says it was ambitious, and all conglomerate funeral home spokesmen are honorable men.

"Locally-owned funeral parlors still charge less than two thousand dollars for a traditional service, while our formerly-local-turned-conglomerate funeral parlor charges over $6000 for a comparable burial, exclusive of what they call the "cover charge," i.e., the casket (about $3500 more), and an additional fee (average of $900 more) for the vault. While the remaining local funeral parlor businesses haven't raised their prices and don't send any of your money across U.S. borders to foreign corporations, yet a conglomerate funeral parlor spokesman has assured you that the FTC is ambitious and has caused universal costs increases in the entire "death care" industry.

"But does regulation mandating honest business practice seem ambitious to you? Overly ambitious regulation should be made of sterner stuff than a requirement of full financial disclosure, but a conglomerate spokesman has assured you that this regulation is ambition, and all conglomerate funeral parlor spokesmen are honorable men.

"I write not to disprove what the conglomerate spokesman wrote, but here I am writing what I do know. Jake Amos is a fine man, a leader in our community. His family owned and operated a distinguished funeral business here in Jackson for many years, but that locally-owned business is history. The Amos family received a fancy sum from the conglomerate for the continued use of their name to aid in squeezing the last dime out of our citizens' pockets during the hour of their greatest sorrows.

"We must needs send our business to the locally-owned concerns that have yet to triple their prices and add insult to injury by pocketing millions in profits and then falsely blaming their wrongs on well-intended government regulation.

"What cause withholds you from doing so, my friends? O judgment, thou are fled to foreign conglomerates, and our citizens have suffered substantial monetary loss. Bear with me, my heart is in the $3500 coffin there, with the FTC, and I must pause till it come back to me."

The day after this article appeared, Jake Amos, the conglomerate spokesman and former president of the once-locally owned funeral parlor Garrott and Amos, vented his rage on the subordinate who brought him a copy of the reporter's article, cursed the reporter for his "venom" and "hatchet-job article," and said, "but since we can't lower our prices, we'll have to provide better service to our customers."

Two years later, when the conglomerate filed for

bankruptcy after losing a multi-billion dollar lawsuit alleging fraud and deceit, the spokesman/former president of Garrott and Amos funeral parlor regained sole ownership of the business and continued making money hand over fist, albeit with substantially lowered prices and vastly improved service to his customers.

Amos offered to spend several thousand dollars a year on ads in the very same newspaper that had humiliated him two years earlier, but only with the understanding that Robertson, the reporter who had slandered him before, be terminated upon the paper's receipt of the first thousand dollar check.

The editor agreed to the deal and took the first check without informing the funeral parlor owner that Robertson had left the business journal six months earlier, had subsequently died of a stroke and been cremated according to his final wishes. The editor also failed to inform Amos that a locally-owned funeral parlor had performed Robertson's cremation at a cost of under $2000, and the reporter's ashes had been spread in the Mississippi Sound, near a condo where he had once spent a weekend with his girlfriend, an English lit professor, penning his rebuttal article to Amos's column which had garnered the reporter numerous awards for integrity in journalism. The article had led to the reporter's employment by a larger market newspaper until his death by stroke during a heated argument with his new editor.

Amos and the business journal editor became fast friends and continued bilking the public (and each other whenever they could) until death came for them as it eventually does for all men. Although a few none-too-flattering words were written about them by another muckraking reporter, those words did them little harm. As the Bard once wisely noted, "after your death you are better to have a bad epitaph than their ill report while you live."

VETERAN'S DAY

She sat gently on the bed beside her sleeping husband. Lying on his side in the middle of their bed, he seemed as peaceful as a sleeping child. But that would change radically, she new, when he awoke to a world he no longer understood.

Alzheimer's disease had reduced his mind to mush, and he rarely knew where he was, who she was, or why he was always so confused.

On the table beside their bed stood two framed photographs; one of a young couple cutting their wedding cake fifty-three years ago; the other a black and white snapshot of him in full military dress on the day he received his Purple Heart for wounds received on Omaha Beach during the Normandy invasion.

He had witnessed the destruction of hundreds of his fellow soldiers that day, and before it ended, vainly struggled to stem the flow of his best friend's blood, holding the boy in his arms as the life's blood rushed from his body onto the blood-soaked bench. All the while, bullets zipped over their heads and whanged off the amphibian carrier that had just deposited them on Omaha Beach. He had been the only soldier on his carrier to survive the day.

For decades she had assumed that his country would never cease honoring him for his service above and beyond the call of duty. But the last military-sponsored social event they had attended while he remained in command of his faculties had disabused her of that notion. To attend a party in honor of all Mississippi veterans of the Normandy Invasion they had driven from Greenwood to the military base in Columbus. The event had been impressive enough, but had ended on a sour note when the brass had refused them entry into the commissary for post-party drinks. Those with military careers were welcomed, but the men who had given four years of their youthful lives to save the world from ultimate disaster in WWII were deemed unfit to attend.

That moment foreshadowed far worse insults to come. Of course, the physical and mental horrors they endured were to be expected in light of his worsening disease and her disabling physical conditions. These led to his crashing their only car into the mailbox, his falling and breaking his wrist when rising from the toilet, his not knowing his own relatives when he saw them. Her crippling arthritis and suffocating emphysema severely limited her ability to help him both during his many accidents and with the simplest of daily activities like showering, taking his meals, undressing, and getting into bed at night. One night he slipped on a sheet and landed hard on the bedroom floor. Unable to lift his six-foot-three, two-hundred and forty pound frame off the carpet, she had been forced to leave him there for the two hours it took the ambulance to arrive. But at least these misfortunes were the natural result of sickness, disease and old age. The government's failure to take any steps to ameliorate their suffering was something else entirely.

For a year now they had lacked sufficient funds to manage their medical problems. Their only son had given his life for his country in the Gulf War over a decade earlier, they had outlived all their brothers and sisters and most of their close friends, and neither his meager retirement fund nor their joint social security retirement proceeds were enough to meet their ever mounting health costs.

And although he had ardently supported President George W. Bush's military actions in the Middle East, his president had betrayed him and rammed a law through Congress that denied him and other WWII veterans all but the paltriest of benefits. Consequently, she and her husband couldn't afford a home caregiver or a bed in a nursing home where he could spend his final days in relative comfort. They had hoped the young new president would right this inexcusable wrong, but like so many of his predecessors, he seemed more interested in fattening the pockets of his major political supporters and increasing the hegemony of his own political party than in offering any real support to the struggling veterans marooned in the boondocks.

The Veteran's Administration had offered them two choices; either divest themselves of their remaining savings and become poor enough to qualify for acceptance into a VA living facility, or they could hold on to their meager savings and continue the living death that old age, disease and an uncaring government had left them.

She had found this particularly galling, knowing as she did that thousands of deadbeats, malingerers, drug users, alcoholics, ne'er do wells, bankers wealthier than Croesus, million-dollar bonus-taking corporate executives, military industrial complex nabobs, and Wall Street thieves had been supported, bailed out or otherwise enriched by their government in Washington. But hard luck veterans and their wives could go to hell as far as their government was concerned, or so it seemed to her.

But now she had created, if not an ideal, then at least a workable solution to their problem.

She leaned across the bed and kissed her husband goodbye. He had been such a gentle and loving husband. The recent fits of violence had not been him at all; they were manifestations of the disease, nothing more. They had shared fifty-three years of all the joys and sorrows marriage could offer, and she harbored no regrets about the life they had made together. No matter how unpleasant the end, the journey had been all she had hoped it would be.

She pulled the covers over his chest and ran her fingers through his thick but graying hair. A wan smile wafted across her lips.

Despite her recent complaints against her government, she new she could always count on the post office. The letters she had sent the day before to her minister, the chief of police, the mayor and the head of the County Board of Supervisors would be delivered within the hour. By the time they bothered to read her words the deed would already be done.

She moved to the other side of their bed and slipped under the covers beside her soundly sleeping husband, taking special care not to wake him. She opened the bottle of pills, poured them into her hand, and washed them down with a glass of water. She lay back on her pillow and touched his cheek one last time.

Now, she told herself, they would have no choice but to care for her husband. Even if his service to his country meant nothing to anyone anymore, now the law would force them to do their duty.

And it wasn't as though he would be begging charity from them. She had set aside enough savings to support one person for at least another five years, if necessary.

They both deserved a better fate, working all their lives, giving their only child for their country, and loving their neighbors as the Good Book commanded. But he had also offered to give the last full measure of devotion to her and the rest of his countrymen on the bloody beaches and killing fields in a foreign land an ocean away from home. He had bled for his country. Had carried a machine gun bullet in his hip and a walked with a limp for the rest of his life. The way she saw it, he had earned a better way out than foundering on the bathroom floor, his eyes filled with uncomprehending terror, his hair flecked with his own feces and urine.

She closed her eyes and whispered a silent prayer. Then she opened her eyes, cast a final glance at her wedding picture, closed her eyes once more, and did the only thing left for her to do.

She remembered.

RECIPE FOR DISASTER

"The Greenwood Kiwanis Club meeting to plan our pancake breakfast event will now come to order," proclaimed club president, Josh Wheatley from his podium in a conference room on the first floor of the Alluvian hotel. "I thank you folks for coming out this morning to help launch our annual fundraiser for disadvantaged children. However, before we begin the meeting, and in honor of the season, I've got a special treat for y'all today. I've asked three of our members to present three Christmas holiday dinner menus handed down by their Deep South families for the past five generations."

A murmur of approval wafted toward the podium from the far regions of the spacious conference room. His fellow Kiwanians settled themselves in their high-backed cushioned chairs and eagerly awaited this unexpected presentation.

"I've asked," the club president continued, "Seth Freeman, Betty Ann Johnson and Hickson David to present their family menus from New Orleans, our beloved Greenwood and Vicksburg, respectively. Seth...."

The sound of chairs creaking and throats clearing accompanied the well-heeled young businessman to the podium. "Thank you, Josh," he said. "My family menu goes all the way back to mid-1850's New Orleans, where outrageously sumptuous holiday meals were served not at home, or in restaurants, but at fancy hotels, where my great, great grandparents and their friends met for Christmas dinners on special occasions during the holidays. I dare say this menu was not the regular fare, but neither was it reserved solely for Christmas Day.

"Delicacies served as appetizers included Broiled Pompano, Oysters in the shell, Rockfish, Normandy fashion Redfish, Lobster Salads, and Codfish Tongues. Popular entrees were Broiled Pompano, Rockfish and Normandy fashion Redfish. If seafood was not the diner's choice, he and his family could choose from appetizers of Calf's Head and brain sauce, and entrees of Leg of Mutton, Westphalia Hams cooked in Champagne, Boned Turkeys and Yankee Chicken Pies.

"Provisions were made for the Creoles among us, of course. Their favored entrees usually constituted Noix de Veau en Bedeau, Tourband de Filets de Volaille, Pigeons en compote, Tenderloin of Beef, Mallard Ducks, Canvass-back Ducks, Wild Geese and Snipes.

"Although you'd recognize most of the vegetables served at these events, many were pastry ornaments with names such as Monument of St. George and the Dragon, Nougat Pyramid, Bunker Hill Monument and Chinese Light-House. Pastry, fruit and other desert options included Charlotte Russe, Champagne Jelly, Parisian Gateaux, Lafayette Cakes, Citron Soufflage, Plum Puddings and Pumpkin Pies. Wines served were often Champagne, Claret, Hock, Madeira, Sherry and Port.

"If all that seems a tad over the top to you, let me conclude by adding that Louisiana Cajuns frequently dined on delicacies that would put most of those to shame, even if they were composed of nutria, alligators, cottonmouths and sac-a-lait."

"What the heck," boomed a husky voice from the middle of the room, "are nutria and sac-o-lei?"

"You would know them," Wheatley quipped as he resumed his seat on the front row, "as giant swamp rats and crappie."

As laughter rippled through the room, Betty Ann Johnson, the town librarian, assumed her place at the podium. "Our family didn't live so high on the hog, or swamp rats, as the case may have been, in the turn-of-the century Mississippi Delta as your folks did in 1850's New Orleans, Seth" she said. "But we didn't have as many alligators to sweeten our pots as did your Louisiana Cajuns."

Another rumble of laughter rose and waned.

"But apparently," she continued with a coy smile, "we managed to have a pretty good time during the Thanksgiving and Christmas holidays, at least by 1890, when my great, great grandmother wrote down this menu from her family's holiday feast. She served baked turkey with oyster dressing and corn meal dressing, giblet gravy, roasted duck, baked ham, potato salad, eggplant casserole, English peas, candied sweet potatoes, cranberry jelly, chow-chow, mustard and turnip greens, corn bread and yeast rolls.

"Desserts included ambrosia, coconut cake, jelly cake, caramel cake with homemade vanilla ice cream, pecan pie, ambrosia and white fruit cake. Beverages served were sweet iced tea and ice water for everyone, Coca-cola, RC Cola and Barq's Root Beer for the children, and for the adults, a choice of Near Beer, unblended Scotch whiskey right off the boat, well-aged Kentucky and Tennessee bourbon, specially imported French red table wine, Arkansas white wine, and for the very adventurous, locally fermented muscadine wine."

"What the heck is chow-chow?" roared a familiar voice.

"It's a relish prepared with celery, onions, carrots, peppers and cabbage," she replied. "Ain't you got no schoolin', Mark Shilling," she asked, grinning widely as she located her seat beside Freeman.

"Heck no," the deep, raspy voice countered. "I matriculated at LSU."

As the laughter and mock booing subsided, Hickson David, owner of a Delta-wide trucking company, strode onto the stage and readied himself to address the members. "I thought I might offer a little something different this morning, first by way of a different holiday, notably, July the 4th."

"God bless America," shouted the now-familiar voice in the audience. "Atta boy, Hickson."

"Thanks, Mark, but I don't imagine many of you will find this particular July 4th holiday one that your forebears celebrated with much relish, if at all. I'm speaking of course, of July 4, 1863, in my former hometown of Vicksburg, Mississippi."

Images of the lengthy Civil War siege of the Gibraltar of the Confederacy by Union infantry, artillery and naval forces sprang to the listener's minds—withered soldiers in butternut and grey standing vigil at their posts; starving townspeople cowering in caves as mini-balls whistled over their heads; dogs and cats hunted and slaughtered for food by starving soldiers and civilians alike; and a lost cause gasping its last breaths in the trenches, ditches and redoubts of the beleaguered City on the Bluff. These images were enough to cast a somber pall over the room, banishing the festive holiday spirit that had so recently carried the day.

"But my ever resourceful forebears and their fellow Vicksburgers were not about to take what the Yankees dished out without a little holiday feasting of their own. So, ladies and gentlemen, without further ado, I offer you, not an old family menu, although my ancestors almost certainly partook of the fare, but the glamorous menu of the Hotel de Vicksburg, courtesy of Jeff Davis and Company.

"Appetizers and side dishes on this menu included mule tail soup, mule salad, mule hoof soused, entrees were mule kidneys stuffed with peas, mule brains a la omelette, mule tripe in pea meal butter and mule tongue a la bray."

Slowly rising peals of laughter reintroduced a festive mood among the Kiwanians.

"As limited as the entrees were," Hickson continued tongue firmly in cheek, "the deserts more than made up for the lack—blackberry sauce, cotton seed pies, chinaberry tarts, white oak acorns and beech nuts. Beverages they were fortunate to enjoy included blackberry tea, genuine Confederate coffee, spring water Vicksburg brand, limestone water late importation very fine, and Mississippi water vintage 1492 Superior."

He paused for a moment, then added, "I trust, Mark, that you require no further elucidation as to the content of such items as mule salad and mule brains."

"Not at all," the crusty old gent bellowed. "The first president of my alma mater, General William T. Sherman, was partly responsible for serving up the Hotel de Vicksburg menu, and I got no p'ticular need for any 'lucidation, confirmation, or further intimidation from you Ole Miss Rebels and Mississippi State Bulldogs. Besides, all this talk of mule brains, chow-chow and sac-o-lei has made me powerfully hungry. I move that we git this meetin' over with and repair to the Crystal Grill where their menu is not as hotsy totsy as what Freeman's folks had, but it's even more varied than the repast Betty Ann's folks enjoyed, and a damn sight more tasty than anything ever served at the Hotel de Vicksburg!"

Few motions in the history of the Greenwood Kiwanis Club had been seconded so vigorously and approved so swiftly as Mark Shilling's, made before his fellow Kiwanians in Greenwood, Mississippi, at the Alluvian hotel, on Wednesday, December 22, 2009.

THE GOOD SHEPHERD

Dave Randall considered his daughter's words while maintaining his best poker face, determined to disguise the anger searing his soul. He had forgone his usual Saturday golf match with his buddies to drive from Greenwood to Oxford to help her move furniture into her dormitory room on the west side of the Ole Miss campus. He had hoped to salvage the day by taking his only daughter to dinner at City Grocery, Yocona River Inn or Taylor Grocery, and induce her to tell him all about her few first months as a freshman at his old alma mater. What he had gotten for his trouble was an aching back and some very disturbing news.

"I just can't believe," he muttered, hoping that neither anger nor sadness was as evident in his voice as it was in his heart, "that Gail would do this to you. Hell, Alison, I though y'all were still good friends."

"No," said his daughter calmly, all the while searching his face for a hint of how her revelation had affected him. "That was a long time ago. Before Frank Odom came between us."

"Right," he nodded. "I remember." Frank had been her first love in high school. The relationship hadn't lasted long but it had turned her longstanding friendship with Gail Moore into acquaintance, at best. Now they had both discovered the hard way that it had devolved far lower than that. "But that wasn't your fault," he blubbered, "and it doesn't justify her blackballing you at the sorority. Thank God you had a viable second choice. I'm so very sorry about this, honey."

"Oh," she said, turning away so he couldn't see the moisture welling up in her eye, "that doesn't matter, Dad. One sorority is as good as another. It's just..."

"Just what?"

"Just that I wanted to be sisters with Martha Gene Gerald. She *is* my best friend. We had planned on rooming together in the house next year. But now..."

Damn, he thought. Having a daughter is so easy for the first thirteen years. Then, boom! The roof caves in. It hadn't been that way with her younger brother, Johnny. He was hyperactive hell for the first seven years but grew out of it and hit his stride in high school, quarterbacking Pillow Academy to the state championship, and making the honor roll three straight years to position himself to pick and choose between all the colleges offering him full athletic and academic scholarships.

Yes, there was the revelation last year that Johnny thought he might be gay. But, well... You raise them to love their neighbor, no exceptions for race, creed or... Lifestyle. Whatever they called it now. Of course, that's not exactly what you had in mind when you taught him that, but...Dammit, he's your son and you love him and that's the end of it. He took the black looks and snide comments like a man until he worked it all out, and so will you, by damn.

Alison had done well, too, despite developing a bad attitude in junior high. Then she snapped out of it and made high school honor roll two years, won MVP in the state volleyball tournament her senior year, and made first chair saxophone player in the band her last two years. But...With girls there's always a 'but,' especially where emotional issues are concerned.

Why did they always seem to hurt so deeply over things that guys generally took in stride? Or seemed to, at least. *And why am I so pathetically useless trying to dry her tears when these things come up?* he asked himself for the hundredth time.

But this time... This was the worst mess yet. One look at his daughter struggling to hold back tears sent his blood pressure rising out of control; he felt his last opportunity to control his temper evaporate like early morning steam rising off a downtown Greenwood sidewalk during an August heat wave.

"Dammit," he barked aloud. "I'll make this right if it's the last thing I do. I'm good friends with the Dean of Women here. We dated at Ole Miss and we're still good friends. By God, I'll fix that little bitch's red wagon if it's the last thing I..."

"No, Dad," Alison blurted, leaping across the dorm room, taking his hand between hers. "I don't want that," she pleaded earnestly. "Please don't do anything like that."

"Why not, for God's sake?" he muttered, his face aflame with anger. "I got the little bitch out of that mess. She would've been suspended her freshman year in high school but for my help! Your mother, God rest her soul, took that trollop under her wing when her parents divorced and took up with other people. That girl just can't do this to you and get away with it, by God. I'll..."

"No you won't, Dad," Alison snapped. Her eyes immediately softened as they met her father's twisted gaze. "That's not how you taught me to act. You remember, don't you? Forgive and forget?"

He turned away from her withering gaze. Outside the dorm window autumn descended upon the campus with thousands of fluttering oak leaves in tow; the sun a reddish disk settling in the western sky behind a cluster of dark clouds and a grove of towering oaks. Ole Miss's campus was one of the South's loveliest, he mused, never more so than in the hazy golden light of dusk, the scent of fall dancing mischievously in the air. She ought to be having the time of her life right now. She shouldn't have to be dealing with a pile of horseshit like this.

He waited until the anger had climbed back into its hole before he spoke again. "I may have mentioned 'forgiving,' Ally," he said calmly, "but there's no way I said anything about 'forgetting.' I believe I told you on more than one occasion that I live in the New Testament but drag a foot through the Old. No, ma'am," he said, shaking his head resolutely, "I can't let this lie. I won't. It's just not right."

"No it's not," she agreed, her voice as cool as an autumnal breeze rustling through the oaks in the fabled Grove within view of her dorm window. "Whoever said life was fair, Dad?"

His anger had already melted into bitter resentment, but now he found his resolve weakening, as well. He measured his words before he spoke. "You're mocking me now," he said without rancor. It wasn't the first time she had thrown his words back at him. Words he had usually spoken to her during on of those crying times when he had no idea what else to say.

"You know better than that," she murmured softly. "I love you, Dad. With all my heart." She kissed him on his restless, furrowed brow.

Now, he told himself, she was using the most effective weapon in her arsenal. A weapon he was powerless to resist. "And I love you, too, angel," he said with mixed resignation and affection, taking her into his arms. "Are you sure that's how you want it?" he asked weakly, knowing the matter had already been decided.

"You know I do," she replied, kissing him on the cheek. "But thanks for being here, Dad. You're the best daddy in the world. You always were."

He turned away so she wouldn't see the tear clinging to the inside of *his* eye, then blinked several times so it wouldn't break loose and roll down his cheek.

I would be the best daddy, he thought, and maybe even the man I ought to be, if I could have *you* back at home with me, girl, for another ten or twenty years.

IT'S TOUGH TO BE A TODDLER

Billie Jean Saylor
6th Grade
Milam Elementary School
My Strongest Memories: No. 3
In 450 words or less

When I was five years old I was jumping on my mom and dad's king sized bed. My curly blond hair was bouncing around and I was having a blast. My mom, dad, sister, and I were all there and my mom was on the phone ordering pizza. "A medium cheese pizza and salad with…" I heard my mom say. "Watch out Billie Jean," my mom tried to warn me. But it was too late.

BAM!!! I had started to jump closer and closer to the edge of the bed, and before my parents could stop me I had jumped as high as my little five year old legs would let me, and landed right BAM on my neck.

On the ground. Crying. I was crying hard and in so much pain I couldn't move my head, so my mom called an ambulance to come get me. I remember the sirens wildly flashing red and blue outside the window, and being carried on a big yellow stretcher two times my size. While I was on the stretcher, still in our house, a man in a medical-looking uniform gently lifted my head up while another put a white, soft, circular thing around my neck. It looked like one of those things you put on a dog to stop them from gnawing a sore spot.

When I was in the ambulance only one family person could ride with me. Dad, some people in medical uniforms, and I rode in the back of the ambulance. While they were loading me in my mom asked my dad "How are we going to pay for this?" She meant check or credit card but my sister, who was only seven at the time, misunderstood and thought we were unable to pay for the ambulance, as in we didn't have enough money. So big Sis ran inside, got her piggy bank, ran out and said "I can pay for it. I just want my sister back!"

Mom and dad thought it was very cute. Then my mom and sister were in the car, close behind us. When we arrived at the hospital I was put in a CAT scan, a big, round, circular, fancy looking machine so the doctors could X-ray my neck. The nurse said "Stay very still like cat woman in the CAT scan and don't move so we can get a good shot."

After the CAT scan they told us that nothing was broken, I had just pulled a few muscles in my neck. I had to wear a brace on my neck for one week during school. It was not really all that bad because it made my neck feel good and I got everyone to sign it!

Mom made me promise not to jump on the bed anymore. Duh! Climbing up on the roof is a lot more fun, anyhow.

DURING THE STORM

ON THE SEA

Three crewmen stumbled across the deck of their three-hundred-and-sixty-five-foot-long ocean-going freighter, struggling vainly to secure two large oil barrels that had slipped through their chain link restraints. Wind whipped furiously about them, lacing their eyes and stinging their faces with sheaths of salt water cascading over the ship's sides. When they reached the first barrel, the ship suddenly lurched forward, its stem dipping momentarily beneath the sea's surface, sending both barrels careening across the deck and slamming into the forward mast.

High above the carnage, on the bridge overlooking the deck, the captain and his officers watched the crewmen's struggles with mounting concern.

"This is a powerful hurricane, Captain," the first officer began, "worse than we were led to believe. Probably a Category Four or maybe even a Five. I thought we could skirt her at twenty knots but she's moving too fast. According the horn card, she's right on our tail. She'll hound us all the way to the coast."

Captain Robert Miller turned to examine the radar operator's small, celluloid card with four printed circles in target design, with the word *eye* centered in the smallest inner circle. He had placed the card over a map of the gulf, moving it in a line that represented the storm's path toward shore.

"And," First Officer Josephs added somberly, "she's packing a lot more action than usual."

By *action*, the captain realized, Josephs meant *cyclones*. Josephs leaned down to view the radar screen while Captain Miller stoically focused upon the scrambling crew on his ship's deck. Flying debris wrecked havoc with his men as several more barrels tumbled off their elevated platform onto the deck. Even at a distance he could see their eyes upturned toward the storm, raw fear etched on their faces.

Then he saw the source of their terror. As a cyclone skipped off the gulf like a top and descended from a roiling swell headlong upon ship's bow.

"Hit the deck!" a sailor yelled as he dove amidst the anchor chains.

Spinning water furiously as it snapped booms and rigging apart like so many twigs and paper mache' sheets, the cyclone ripped planks off the deck and lifted two crewmen like limp rag dolls, slamming them into a cabin section bulkhead. It spun two three-hundred-pound barrels like so many feathers in the wind then dumped them into the sea.

"Evasive action," shouted the captain.

"Aye, aye," Josephs replied, moving swiftly to comply. *If it won't go away, get the hell away from it as fast as you can.*

Then, just as quickly as it had appeared the cyclone vanished. But before the officers could relax, the radar operator raised his voice in alarm.

"Vessel approaching from the rear, captain!"

Josephs trained his binoculars onto the gulf's surface. A fifty-foot-long commercial shrimp boat forty meters distant hurtled directly toward them, driven along by the hurricane's winds, completely out of control.

"Do what you can, Mr. Josephs," the captain said calmly. This was the time, he silently reminded himself, to show calm in the heart of the storm. This was the first hurricane at sea most of his officers had experienced.

But many of them, he knew, had grown up in Mississippi, Louisiana, Florida and Texas, and knew all too well what a storm like this could do to their friends, relatives and neighbors on the coast, languishing at ground zero in the path of the storm of the century.

God help them, Captain Miller prayed silently for those facing a monster the likes of which they had never imagined in their wildest nightmares. *God help them all.*

*   *   *   *

IN THE AIR

"Look at that," copilot Jerry Saucier marveled as stared out his cockpit window. Outside their WC-130 Hercules aircraft a flock of seagulls floated serenely in the monster hurricane's eye.

"Looks as if we've got company," said Captain Drew Stone as the hurricane hunter pilot peered out Saucier's window at the seagulls and the blue and peaceful skies surrounding their plane. But beyond those skies ominous dark clouds hovered menacingly in the distance. These were part of a surreal-looking miles long ring of thunderstorms that made up the monster's eyewall, a magnificent black column rising from the glassy sea's surface to ten thousand feet above the gulf. Below them, the gulf appeared as calm as a backyard swimming pool on an airless December evening.

"Too bad," Saucier nodded, "we can't stay in here wit' em."

"Yep," Stone grimaced. "Prepare for eyewall penetration."

"Nothin' like goin' home, eh, Captain?"

"Guess again, Louisiana. This squadron works differently than the rest."

Saucier frowned. "Whatchu' talkin' 'bout, Captain?"

Stone smiled for the first time since they had taken off at Keesler Air Force Base in Biloxi three hours earlier and tracked down the monster hurricane's eye in the center of the Gulf of Mexico. "We penetrate the wall six times to get three readings of wind speeds and barometric pressure at three different elevations."

Saucier turned a sickly shade of green. "Three readings? Jesus, Joseph and Mary. I resign."

"Too late, hotshot. Wall penetration in ten seconds."

Turbulent skies and shrieking winds greeted the aircraft as it slammed into the inner eyewall. Pelting rain and two hundred miles per hour gusts buffeted the plane like a kite at the beach.

Stone was ordering the dropsonde technician to prepare to launch the instrument into the storm when Saucier cried, "Tornado at two o'clock!"

"Go left," Stone barked as the tornado dipped down from above them and struck their right wing. The plane shuddered as if struck by an anti-aircraft round as the twister gripped the wing.

"She's not responding," Saucier shouted above the howling winds.

"Hang on," Stone blurted. "Dive, Sergeant, now!"

They strained against their steering rigs pushing them forward. Behind them, navigator Henry Wingate stared calmly out the cockpit window at the whirling gray funnel a few meters away. "This isn't good," is all he said.

The plane finally lurched downwards and veered away from the tornado.

"Close call," Stone sighed. "Everyone okay?"

"Everyone reporting in good condition," Saucier replied, gaping out the right cockpit window. "But we got some trouble out dere, Captain."

"Oh? How's the wing?"

"It's fine, now. It was flappin' like a pelican's wing back dere. But look at dat," he pointed anxiously out his window.

"One prop is gone."

"What?" Stone blinked. "You mean it's not working?"

"No, Captain. I mean it's not dere!"

*   *   *   *

ON THE LAND

"It's for you, Bob," said his wife, handing him the phone. "It's the police."

The architect took the receiver, thanked his wife, and said, "Just won't give up, eh, Myrtle? Hello, Bob Wilson here." He nodded in recognition of the voice on the other end. "Yeah, chief, I know why you're calling. And you knew my answer before you called."

Myrtle returned to the living room wet bar to pour one of her guests a drink and Wilson seated himself in his recliner to continue his phone conversation. "It's the same answer I gave you the last two times. I designed this house myself. It's hurricane proof, I tell you. Hurricane proof."

Wilson laughed at the chief's reply and gave a 'thumbs up' sign to Myrtle, whose grim visage evinced more than a slight degree of concern. This was, after all, the third time the chief had phoned her husband. She glanced at the TV. The emergency broadcast radar map showed a storm converging on the coast with tendrils reaching from Florida to Texas.

Wilson studied his fellow revelers faces as he listened to the chief's dire predictions. They had believed him when he assured them he had designed his beach-front-facing house to be entirely hurricane proof, but three hours into their hurricane party they needed reassurance in light of recent developments in the gulf. "Well, chief," he said confidently, "I guess we're going to find out in a few hours, aren't we? Because we'll all be riding out this storm right here, just like we did in '65 and again in '69."

He grinned at his wife who poured herself another drink. "Chief, you're a fine public servant, and an even better friend.

You may rest assured of two things. One, I'll support you for mayor if you ever decide to run, and two, we'll be here during the storm and long after it's over. Hey, did I tell you I built this son-of-a-buck to be hurricane proof? Heh. Heh. Uh, what's that? Why?" Wilson listened more intently, as if he hadn't heard the man clearly the first time, or couldn't comprehend what he'd said. "Forget it," he suddenly roared and slammed the phone into its cradle.

"What did he say, Bob?" Myrtle asked, gamely disguising her rising anxiety.

"Nothing worth repeating."

She waited until her friends' conversation drifted on to safer subjects before approaching him again. "What did he say, Bob?" she whispered.

He shook his head as he surveyed the tops of his shoes. "Something...I don't know. Not like him, at all."

"What? Tell me."

"He said, 'can I have the names and addresses of your closest relatives on the coast'."

"Why?"

"So he could contact them after the storm to help identify our bodies."

Two hours later, Myrtle signaled her husband from across the room. He patted a buddy on the shoulder and moved casually across the new carpet to commiserate with his wife standing near the front door.

"Look at that, Bob," she said, the agitation in her voice clearly more evident than it had been before the Biloxi TV station had been knocked off the air by what the Gulfport radio station had reported as hundred and twenty miles-per-hour winds. "There's water coming in under the front door."

He shot her an impatient look. "Hey," he groused, "I said our house was hurricane proof, not water proof. I've already stuffed ten towels down there. We're going to take some water, regardless."

"Well, do something, Bob." Her foot tapped a staccato beat on the wet carpet. He thought of a hooked fish angrily slapping its tail on the deck of his boat.

"Oh, all right," he shrugged, setting his drink on an end table. "I'll check it again. But when I open this door I may not be able to close it again, with all this wind."

Wilson retrieved several of the wet towels crammed under the door, all soaked completely through. "Bring me some more towels, will you, Myrtle?"

"Sure."

One of their friends watching Wilson laboring over the towels decided it was time to intervene. "I don't know that I'd open that door, Bob," he said. "I'd just keep the inside towels dry and worry about whatever's going on out there tomorrow."

"Humff," Wilson scoffed. "You think I wanta' spend the rest of the day listening to her complain about her precious dadgum carpet, Edgar?"

Edgar replied with a blank stare. Wilson rolled his eyes, took the dry towels from his wife, unlocked the front door, gripped the knob and pulled it slowly toward him. He peered out across the threshold into the darkness enveloping his beloved Gulfport beach.

His mind had barely grasped the fact that the dark wall rushing down upon him was a thirty-five foot tall tidal surge when it blasted him backwards, shattered the front wall of the house and swept them all away with the rolling, surging tide.

MY HOW TIMES IS CHANGED

"Ladies and gentlemen, I give you Senator Josh Hamilton."

The distinguished-looking sliver-haired U.S. Senator rose from his seat on the stage, waved to the audience, shook the emcee's hand and strode purposefully toward the podium. He waited patiently for the crowd's obligatory applause to rise to a crescendo then fall off to an acceptable hum. Breezed through the obligatory greetings and thanks and began his speech. Although he used no notes, he spoke with the ease of a man accustomed to public speaking and genuinely happy to be home among family and friends.

"Most every boy growing up in the Mississippi Delta," he said, "recalls plumbing the depths of their hometown streams; the rivers as prominent in the Delta as bulging blood vessels on a weight-lifter's arms. In another time they were no less than the life's blood of our cotton-drenched alluvial plain, before the Northern industrialist's railroad consigned the southern planter's steamboat to entrepreneurial extinction.

"The principal stream of my childhood was the oak-lined Tallahatchie, which joins the Yalobusha near downtown Greenwood to form a river with the extraordinary name of Yazoo. My north Greenwood backyard ended where the Tallahatchie's southern shore began, and my buddies and I made like Hernando DeSoto and Jim Bowie every chance we got, seeking our fortunes exploring our stream's vine-covered banks and tussling on its mussel-flecked sandbars for the honor of being the first of the day to make Bobbie Gentry's myth a reality and leap off the nearby Tallahatchie Bridge."

The senator paused, enjoying a moment of reverie. "But the biggest mission we ever undertook," he continued, "was hiking the five mile trek to the Civil War battle site located on that stream's south bank a few miles west of Greenwood. There at Fort Pemberton we slogged through brambles, vines and mud exactly 300 more feet along the shore, then slipped beneath the river's brown, silt-laden surface in search of the remains of that ill-fated vessel, *Star of the West*. In 1863 'our' valiant Confederate boys had sunk her there while defending their besieged homeland against invading Yankee marauders.

"I say 'ill-fated,' because the *Star* failed to relieve Fort Sumter when President Lincoln sent it to Carolina for that purpose on January 9, 1860. Confederate officer Earl Van Dorn's company captured it shortly thereafter on the Texas shore line, according to more legend than fact, by virtue of a ruse that tricked a vastly superior Yankee force into surrendering their ship without a shot. Confederate forces at Fort Pemberton scuttled her in the Tallahatchie to block the Union fleet's attempted backdoor invasion of Vicksburg. Ill-fated or not, to me and my childhood companions, she was the great star which fell upon the Delta, whose flaming demise still fueled our imaginations exactly one century to the day after Rebel soldiers pulled her plugs and began her final descent beneath the waves on March 11, 1863 at 10:00 AM.

"The sinking was precipitated by General Grant's decision to approach Vicksburg via a route along the Tallahatchie which began in Grenada and was to end at the Mississippi. Warned by southern spies of the flotilla's progression into Moon Lake, one-armed Confederate General William W. Loring ordered a few civil engineers, two hundred slaves, and fifteen hundred civilians to hastily construct a breastwork of logs, fence rails, sandbags and cotton bales on a patch of land three miles below Greenwood. Loring chose the spot because it overlooked a bend in the Tallahatchie with the river wide enough to accommodate only one boat at a time.

"Three hundred yards upriver from the hastily erected and newly christened Fort Pemberton, the Confederates positioned the *Star of the West* in midstream. Her captain, Lieutenant A.A. Stoddard, ordered the crew to drill 250 holes in her below-water hull and plug them with oak bungs.

"When the Union fleet under the command of General L.R. Ross appeared on the river a few miles upstream, Confederates pulled the ship's plugs and sent her to the bottom, her masts still protruding ominously above the Tallahatchie's surface. When the Federals attacked, Rebel sharpshooters and their lone cannon treated their opponents to a frightful, hot-shell reception. As one Confederate later reported, the Yanks "met with such a warm reception from our cannon planted along the south bank of the Tallahatchie…that they were glad to retire."

"But the Federals returned on the 13th and an all day battle ensued. "Give 'em the blizzards, boys," shouted General Loring, and his men rained hell down upon the Union fleet. Unable to land his men because of springtime flooding, Ross again retreated. On March 16, the Federals returned for one more battle, but within twenty short minutes, Confederate lead incapacitated the Union gunboat, Chillicothe and claimed 31 Union casualties. The victorious Rebels suffered less than a dozen dead and wounded. When apprized of the stunning Confederate victory at Greenwood, Grant abandoned his backside approach to Vicksburg and made plans to take Vicksburg by land.

"Through the years, we saw the Star's upper hull languishing above the river's waves every spring, but treasure-seeking history lovers and safety-conscious pleasure boaters made off with most of the hull's planks. Only the lower section remained to haunt the river bottom and entice young boys such as my pals and I to brave a surprisingly swift current, ever-patrolling cotton-mouths, ubiquitous alligator gars and almost certain parental rebuke, solely for the pleasure of touching the Star of the West's hallowed hull.

"As I recall, the diving part of our excursions lasted no longer than a New York City skyscraper elevator ride, although the debates over whether the souvenirs dredged up off the bottom were remains of logs, cotton crates, or the Star of the West's hull often raged for the four or five hours we spent hiking down Park Avenue and the venerable Grand Boulevard toward our homes on Robert E. Lee Drive. While countless others squandered precious hours of their youth aimlessly gazing at unreachable stars, I spent a treasured part of mine seeking the sunken remains of history, of a fallen Star that always remained a few inches outside my grasp.

"I seek that fallen star still, in the constellation of my imagination, where she shines as brightly as she did during my youth, sparkling brilliantly alongside Chief Greenwood Leflore's vanished mansion, Malmaison, the long silenced guns of Fort Pemberton, and the elusive grave of bluesman Robert Johnson. An old southern gentleman once told me that I would never see the stars so clearly anywhere else in the world as I would while lying flat on my back in a barren Delta cotton field. As I reflect upon my childhood experiences in the legend-drenched Mississippi Delta, I fancy now that I understand what he meant."

The senator smiled broadly as he raised his hand in acknowledgment of the crowd's tumultuous applause. As with all his recent speeches, he offered nothing about his rumored retirement from office, but merely stepped back from the podium and unceremoniously seated himself beside his wife, daughter and grandson.

In the middle of the third center row of the audience, an elderly white man dressed in overalls, white cotton shirt, and work boots, clutching a dirt-stained cap in his hand, tapped the shoulder of the youthful, charcoal-grey-suited, bowtie-wearing black man seated directly to his right.

The young man turned his head. "Yes sir?"

"Fine yarn, he tole, don't ya thank, young feller?"

The young man noted the farmer's sun burnished, wizened face, cigarette-tarnished teeth, sandy brown crew-cut hair and mole-splotched hands, then replied without emotion, "Sure. Don't you?"

The farmer rubbed his chin with one hand as he placed the old cap on his head with the other. "Eah. I reckon so. Ain't never heard one like that before, I'll give him that much."

"How's that sir?"

"Differn't. Jus' differn't, that's all."

"Yes sir." The young man gave a furtive glance over his shoulder hoping to locate his wife in the throng offering well wishes to senator. Unable to find her in the milling crowd, he turned to face the farmer.

"Well, young feller," the old gent said, "You ain't asked but I'll tell ya anyhow. This is a politician speaking, you see. He ain't tole narn' lies, ain't bragged on hisself about what he done in Washington, not onest. He ain't promised nothing to nobody, ain't kissed no babies," then with a conspiratorial whisper he added, "nor no ass neither."

The young man laughed and leaned closer to his older companion. "He jus' talked 'bout something that sho 'nuff happened over a hunnered year ago, and yapped a bit about what he and his buddies did when they wuz young and livin' here in town."

The young man smiled warmly. "Liked that part, did you?"

"Ain't said that. But I will tell you one thang."

"What's that, sir?"

"I see why he's hangin' 'em up."

"Oh, yeah? Why's that?"

"Shoot, boy, don't take this the wrong way. Myself, I'm like an old hound dog; got plenty of heart but jus' ain't got the legs. The senator got a different problem."

"Oh?"

"Yep. You see, when the runt in the litter sees it ain't goan' get no mo' milk, it jus' wanders off in the woods to die. Grown man's got that much sense, I reckon"

"Sir?" blinked the young man. "I'm not following you."

"Humpff," the older man half-chuckled as he rose from his seat. "Man in Washington don't lie, don't brag, don't try to re-write the past, don't brown no noses. And worst of all, say he got a happy childhood in Mis'ssippi. Now who you reckon in the halls of Congress goan' want to have anythin' to do with a feller like that?"

The farmer nodded knowingly to the young man then ambled gingerly down the row toward the auditorium's side exit

MERCY OF THE GODS

So I'm sitting at a table in Webster's Bar and Grill a few feet from the bar having a frosty mug of Michelob Ultra Amber, the perfect blend of slightly watered-down dark beer taste and low calorie refreshment, when the big goon starts yapping about how worthless the Choctaws have always been and will always be, and how the state had better not allow them to build a casino in Leflore County. "This would," he pontificates loud enough to be heard across the county line ten miles away, "bring a bunch of drunk fucking Indians to town and do more to tarnish Greenwood's future than the jigs have done since the government rammed integration down our throats."

Not that impersonally spouting off such hateful language in a public place isn't bad enough, but this time, it's being foisted directly upon three Choctaws seated at the opposite end of the bar. I figure the goon is sending a message to their chief through the chief's nephew, the shortest of the three in the group.

Most white or black folks would take umbrage at such insults and open up a can of whoop-ass on the goon, but not these Choctaws. They're a peaceable, generally non-confrontational sort, resorting to violence only when given no other choice.

But *I* may do something about it. For two very good reasons. First, I know how those fellahs feel, having to sit there and take that crap. I've seen it a million times, and usually at the hands of some world-class jackass like this redneck goon. Whether it's the back alley thug beating up an unsuspecting passerby, the school bully wailing away on the math nerd, the gang initiate raping the helpless girl, or the human waste of protoplasm back at my high school who laughed at me because of my deformed leg and the goofy way I limped along with my wooden cane.

"Get the lead out, crip," he shouted. Made a special point of making sport of me in front of the girls, as if that was going to suddenly change their minds about him and convince them to shower him with their panties. Then he'd catch me alone outside the cafeteria and snatch my lunch money. I'd always put up a fight and he'd invariably bust my lip.

Oh...I cried to my mother about it once and she comforted me as best she could. But when my father got wind of it he hauled me up to my room and gave me the belt. Said it'd toughen me up. That I'd need to be tough on account of my disability. I'd thank him later, he assured me.

Wrong. But that bully wasn't the worst I've ever seen, and nor is this only-good-Indian-is-a-dead Indian goon here at the end of Webster's bar. When the courts integrated Greenwood High School back in '71, we had a real bad one there, too. He was the worst I've ever seen.

The blacks had sent two guinea pigs to our school that first semester. A "slow" boy and a very pleasant but frail and sickly girl. She wore thick glasses and coughed up phlegm all morning long. I guess the blacks thought the redneck bullies would take pity on those two and lay off for a change, and for the most part they were right. But nothing stops that spectacular brand of blockhead from showing his true colors whenever the perfect opportunity arises.

"Go back to Africa, you damned apes," that one shouted whenever no teacher or hall monitor was in sight. "Or get a job as a diving suit with that thick black rubber skin of yours." A few idiots laughed, but mostly everybody knew the score and just wanted to get on with it. Change was in the air, and if you thought that was a shit sandwich, all you could do was step up to the plate and take a big bite. Either move on to the greener pastures of the white flight private school or conduct yourself like a civilized human being for four years and get on with your life. You might even make a few new friends and enjoy the whole thing as I and most of my buddies did.

But for those two brave souls, innocent black children seeking only what other Americans took for granted— a free, worthwhile education—they had hell on wheels whenever that jackass caught them by themselves.

In college it was the fraternity boys who took the goof balls, sci-fi geeks, effeminate-and-presumed-gay guys, habitual chess players, and boys who grew up poor with little or no training in the social graces, and sequestered them in a room set aside for making not-quite-subtle-enough fun at their expense. One of their victims, a guy from Yazoo City who went through fraternity rush with me, slit his wrists after taking a ride on the goob train at the SAE house.

The sorority girls acted even worse. I remember when they cut one freshman out of rush the first day because she weighed two hundred pounds and had a face with three chins that was pocked with acne. The girl overdosed on sleeping tablets and had to be rushed to the ER to have her stomach pumped. She left the university the next day, and we heard that she died of a drug overdose two years later.

In the working world, the bullies are more subtle about it to be sure, but for those of us on the receiving end, it hurts just the same. Whether its an employer giving the sexy woman a promotion the ugly one deserved, the snubbing of obviously poor patrons by department store clerks, or the ridiculing of people of other races, creeds or national origin in tactless letters-to-the-editor, it still hits home like a fist in the gut.

Yes, I've seen this sort of thing a thousand times before. And sure, the bullies and lame brains are all sad stories themselves. They're often formerly abused kids or the victims of snobbery and prejudice themselves. But rather than feeling empathy for their fellow sufferers they choose to vent their anger upon them. Making themselves feel better, I guess, by making someone else feel worse.

And despite their blustery show of strength they're all cowards at heart. The goon here in Webster's, for example, wouldn't have the guts to use the word "jig" if three black Delta State football players were partying at the bar. And he's only messing with the Choctaws because he and his buddies outnumber them ten to one tonight. So now he's enjoying himself by making a very public show of not having learned his Sunday school lessons as a child.

But somebody needs to teach guys like him a lesson. Lord knows Jesus tried. He lived and died the way he did so they'd eventually get the point. But most of them simply don't. And that's where my second reason for intervening comes in.

Jesus wasn't the only demi-god who fought for humanity, who strove to aid the weak and helpless in the painful struggle of life. While most of the other gods proved indifferent to human suffering, two other noble demi-gods took up their cause.

The Greek god Hercules was one, and Thor, the Norse god of thunder and fertility, the other. They fought, and ultimately died, sacrificing themselves in the cause of humanity. Hercules gave his life at the end of his many painful labors, and Thor died during his fatal struggle with the evil Midgard Serpent, a beast so large it could wrap itself around the Earth's midsection. According to the myth, in the time of Ragnorak, the end of the gods, Thor slew the beast then died moments later from wounds suffered in the struggle.

Well, Jesus and Hercules may be residing in heaven and Mount Olympus, but the god of thunder is back. That's right.

You heard me. I am Thor, god of thunder, lord of the living lightning. Not a Germanic mythical god of yore, nor a 21st Century comic book character and idol of millions throughout the world. No, I am the god Thor reborn! Here in the flesh, albeit in mortal guise as a weakling human with a bum leg who hobbles around on a cane.

And here's the thing. All I need to do is stamp that cane upon the ground, and in a blinding flash, the lame weakling is gone and the all-powerful thunder god lives, with silver winged-helmet, flaming red hair, steel-plated armor, fur cape and a magical Uru hammer forged by the king of the gods, Odin himself.

The hammer grants me both the miracle of flight and the power to fire lightening bolts at my enemies. A magic Uru belt grants me the strength of fifty mortals, and my immortal heart endows me with courage worthy of the gods. And most relevantly here, the will to protect those humans unwilling or unable to defend themselves from the forces of evil. Or at least from goons like this jackanape hassling Choctaws in Webster's Bar and Grill.

But out of respect to my human parents, Sunday school teachers, and other well-intended mentors, I always try the Jesus method first.

I don't have to wait long.

"Like I said before," the goon barks, "I sure hope they aren't so stupid as to put a casino five miles up the road to let these damn redskins loose on hard working folks like us, drinking and driving and killing more people than they ever did with tomahawks."

What a wit. Shakespeare will rest easy tonight.

For their part, the Choctaws focus on their conversations and ignore the goon. But not me; not tonight. The gods have charged me with a responsibility to help those less fortunate than myself. And I always do my duty.

"We heard you the first time," I announce without the least hint of challenge in my voice. That's what Jesus would do, I figure. Speak out fearlessly but with ill will toward none. Diffuse the situation and send everybody home happy.

The goon whips his neck around and focuses upon the little man with the glasses cradling a cane at the table directly behind him.

"What's that?" he snaps. "You got something to say, bub?"

"Sure," I say rising from my seat and hobbling slowly toward the bar. "I want to say that I'd like to buy you a drink."

"Oh, yeah? Why's that," he bellows, sizing me up one more time just to make sure I'm not packing, not a legitimate physical threat, and that my cane is not made of heavy-enough material to crack open his skull open with one blow. It's not. My cane's made of porous wood no thicker than the goon's muscle-bound index finger.

"Because it sounds like you've had a bad day," I hear myself explaining, "and I thought I'd try to brighten up your day."

"Oh, yeah?" the goon scoffs, malevolence dripping off his beer-soaked tongue. "Well I thought I was having a good day," he yowls to his buddies, "till Randy here tells me about those damn Choctaws trying to put up a got-damned casino hereabouts. Now I feel like hell. What you got to say about that, buttercup?"

I ignore the insult. I'm sure that's what Jesus would do, and besides, what does a god of thunder care about the babblings of lamebrain morons? And for that matter, why should I, even in mortal guise, care what he thinks? I mean, mortal though we humans are, we share common traits with the gods, don't we? A shared capacity for love, hate, greed, lust, pity, mercy, resentment. And most of all forgiveness. Shouldn't we indulge fools at least as patiently as our counterparts on Mount Olympus or in Asgard?

So I said, "I'm hip, big fellah. But hey, these Choctaws are my friends (a lie, yes, but surely in a good cause; let the gods who've done less cast the first stone). And I wanted to ask you to hold it down a little. There's no sense in making anyone feel unwelcome here in Websters, is there? What a festive place this is, especially now that it's all decked out in holiday dress? Surely you don't—"

Without so much as a 'by your leave,' the goon grabs me by the collar, jerks me into the air, pulls me so close I can see the pores in his skin, smell what he ate for dinner on his breath and give him an Eskimo kiss if I were so inclined.

"What the fuck did you say, boy?"

Believe it or not, I didn't fear him at all. I was a mere rap of my cane from becoming the most powerful force in the known universe. "I believe I was clear," I said coolly . "I asked you to stop insulting my friends. If that's quite all right with you."

He blinked with disbelief, as if I had told him I was an emissary of the gods, come to take him up to heaven for a three hour tour. If only he knew...

"It ain't all right with me, you little worm," he growled. "Are you looking for trouble, bub?"

"Not really."

"Then why are you standing on my feet?"

Now it was my turn to blink. I looked down, and sure enough, he had set me down atop his own feet. Sometimes they're hell bent on a scrap and just don't give you any choice but to fight or flee.

Thunder gods don't flee.

"I'm going to say it one more time," I persisted with the near-exhausted patience of a junior high school principle facing down the school bully for the umpteenth time. "Either you leave my friends alone or face the consequences of your actions."

"I'll take my chances," he snarled and spat right between my eyes. As his phlegm oozed down the bridge of my nose I struck the ground with the cane dangling from my right hand. A blinding light, brighter than a nuclear explosion, announced my transformation from a 130-pound weakling to the most powerful being in Leflore County.

The flash blinded him for a moment, and when he finally opened them, he couldn't believe what they assured him was the case. Standing before him was a six-foot-six, two hundred and fifty-pound thunder god, replete with rippling muscles as hard as steel, winged helmet, gleaming armor, a coat of mail that sparkled brighter than the Christmas lights reflecting off it, flowing fur cape, flaring nostrils, and most significantly, the fierce, raging, merciless eyes of an immortal Asgardian warrior.

"What...the...fffff..." was all the goon said before my alter ego grabbed *him* by the throat and with a flick of his mighty wrist, flipped the goon over his shoulder like a tequila drinker tossing a pinch a salt into the air. The goon crashed to the hardwood floor and tumbled down the steps that led from the bar to the dining room. There he collapsed into a broken heap, almost entirely unnoticed by the restaurant's patrons, who had not yet taken their bulging eyes off the thunder god in their midst.

I turned, bounced down the steps, raised my Uru hammer and leveled it in the shattered goon's general direction. "Let this be a lesson to you, mortal," I proclaimed in my deep, booming Asgardian voice, "that Thor stands ever ready to defend those who suffer at the hands of misguided evildoers."

The goon, still a near unconscious heap where I had deposited him, groaned, but remained perfectly still. Lesson learned, I told myself and....

*   *   *   *

Greenwood Leflore Hospital ; Emergency Room Summary 12/4/2010

Provider: Kay Ballard, RN

Patient brought in on stretcher by EMT providers. Still unconscious, probably the result of concussion. Severe contusion above the right eye socket. No longer hemorrhaging. Patient sustained a blow to the head, apparently in a fist fight in Webster's restaurant at 09:35 PM. According to witness who presented herself at the emergency room, patient, who had been grasped by the collar and lifted off his feet by the assailant, a much larger man, had raised his cane to strike the larger man when he received a fist blow to the face, causing the damage detailed in this report. The cut over the patient's right eye believed to be caused by his glasses when struck by the assailant; the witness turned in a pair of shattered eyeglasses believed to be patient's. She left other items of patient's property with the ER nurse. Patient will be assigned a room and treated for concussion and contusions. 11:43 PM

* * * *

Okay, so by now I guess you know I'm not really the god of thunder. I didn't turn into Thor last night when I stamped my cane on the floor of Webster's Bar and Grill. What's worse, the goon told the police he hit me in self defense when I raised my cane to strike him. I don't remember that part, but I suppose it could be true. I guess it's also true that, although I refer to redneck bullies as idiots, I'm the bigger idiot for believing that just because Thor, the god of thunder, is able to overcome injustice with a swing of his mighty hammer, I, a cripple, can also accomplish the same thing with a measly, hollowed out, wooden cane. No one needs to remind me that my fantasy about *being* the god of thunder is the most idiotic conceit since Adolph Hitler convinced himself he knew more about waging war than Irwin Rommel.

Maybe Jesus was right after all, and I should learn to turn the other cheek and let the Choctaws, blacks, geeks like me and other victims of hatred or contempt work these things out by themselves. Now that I think of it, the Choctaws at Websters were actually doing a pretty good job of ignoring the goon before I horned in. Also, I probably shouldn't be judging the goon or anyone else, and should leave the condescending tone to the gods, who can get away with taking a condescending tone with anybody they want because, well, they are the gods, after all.

I'm only mortal. And no one realizes that better than I after waking up with a busted head and pounding headache that guys like me always get when we pick a scrap with guys outweighing us by a hundred pounds of hard core muscle.

Even so, some god somewhere smiled on me despite all my arrogance, stupidity and the pointless suffering I brought on myself. Tell you the truth, it's such an unbelievably extraordinary turn of fortune that I'm having trouble believing it myself.

The girl who brought what was left of my glasses to the ER was someone I've had a crush on for years. Well, at least a year and a few months, anyhow. She works in my office, a few cubicles over from mine, but I figured she never even knew I existed. Maybe she didn't before, but she surely does now.

You see, when I woke up in the hospital room early the next morning, she was sitting right there beside my bed, reading the comic book she had rescued off my table after my near suicide attempt left me unconscious on the restaurant floor. I was a little embarrassed that any girl who cared enough about me to follow the ambulance to the hospital to return what was left of my shattered glasses, and who had seen what she apparently thought was my courageous act of defending the Choctaws, had to find out that my reading material for a Friday night on the town was neither a best-selling novel nor a book of philosophy by the world's greatest thinker, but a comic book about a costumed super hero with long blonde hair, a magical hammer and a Shakespearean dialect. No, not even Superman, Spiderman or the Hulk, or another of the cool guys in comic lore, but Marvel Comic's one and only mag about my beloved hammer-tossing Avenger.

But as luck would have it, she too was a fan of that rascally thunder god and his mortal pals, the Avengers: Captain America, Iron Man and the Hulk.

Too good to be true, you suspect? He's fantasizing again, you say? Did I forget to mention she's a Choctaw? One of the most beautiful I've ever seen with raven-colored hair, lovely olive-shaded skin and a figure worthy of the attention of the gods. And get this; her brother was one of the three I defended at the bar, one who had endured a lengthy succession of insults and abuse from the goon and countless other insensitive clods like him. I figure my actions cast me in a pretty heroic light so far as those Choctaws were concerned.

Maybe she was making up the part about being a Thor fan, but I gotta believe her when she rattles off the names of every Avenger from the Vision to the Scarlet Witch. She even named a few of the West Coast Avengers I had forgotten, albeit not without good reason since I never read that rag in protest of their trying to steal the limelight from my glorious New York City heroes.

Anyhow, this Choctaw girl—her name is Nellie—she and I are now an item. Somewhat ironically, our first date took us back to the scene of the crime, now renamed Webster's Restaurant and Patio Bar, undoubtedly in hopes of attracting a better sort of patron that doesn't slug it out with goons on Friday nights.

Did I tell you that Websters is located a stone's throw from the Yazoo River levee? It is, and she told me that the Choctaws named it the Yazoo, meaning 'River of Death', because they believed the Yazoo, or at least the part of it near where Websters is today, was cursed by their god, the ever vigilant Great Spirit.

Which brings me to a less than comforting thought... One I really hate to think about, especially during the Christmas season, and also the Thor-worshipping Celtic season of light. But I may as well face this daunting prospect with the same deluded courage that prompted me to stand up to the mighty and powerful goon.

What I'm wondering is—have I been worshipping the wrong gods all along?

THE DRINKING PARTY

"So Senator Phaedrus," Judge Callais grumbled, "where is your buddy, that do-gooder, Socrates? And why is he always late to all of our Saturday evening dinner parties at Giardina's?"

Phaedrus' eyebrow arched heavenward. "Socrates a do-gooder, Callais?" he asked incredulously. "Why Judge, he could drink you and me under the table and get up the next morning and do it all over again."

"Of course. He's done it many times before. Alcohol has no effect upon him. He's not human, that man."

"That's true, Judge," the youthful Autolycus agreed. "He's old as dirt and walks five miles to Greenwood High School every morning to teach his APAC classes, then jogs home every afternoon after coaching the baseball team or walking 18 holes of golf at the Country Club."

"And he's quite the dancer, too," Chrysilla added.

"Is that so?" the judge frowned. "I know you're quite adept at the piano, Chrysilla. But what makes you such an expert at dancing?"

"Experience," she responded without hesitation. "Socrates chaperones the Graduation Dance every year and dances with every teacher and student that can keep up with him. Fast dancing, too. He never tires. And he's ancient."

"Do you hear that, Judge?" Phaedrus deadpanned. "According to your son's girlfriend, your contemporary is ancient."

"Yes," Callais groused sardonically. "Old as dirt. I hope you aren't running low on funds at college, this month Autolycus. I'm not in the habit of rewarding insults with a free dinner."

"Stop it, Dad."

"Now," Callais griped with mounting impatience, "where is that Socrates? I'm getting older *and* hungrier by the minute. And where is Agathon? Didn't I hear that he won some award at the Greenwood Arts Festival for his new play? A comedy about Mississippi politics?"

"Mississippi politics?" Phaedrus roared. "It must be a tragedy. Anyhow, they're both coming. They..."

"Hello, all," Agathon called from behind the curtained entrance of the booth where the revelers had been seated for the past thirty minutes.

"Speak of the devil," Callais said with uncharacteristic pleasantness. "Welcome Agathon. Let me be the first to congratulate you on the Festival drama award."

"Thank you sir," Agathon replied sheepishly, "but you should save the congratulations for Autolycus. Taking nothing from a local festival award, garnering All-American laurels for the SEC baseball champions is something else entirely. "

Callais smiled broadly. "Well said, Agathon. Hoddy Toddy and all that. But where the hell is Socrates? We thought he was coming with you."

"He was behind me just now as I entered the lobby. I'm afraid his lateness is all my fault."

"How's that?"

"I had heard something of one of his recent talks at the Rotary Club," Agathon admitted apologetically, "and made the mistake of asking him the difference between true goodness and apparent goodness. Sorry, Judge."

"You've done it now, Agathon," Callais chided with unrestrained resentment. "Socrates has the most irritating penchant for stopping anywhere he happens to be and losing himself in Cloudcukooland, debating some abstract concept with himself or with his *daemon*, or whatever he calls that voice in his head he claims to hear. Sounds weird as hell to me."

"I don't know what to make of that comment, Callais," Phaedrus scolded. "A judge who thinks hearing from his conscience now and again is weird. Sounds frightening to me."

"Very funny, Senator. A case of the pot calling the kettle black."

"Touche', my friend."

"Hallo all," Socrates hailed as he turned the corner, swept the curtain aside and entered his companions' booth. "Sorry I'm late."

"What were you thinking about out there, teacher," Autolycus asked.

"It was nothing, really," Socrates replied casually.

"Don't buy that, son," Callais quipped. "Now that he's here, maybe you should consult friend Socrates on any questions you have about the mysteries of life. I'm told he knows something about everything. Come here, Socrates, and sit between Autolycus and me, so that we can be near you and enjoy the benefit of every wise thought that entered your mind out there in the lobby, about which I'm sure you gained a better understanding, or you'd still be out there mulling it over while our bellies debated the meaning of hunger."

Socrates smiled as he took the empty seat between them. "If only wisdom could be gained by osmosis, Judge; out of the wiser man into the slower one, just as water seeps through the irrigation ditch to sustain our parched cotton crops in summer. If that were so, Callais, I would spend every minute at your side, and let you fill me to overflowing with the stream of knowledge you've acquired from years of study and your exertions on the bench."

"He's full of something, Socrates," Phaedrus laughed, "but I'm not sure what that might be."

"You're mocking me, Socrates, I know," the judge scowled. "But this evening we'll find out who is truly the wisest."

"That's no contest, Callais," Socrates nodded. "You're absolutely right to suggest that you know more than I. I'm painfully aware that I know absolutely nothing, and that the sum total of my wisdom lies in the fact that I'm aware of my ignorance. I could never teach Autolycus anything he didn't already know himself. I certainly didn't teach him anything about hitting, something he surely knew from birth."

"That's very magnanimous of you to say, Socrates," Callais said with no sincerity whatsoever, "but we don't have the time now to hear another of your spiels about how you're just a midwife, bringing your students' ideas to birth, or whatever it is that you're always going on about. Right now, we're better occupied with dining on some fried oysters, delectable veal, grilled catfish or divinely prepared filet mignon. Buzz that waiter, Phaedrus. We can't have the professor going on too long without the oil of conversation, the philosophic wine, or as my minister would say, the devil's own brew."

Phaedrus pressed the buzzer and turned to address Socrates. "I've a question for you, old friend. You always catch the winning bass in our annual Rotary Fishing Rodeo on Callais' private lake. Which is the best fish attractant for bass?"

The older man rubbed his chin for a moment. "Fish attractant? What is that?"

"Oh, you know very well what he means, Socrates," Callais carped bitterly. "That bottle of fish scent we spray on our lures to attract fish. Oh, yes, I see from your doubtful expression that you're about to tell me that learning how and where to cast a lure is the surest method to land bass."

"You see, Phaedus," Socrates nodded. "Let the record reflect that Callais knows what I'm going to say even before I do. If that doesn't convince him he's the wiser, nothing else will. However, I would like to remind you, my friends, that you wouldn't put on a woman's scent to attract a woman, so why rely on a fish's scent to attract another fish? Wouldn't your time be better spent learning the art of love if a woman's attention is what you seek?"

"Good point, Socrates," Callais admitted. "What should we men smell of if we wish to attract women?"

"Why, true goodness, of course."

"And where should we find that, teacher," Autolycus asked.

"You should tell us, young man. You seem to be the only one of us here with a woman, the lovely and talented Chrysilla."

"Don't evade the issue, Socrates," Callais prodded. "Answer the question, *teacher*."

"Not in a bottle of cologne, for certain."

"Then where?"

"Where the philosopher said: 'Good company with teach you, bad will rob you of even the good sense you had'."

Phaedrus placed his hand on Socrates' shoulder. "Good company notwithstanding, old friend, is goodness something that can truly be taught? Or does one come by it naturally? Born with it, as the Calvinists believe?"

"Anything may be taught," Socrates nodded. "Given a good enough teacher and a student willing to learn. Chrysilla wasn't born playing the piano, but as you've all seen, she applied herself and became an accomplished concert pianist. As for goodness, anyone wishing to acquire it will do so, provided they sufficiently discipline themselves for the task."

Judge Callais assumed his familiar superior attitude. "If that's your viewpoint, Socrates, why don't you teach your wife, Xanthippe, to be a less troublesome wife. For if you're to be believed when drinking, she's the most difficult wife in the Delta."

"Because I notice that people who want to become good equestrians don't keep the most docile horses on hand, preferring the more high-spirited ones because they believe if they can get along with those, they will easily handle the others. I've chosen Xanthippe because I'm certain that if I can get along with her, I can get along with anyone."

"Well, Socrates," Callais said, "I see you liken your wife to a horse, but I'd wager that she would say you're the one who most resembles a horse's rear end."

"Wiser *and* wittier that I you are, Callais. I rest my case. You're right, of course. But if we can begin with the proposition that goodness can be taught, would anyone here deny, in the presence of these two young people, that we should pride ourselves in our ability to instill goodness in others?

"Okay, Socrates," Callais snorted, "let's all head to Cloudcuckooland for another riveting abstract discussion on morality. I greatly enjoyed my abstract legal discussions with professors in law school. By all means, let's have one about morality."

Socrates gave a subdued smile. "Excellent thought, Callais. But let me assure you that our discussion will have nothing to do with abstract concerns. While I certainly agree that the law is one abstraction piled on top of another that no one can possibly understand except the lawyers, I intend to avoid such discussions like the plague."

"Very funny, Socrates. But what will our discussion have to do with the price of tea in China?"

"Only everything, my friend. Don't you agree that if every law school professor spent as much time instilling goodness in his students as he did teaching arcane knowledge about particular subjects, society would benefit in the long run? If someone practices honesty in law, medicine or business, as well as in all personal relations, wouldn't that person be a greater success in his chosen profession or business and infinitely more pleasing to his or her family and to God as well? And if this is so, shouldn't we feel an urgency to ferret out what is the good and what is not the good so we can teach it wherever we go?"

Callais groaned and raised his hands in surrender. "All right, Socrates. I concede the point. Let's discuss what you say, by all means."

They discussed the definition of the good while enjoying a fine repast and enough whiskey, wine and beer to keep the mood as jovial as a Delta wedding reception. Notwithstanding the good time had by all, unhappy with Socrates' usual method of asking questions and providing no answers, Callais demanded that they switch gears and define an easier concept— friendship.

"That *is* an easier one," Socrates agreed. "Even I can answer that. A good friend cares about his friends, delights in nothing so much as in good friends, rejoices no less in her friends' good fortune than in her own, is never weary in contriving that his friends may have good fortune, and believes that the best quality in a person is to outdo his friends in acts of kindness and her enemies in acts of hostility."

"I'll buy that, Socrates," Callais conceded. "If you won't define 'good' at least you came close to defining 'good friend.' Care to try defining 'beauty?' That's the other subject you're always blathering on about. Just this once, though, I'd like to hear you answer this question outright, if you please."

Lenaia, who had just arrived and had been listening to the conversation on the other side of the booth's curtain, suddenly whipped it open in and bounced into the room. "So you want to know about beauty?" she demanded to the startled Callais. "Or more specifically what Socrates taught us about beauty?"

"Well, I... Well, yes, Mother Lenaia, I do."

"Then bend your ears," their priest said, "and I'll be glad to enlighten you."

They all settled back in their seats as Lenaia spoke as if she were delivering another homily at the Episcopal Church a few blocks down the street. "Right after my sixteenth birthday my parents moved to Greenwood from Tupelo and enrolled me at

Greenwood High School. I was a socially insecure girl from the hills and didn't know a single girl in my class. The first to befriend me was Theano, and one day after school, she took me out to a bend in the Tallahatchie River where, from behind the trunk of an giant oak on the riverbank, we spied on some boys in our class skinny dipping downstream. That was the first time I saw Alcibiades. Oh… His body was so beautiful. Unlike anything I had ever seen or imagined. Even in the movies. I couldn't sleep for three nights and my mother worried I was smoking marijuana or something worse. She was right, of course. I was hooked on something worse; I was hooked on love. Fortunately, Cupid answered my prayers and Alcibiades asked me out the next week. He brought me here to Giardina's for dinner and I felt like the luckiest newcomer in high school history."

Lenaia paused for a moment, assuming a more somber expression. "Until a few months later when Alcibiades got his draft notice for Vietnam. I was crushed, my friends. Inconsolable. Destroyed. I had found my Trojan Horse, for sure. That was when I enrolled in Socrates' honor class. He introduced me to new friends and showed me that physical beauty was by no means restricted to one person. That Agathon, Theano and many others were more beautiful than I had realized. Then he showed me the beauty of a sunset on the Yazoo River, of the birds and trees, waterfalls and lakes. If that kind of beauty was what I sought, he told me, I could find it almost anywhere in the world.

"Then he taught me about the beauty of the soul. Socrates, the old procurer, introduced me to an elderly black man named Aristodemus. Yes, Callais, your caretaker, Aristodemus, who was helping launch a Leflore County Head Start program for disadvantaged youth with tutoring, mentoring, teaching or whatever they needed. Of course, old Aristodemus was by no means a specimen of great physical beauty like Alcibiades, although he was certainly better looking than Socrates."

Everyone in the booth laughed, Socrates loudest of all. "But," Lenaia continued, "they both taught me what I needed to know about justice, charity and what Socrates called 'moral beauty.' And then Socrates taught me about the beauty of knowledge. How the tiresome thing about ignorance is that those who lack beauty, goodness and wisdom are perfectly satisfied with themselves and can't fix what they don't know is broken. Then he taught me all he could about science, math, literature and philosophy. I know some say that the beauty of a tree surpasses that of a well turned phrase, or a stunning work of art, or the perfect mathematical equation, but I beg to differ on that point."

"Why, that's bordering on sacrilege, Lenaia," Callais grumbled. "And you, a priest, agreeing with Socrates that man's knowledge of beauty rivals that of God's conception of it? Why you ought to—"

Lenaia silenced him with a raised hand. "What is the beauty of a stream, Judge Callais, if one lacks the capacity to appreciate it? Anyhow, after teaching me about physical beauty, moral beauty and the beauty of knowledge, Socrates taught me about absolute beauty. Divine beauty. So that after I had learned how to make my way in the world, I could learn to become acceptable to God. In divine beauty lies the answer to any question, the solution to any problem. As you suggest, Callais, the words of man are as dust in the wind compared to the truth and beauty contained in the words divinely inspired by God."

"And that's when you became a priest?"

"Yes, Agathon," she replied. "That's when I applied to divinity school. I became a priest, you a playwright, Phaedrus and Callais lawyers, Alcibiades an athlete and general, and Pausanius and Theano college professors. And everything we ever accomplish, everything we ever become, we owe to—"

"Socrates! Socrates!" Callais crowed sarcastically. "You all owe *everything* to Socrates. That's all very well and good, I'm sure. But while you told us what he taught you about beauty, I don't suppose he ever told you how much you sacrifice by way of practical knowledge of the world when you shuck it all to go live in the clouds with Socrates and his beloved *daemon*. No offense to your profession intended, Mother Lenaia."

"None taken, old friend."

"But," Callais argued, "Socrates still hasn't answered my question about the meaning of beauty, at least not in any way that's relevant in the practical world."

"How about it, Socrates," Chrysilla asked. "Do those who abandon all other kinds of beauty for absolute beauty lose anything in the bargain?'"

"Do you not see, my friends," Socrates entreated as he finished his fourth glass of wine, "that in this place alone, in the spiritual place where absolute or divine beauty can be seen, it is possible to discern true goodness—not mere reflected images of goodness, but true goodness itself. And those who've successfully nurtured this capacity to perceive absolute beauty will have the privilege of being loved by God; they will become as far as possible for humans, immortal!"